MOMENT OF TRUTH

"That was a sneaky way to get a dance with me," Gaiety said to the man who had just cut in on her first partner.

"A determined man uses whatever means at his disposal. Surely I deserve one dance."

"Why would you think that?" she asked. "I don't even know your name."

"I'm wounded. I was certain you would have asked someone to tell you by now."

She looked into his eyes. He was lying. "No, you weren't. You knew I wouldn't ask."

He smiled. "True. But I had hoped I might be wrong," he said as the music came to an end. "Shall I remain a stranger to you then?"

"I think so," she said hesitantly, although she didn't want to go home without knowing his name.

"And why is that?" he asked, as the dancers started leaving the floor.

"You presume too much. A gentleman would never have been as forward as you have been. A gentleman wouldn't have been poaching on our land, and a—"

"A gentleman wouldn't have touched your lips with his finger or looked so deeply into your eyes. He wouldn't stand before you nameless and tell you he wanted to kiss you."

"That's right," she answered, knowing she was being drawn closer to him with each word he spoke.

"So you don't believe I'm a gentleman."

"No," she whispered, as her eyes rounded with sudden recognition . . .

CAPTURE THE GLOW OF
ZEBRA'S *HEARTFIRES!*

CAPTIVE TO HIS KISS (3788, $4.25/$5.50)
by Paige Brantley
Madeleine de Moncelet was determined to avoid an arranged marriage to the Duke of Burgundy. But the tall, stern-looking knight sent to guard her chamber door may thwart her escape plan!

CHEROKEE BRIDE (3761, $4.25/$5.50)
by Patricia Werner
Kit Newcomb found politics to be a dead bore, until she met the proud Indian delegate Red Hawk. Only a lifetime of loving could soothe her desperate desire!

MOONLIGHT REBEL (3707, $4.25/$5.50)
by Marie Ferrarella
Krystyna fled her native Poland only to live in the midst of a revolution in Virginia. Her host may be a spy, but when she looked into his blue eyes she wanted to share her most intimate treasures with him!

PASSION'S CHASE (3862, $4.25/$5.50)
by Ann Lynn
Rose would never heed her Aunt Stephanie's warning about the unscrupulous Mr. Trent Jordan. She knew what she wanted—a long, lingering kiss bound to arouse the passion of a bold and ardent lover!

RENEGADE'S ANGEL (3760, $4.25/$5.50)
by Phoebe Fitzjames
Jenny Templeton had sworn to bring Ace Denton to justice for her father's death, but she hadn't reckoned on the tempting heat of the outlaw's lean, hard frame or her surrendering wantonly to his fiery loving!

TEMPTATION'S FIRE (3786, $4.25/$5.50)
by Millie Criswell
Margaret Parker saw herself as a twenty-six year old spinster. There wasn't much chance for romance in her sleepy town. Nothing could prepare her for the jolt of desire she felt when the new marshal swept her onto the dance floor!

Available wherever paperbacks are sold, or order direct from the Publisher. Send cover price plus 50¢ per copy for mailing and handling to Zebra Books, Dept. 4446, 475 Park Avenue South, New York, N.Y. 10016. Residents of New York and Tennessee must include sales tax. DO NOT SEND CASH. For a free Zebra/ Pinnacle catalog please write to the above address.

STARLIGHT

GLORIA DALE SKINNER

ZEBRA BOOKS
KENSINGTON PUBLISHING CORP.

ZEBRA BOOKS are published by

Kensington Publishing Corp.
475 Park Avenue South
New York, NY 10016

Copyright © 1994 by Gloria Dale Skinner

All rights reserved. No part of this book may be reproduced in any form or by any means without the prior written consent of the Publisher, excepting brief quotes used in reviews.

If you purchased this book without a cover you should be aware that this book is stolen property. It was reported as "unsold and destroyed" to the Publisher and neither the Author nor the Publisher has received any payment for this "stripped book."

Zebra, the Z logo, Heartfire Romance, and the Heartfire Romance logo are trademarks of Kensington Publishing Corp..

First Printing: January, 1994

Printed in the United States of America

This book is dedicated to Liz, Frances, Marty, Dolores, Gerry, Sandra, Sharon, Hortense, and Meryl Sawyer for their generous support of my work and unfailing friendship.

Prologue

Georgia: 1836

He'd die before he'd marry her. Aston's gaze darted back and forth between the two men holding rifles pointed at him.

"Let me kill him, Pa," Josh said. "I ain't sixteen yet. They won't hang me."

"Won't hang me, neither," his father told him in an unhurried voice.

"She's lying!" Aston protested again, his whole body shaking with outrage. "It's not my baby. I swear I've never touched her."

Aston glanced over at the confident-looking girl standing beside her father. There was no denying that she was pregnant, and it didn't take long to figure out why she'd blamed the baby on him. His father was the wealthiest man in the county.

Ambushed as he was leaving town, Aston had been forced at gunpoint to come to the church with Dewey Talbot and his son, Josh. Aston had heard talk of how free Theodora Talbot was with her body. And it wasn't that he hadn't been interested. In fact, he'd expected to have his turn with her eventually. But he hadn't.

"She told us you wouldn't admit it," her brother said, as he lifted his rifle a little higher, pointing it at Aston's chest.

"Didn't expect him to. They never do," her father added, before turning his attention back to Aston. "But you're going to marry her just the same. I won't have you ruining my daughter, then leaving me the brat to feed. Now, you say 'I do' or I'll pull this trigger and splatter you all over this church."

The click of a hammer being pulled back tightened Aston's gut, and he turned to his only hope. The preacher, lips trembling with fear, cowered behind the communion table. His gaze darted nervously from the girl to her father and brother. Aston knew the preacher wasn't in any better a position than he was, but he had to try one more time. "Tell them they can't make me marry her," he demanded.

"I—he—he's right—" The minister stumbled over his whispery words.

Theodora's father placed the barrel of his rifle behind the minister's ear. "I 'spect you better not say anything but them wedding vows. Now, get on with it."

"She's lying, I tell you," Aston said again, frantic for them to believe him. "I know she's been with most of the boys around here, but I'm not—"

The butt of Josh's gun struck Aston just

above the eye, knocking him backward. Sparkles flashed before his eyes. He groaned, swaying from the pain in his head.

"Don't you talk about my sister that way. She ain't no whore." Josh shot a glance toward his father. "Let me kill him, Pa," he said again.

The blow to his head calmed Aston enough for him to realize talking wasn't going to get him out of this marriage. The Talbots had made up their minds that Theodora was telling the truth and he was lying. Aston didn't believe Theodora's father would shoot him, but Josh was young and foolish enough to pull the trigger. Marrying poor white trash wasn't what Aston wanted for himself at age seventeen, and he didn't think Theodora could be more than fourteen.

But Aston knew the only way he was going to leave the church was either married or dead. It was his choice. He took a deep breath and decided he'd rather be married. He turned to the preacher and mumbled, "I'll marry her."

With rigid control, Aston listened to the preacher and answered at each appropriate time until he was pronounced married to the young girl with the stringy brown hair and swollen stomach.

Dewey Talbot picked up a small bundle of clothes that had been tied together and threw them at Aston.

"She's yours. Take her home with you." He cut his clear blue eyes around to Theodora. "I did what the good Lord expected me to do. I made him marry you, but I'm through with you now. I don't want to see you again."

"Papa—"

The door of the church burst open with a bang. Howard Rutledge and three of his men rushed inside, guns drawn. Josh raised his rifle.

Seeing the fear in Josh's face, Aston pushed Theodora aside in his haste to stop her brother. "Don't shoot!" he cried, but his words were lost in the deafening sound of a rifle blast as one of his father's men fired. The bullet struck Josh in the chest.

"No!" Dewey yelled, as his son stumbled backward and fell to the floor. Dewey raised his weapon, but three bullets hit him in the chest and stomach before he could get off a shot. He dropped the rifle and crumpled to the floor.

Theodora covered her ears with her hands and screamed as she scampered for the far corner of the room. She fell to her knees and whimpered, "Don't shoot me! Papa made me say it was you. Don't shoot."

Aston jerked the rifle out of one of the men's hands. "Nobody's going to hurt you," he told Theodora, as he bent down to look at her father and brother.

Both Talbot men were dead. Aston looked up at his father and the men he'd known all his life. He was shaking. He was sick to his stomach. "Why did you shoot?" he yelled up at them.

"That boy aimed, son. It was him or us."

Aston winced and shook his head, not wanting to believe what had transpired. "Josh didn't know what he was doing," Aston said, trying to vindicate the young man.

"Old Ben saw Talbot and his boy stop you just outside town and followed you here to the church. He had an idea of what was going on, so he rode over to the sawmill to get me. I couldn't let you marry that girl."

"You're too late," Aston murmured. "We're already married." His fists tightened as he looked at the two dead men, blood darkening their shirts.

"Sonofa—!" Howard cut his word off short as if remembering he was in the house of the Lord. He shook his head in disbelief. He looked over at the girl who was sobbing pitifully. "Don't worry, son. I'll take care of everything." He shot a quick glance to the preacher. "No one will ever hear about this."

"No! You've done enough," Aston rose to his feet. He faced his father with a purpose in mind. "She's my wife now. My responsibility. I'll take care of her."

"Is that your bastard she's carrying?" Howard asked, disgust sounding in his tone.

Aston had never lied to his father and he couldn't now. "No. I've never touched her, but the baby will carry my name."

"I won't have a—"

"It's not up to you, Pa," Aston interrupted. "It never was." His gaze strayed over to the two dead men. "Damn it, Pa, why did you have to kill them?"

One

Georgia, 1848

She was back. Gaiety couldn't have wished for anything more than to return to the home she barely remembered. She stood on the front porch of the newly restored clapboard house and looked out over the grassy lawn. In the distance beyond the freshly painted, arched entrance gate which read "Lilac Hill," tall Georgia pines shot up toward a clear blue sky. Twelve years ago, when she left this house, she was Avalina Talbot. Yesterday she had returned as Gaiety Smith.

Gaiety knew her adopted father wasn't happy that she wanted to return to the South and had forbidden it for the past two years. But last winter, when the doctor had told him his rheumatism wouldn't bother him as frequently if he moved to a warmer climate, she immediately started trying to convince him to sell his ironworks shop and move into the house that had once been her home.

A gentle hand touched her shoulder from behind and she turned to see her father standing behind her. She'd been so deep in thought she hadn't heard him come outside.

"Are you happy now?" he asked.

Gaiety smiled up at the robust man with thinning hair and aging blue eyes. "Yes, Papa. It's beautiful here."

He grunted good-naturedly. "I should have guessed. Even after twelve years in the North, you still feel the South is your home."

She patted his hand. "There'll always be a sadness in my heart because we couldn't find Titus, but in time, maybe that will pass."

Lane Smith sighed. "You don't know how many times I've wished the lady at the orphanage had made it clear to me you had two brothers and that even though Josh was dead, Titus was very much alive and he was the brother you cried for."

"I know, Papa. But as we've discussed before, since you asked for a girl, she was probably worried you wouldn't take either of us if she told you I had a younger brother at the orphanage."

"I would have adopted him, too."

Gaiety reached up and hugged him. She loved her adopted father. He'd been so good to her. "You spent a lot of money trying to find Titus. I think I knew it was hopeless once we discovered the orphanage had burned shortly after I left. At least you were able to buy Lilac Hill for me. I've always been very happy you did that."

A wrinkle appeared on her forehead. She knew Aston Rutledge was desperate to buy the thirty-acre farm. He'd approached her father a few years ago when all of the South had been in a drought. The land was valuable because the five-acre pond on Lilac Hill was fed by an underground spring. It hadn't dried up, like most of the other ponds in the area. He wanted the land so he could keep his livestock watered.

"Right now, there's nothing I'd want more than a brother to help look after you when I'm gone."

"Gone?" She gave him a stern look. "Hush that kind of talk. You're not dying."

"I know the doctor says not. But some mornings when I can barely get out of bed because my bones don't want to move, I feel like I'm going to."

Many times Gaiety had wished she had the affliction instead of her father. She hated to see him suffer. The only thing she could do for him was encourage him. "That stiffness will get better, now that we're here where it's warmer. Just wait and see what the summer sunshine does for you."

"I am moving a little better already." He rotated one arm up and over his head while holding his shoulder and then rotated the other. "It's hard to believe we left snow on the ground in Connecticut not two weeks ago and here, south of Savannah, we're comfortable outside without a winter coat."

"I knew you'd like it here, Papa." She smiled.

"Don't try to act like this is my first trip south, young lady. You know good and well the reason I was reluctant to come here."

Gaiety took a few steps away from her father, the skirt of her rose-colored dress swishing about her legs. She heard birds chirping in the distant trees and a mid-morning breeze stirred the early-spring air. "I want to make Aston Rutledge pay for destroying my family. I've never hidden that from you."

Lane Smith grunted and moved to stand beside his daughter, his robust frame towering before her. "And I've never approved. How many times have we had this conversation?"

She stared straight ahead, not wanting to meet her father's eyes. She didn't want to see his disapproval.

"Gaiety?"

"Many times," she answered.

"And what did I tell you?" Gaiety started to walk away, but Lane grabbed her upper arm and forced her to face him. "Let me hear you say it so I'll know you haven't forgotten." His tone was firm, yet gentle.

Gaiety took a deep breath and recited, " 'Revenge is a hard thing to carry out, and even harder to live with, once it's accomplished.' " She tried to move away from him, but he held her firmly.

He fixed his gaze upon her face. "The rest."

She sighed. "Papa?"

"I want to hear the rest of it."

" 'Revenge is never pretty, but it's especially ugly coming from a lady.' "

"Don't forget that, Gaiety. Now, I'll hear no more about revenge." He let go of her. "Living here, we're bound to run into Mr. Rutledge now and again. Since he's our closest neighbor, I fully expect a visit from him. I don't want you doing anything other than behaving like the proper young lady Mary taught you to be."

Cold resolve settled upon her shoulders as sunshine lit upon her face. "I want to meet him, Papa," she said earnestly. "I'm all that's left of the family he destroyed twelve years ago. I think it's only natural for me to want to see what he looks like."

"And I've agreed to that much." He pointed an arthritic finger at her. "But no more."

"Papa, when we were in Connecticut, you told me that no one here knows that you bought Lilac Hill for me. Is that still the case?"

"It's true. And that's the way it has to be. I don't want anyone to know you were once Avalina Talbot. What happened to your family was horrible, no doubt about it. I don't want you subjected to the questions and stares that would surely come if anyone knew your beginnings. As far as the people here know, I bought this land years ago to use as a second home someday. That's all I intend for anyone to know about us. Against my better judgment, I agreed to move here. Now, when you meet Mr. Rutledge, I'm depending on you not to create a scene."

"I understand, Papa. I ceased to be Avalina Talbot a long time ago." Gaiety said the words her adopted father wanted to hear, but knew they were not true. Deep inside herself, she'd never forgotten her father's and Josh's deaths.

"Good. That's my girl." He smiled.

"I'll be coolly polite whenever I meet Aston Rutledge."

Lane laughed heartily. "You, be polite to Aston Rutledge? It'll never happen. I just hope you don't throw yourself on him and try to scratch his eyes out."

Gaiety joined his laughter to cover the guilty feelings her father's words evoked in her. Lane Smith obviously knew her thoughts better than she wanted him to.

She had plans she didn't want her father to know about. For now she was content to let Aston Rutledge think of her as Gaiety Smith, but when the time came, she would let him know her name used to be Avalina Talbot.

"We've only been here two days. Soon the invitations will start coming, and I have a feeling you'll be too busy getting ready for parties to think about anything else."

"And as you said, we may have our neighbor Mr. Rutledge stopping by to welcome us to the community."

Lane looked over Gaiety's shoulder to the lazy blue sky. "It's my hope that once you've seen the man your fascination with him will cease."

"I'm not sure fascination is the correct word, Papa."

He grunted, then lowered his gaze to her face again. "I am. Even though you've never met the man, he holds you transfixed with an irresistible power. Just remember, Gaiety, you have five months. If the end of summer rolls around and you haven't picked a husband, I'll decide on one for you."

Gaiety looked up at her father and smiled. "I'll do my best to find myself a husband. But I don't understand why you are in such a hurry to get rid of me."

His features softened. "It's not that and you know it. I'd like nothing better than to keep you with me for the next ten years. It's a shame, but the best marriages are made before a girl reaches eighteen. You're past that now."

"Don't worry, Papa, we'll find me a suitable husband. But he has to live nearby so we can visit often. I've lost one father. I don't want to lose you."

"You won't. Not for a long time."

She smiled. "I'm going to enjoy being back at Lilac Hill. Thank you for agreeing to come."

"Just don't make me regret it, Gaiety."

"I'll try not to," she said, but knew she wasn't being entirely truthful. She looked out over the lawn. A gentle breeze ruffled the shrubs and swept across her face. "It's such a beautiful day I think I'll walk down to the pond and see if it's changed."

"Have Maine go along with you."

"I don't need a driver. I plan to walk."

"Very well. Take Mimi with you."

She looked back at him. "I don't want her along, either. Papa, I'd like to go alone this first time, if you don't mind."

"I don't think that's a good idea."

"I'm sure I'll be all right. No harm can come to me here on our land. I promise I'll have Maine drive me when I visit Josh and Papa's graves tomorrow."

"All right, but if you're not back in an hour I'll come looking for you. I wish your mother were alive," he said. "I've never been able to handle you the way Mary could," he mumbled to himself as he opened the door and walked inside.

Gaiety looked down at her long-sleeved rose-colored dress and decided she didn't need to change for her walk. She had on her day corset and a pair of good walking shoes. The sun hung high in the sky, but with the breeze, she didn't have to worry about getting too hot, so she decided to go without her bonnet. Surely, one day in the sun without covering her head wouldn't make her skin blotchy with freckles. And if the water wasn't too cold she just might take her shoes and stockings off and wade in it. When she'd lived here as a little girl, the only washing she'd ever had was when Theodora had taken her and Titus to the pond and let them play in the water.

She sighed and headed toward the pond. Theodora and Titus were part of the reason she wanted to go alone. To remember a time long ago, when she lived on this land with her other family.

Gaiety had no trouble finding her way. The clump of hardwood trees, then the clearing, were as fresh in her mind as if she'd been down the path just yesterday. She walked quietly as she neared the water's edge. From a distance not far away, a movement caught her eye. She saw a man standing on a rock with a pole and line in the water. She stopped, startled for a moment. Her pulse quickened. She hadn't expected to find anyone on her land. The sun glared in her eyes so she couldn't get a good look at him.

"Hello," he called to her, his voice friendly.

Holding up her hand to shield her eyes from the sun's rays, she asked, "Who are you and what are you doing here?" She was a little irritated that he should presume to be so friendly while trespassing on her land.

He held up the fishing pole and looked at her with amusement lurking in the upturned corners of his mouth. "What else? Trying to catch fish for my supper."

"I don't believe you asked permission to fish in this pond," she said with all the authority she could muster.

"I wasn't aware I needed to ask permission.

People from all over the county have been fishing in this pond for ten or twelve years."

Feeling no immediate fear of the stranger, she lifted her skirts and walked closer to the bank so she could look at him without the sun in her eyes. With that teasing grin, he didn't look or act dangerous, but she still found herself wondering if her father or Maine could hear her should she need to scream for help.

"That may have been true in the past, but not anymore," she said. "My father has had the house restored and we're living here now."

"I'd heard a family would be moving in, but I hadn't expected to encounter anyone today."

She took a closer look at him. He wasn't an unpleasant-looking man. In fact, he was quite handsome. "We arrived just yesterday," she said, and immediately wished she hadn't. It wasn't proper for her to be carrying on a normal conversation with this stranger.

"Not that it's any of your concern," she added quickly, in a less friendly manner. "From now on you must ask permission before you fish this pond. We won't allow trespassers or poachers on our land any longer." She hoped she sounded firmer this time.

The man smiled again. And even though she didn't want to, she liked his smile. It was genuine. There was also something pleasing and captivating about it. He was teasing her, playing with her. He didn't appear to be laughing at her this time—just enjoying the conversation. She noticed, too, that he didn't have the look of a vagabond. His brown breeches and white shirt were clean. His hair was a little longer than what was usually considered acceptable, but she found that it made him more attractive, not derelict. But he'd said he was fishing for his supper, so he had to be a man of meager means. And a man she shouldn't be passing the time of day with.

The thought that she was drawn to a man who had to catch his own supper irritated her. And her father would be horrified to hear of it. Not only that, she had to remind herself this man had interrupted her time alone. There were so many things she wanted to remember, now that she was back home.

"I suppose you want me to leave," he said, as he reached down and pulled a string of four or five fish out of the water.

Gaiety cleared her throat and straightened her shoulders. "Yes," she said firmly. "As I stated before, we can't allow poachers, now that Papa and I are living here." Besides, how could she think about the past with this man watching her so closely?

He started toward her, the string of fish dangling from one hand and his pole and line in the other. "And I'm to ask permission before I fish here again."

"Yes," she said, thinking she liked the way he walked, the way he carried himself with his shoulders back. This man was no ordinary vagabond or poacher. He was too self-confident, too much in control. "All you need do is go up to the back door of the house and speak to the cook."

The smile still in place, he asked, "You want me to go to the back door?"

"Of course." She found herself backing away as he came closer, but not because she was afraid. When the heel of her shoe sank into the soft mud near the water's edge, she stopped. She had to be careful. Another step and she knew she'd be in the water.

The man stopped in front of her and said, "I have enough to share." He held up the fish and she saw that he had several good-sized bream and a couple of catfish dangling from the string.

"No—no, thank you," she said. "I'm not fond of fish. Just be on your way." She was suddenly nervous with him being so near.

"I won't hurt you," he said in a soothing voice as his gaze scanned her face. "Don't be frightened of me."

She moistened her lips and said, "I'm not. It's just that I shouldn't be carrying on a conversation with a stranger. It's not proper."

"You're right. It's not." He bowed slowly. "I'll ask permission before I come to your pond again." He started toward his horse, tied to a nearby tree, but turned back to her and said, "And I'll be sure to use the back door."

Gaiety kept her gaze on the stranger as he mounted. He looked back twice as if to make sure she was still watching him. She let out a deep breath when he finally disappeared from sight.

The man disturbed her more than he should have. And she realized what disturbed her most was that she hadn't been frightened of him, she'd actually been drawn to him. She turned away from the spot where he'd disappeared and looked out over the dark blue water of the glassy pond. How could she think on the past after her encounter with that man? Her mind wanted only to replay the things he'd said, the way he'd smiled, the soft, masculine tones of his voice. If she found him on their land again, she'd have to tell her father.

Gaiety stood on the soft bank, her shoes sinking farther into the mud, and closed her eyes, determined to put thoughts of the stranger from her mind. She wanted to recapture feelings from days long since past. She wanted to bring to mind memories that seemed to fade a little more each day. She wanted to remember the facts, not the distorted patches of the past that occasionally flashed through her mind. As hard as she tried to keep it from happening, her first family was slipping from her memory.

It was wrong for her to forget about her papa, Josh, Theodora, and Titus. But how could she keep them from fading away completely? Their only legacy to her was the impact they had made on her life. What could she do to preserve that memory? What would be her memorial to them?

Her father had been a quiet man of few

words. He'd spoken slowly and seldom raised his voice. Josh she remembered as more temperamental. She recalled one night when he'd become very angry with Theodora and left the house, not returning until the next day. But there were the good times when Josh would play with her and Titus. He would throw her over his shoulder and pretend she was a sack of potatoes.

Theodora was quiet, like their father. Gaiety remembered that Theodora enjoyed going for walks down to the pond when Josh and their papa were in the fields. Sometimes she was nice and would let Avalina and Titus go with her. At other times, she made them stay in the house with the door shut.

Dear sweet Titus, Gaiety thought, was the one she dreamed of most often, but remembered the least about. Had his eyes been bluish-green like her papa's, or were they more sky blue like hers? Had his hair been thick and straight like hers, or did it have a bit of curl? He was only four the last time she saw him and he had just learned to say "Avalina" correctly, but Gaiety couldn't remember the color of his eyes. It wasn't fair that her memory was failing her.

Titus would be here with her today if Mrs. Conners from the orphanage had told Lane and Mary about Titus. She would always wonder if the woman had confused Titus with Josh or had intentionally told the Smiths that the brother she cried for was dead.

Gaiety looked at the pond but didn't see it. She had snatches of memory from the orphanage about dark corners and older children hitting her, pulling her hair and kicking her. She'd been weak and afraid. She was glad to leave the orphanage, but she hadn't wanted to leave Titus behind. When Lane and Mary adopted her, all she could do was cry for her brother. It took several months, but through their strength and love she'd learned to trust them and open up to them. That's when Lane had realized that she had two brothers. Because of her fear, Titus had been lost to her forever, just like the rest of her family. She vowed never to be afraid of anything again.

Lane liked to say she was stubborn, but she wasn't. She liked to think of it as strength. Her father would have to realize that when the time came.

Gaiety squeezed her eyes shut and her hands made fists. It was all fading and she didn't know what she could do to bring it back. How could she tell the man who had rescued her from the orphanage, the man she now loved with all her heart, that she was losing her first family? Could she tell him she wanted to keep those memories alive without hurting him? And that she intended to find a way to make Aston Rutledge pay for their deaths?

When Gaiety returned home, she saw a carriage in front of the house. Her spirits lifted.

Already they had their first guest. As she started toward the front steps, the door opened and Maine came stalking out.

"I was just on my way to look for you. You have a visitor." The tall, solidly built man whipped his hat off his head as he waited for her on the porch.

"Thank you, Maine. I'll go right in."

Mimi, her maid of three years, was waiting just inside the front door for her.

"You have a guest, Miss Gaiety," Mimi said, clasping her hands together under her chin. Her brown eyes sparkled. "She's a pretty lady with a sweet-sounding voice. Dressed real nice, too. She said for me to tell you she's Miss Elaine Harper," Mimi finished, then took a much-needed breath.

Gaiety didn't have to be excited about their first visitor, Mimi had enough excitement for both of them. "Did you offer refreshment?" Gaiety asked, as she looked at her hair in the gilded mirror hanging over a finely crafted Hepplewhite side table decorated with inlaid ivory medallions.

"Yes, Miss. I gave her tea with a ball of apple cinnamon in it and some of those sweet cakes Helen baked when we got here yesterday. Miss Elaine's driver is in the kitchen having a cup."

Gaiety turned quickly to Mimi and asked, "Is Papa with her?"

"No, Miss. He's napping in his room. Said he hasn't rested from that long journey from

Connecticut. He doesn't want to be disturbed until dinner."

Wisps of hair had fallen out of her chignon. A quick glance down at the petticoat mirror showed muddy shoes. She couldn't meet her first guest looking so disarrayed. "Drat," she muttered.

Mimi's bright eyes rounded in surprise before a stern look stole over her young face. "You know your papa doesn't like for you to—"

"Not now, Mimi," Gaiety said, cutting into her sentence. "Go tell our guest that I'm home, and that I'll be joining her in five minutes. Then hurry upstairs and help me change into a clean dress and shoes." Gaiety lifted her skirts and took the stairs two at a time.

Five minutes later Gaiety had repaired her appearance and was walking into the sunlit parlor attired in a melon-colored dress. "Good afternoon. I'm sorry you had to wait so long. I'm—"

"Gaiety Smith," the smiling young lady said to her, as she rose from the brocade-covered settee, the folds of her crisp blue skirt falling to the floor. Her green eyes sparkled with friendliness. "I know all about you. Everyone in the area has been talking about you and your father for months now. We've all been waiting for your arrival. I'm Elaine Harper, and I'm so pleased to make your acquaintance. I do hope your papa didn't suffer too much on the journey."

For a moment Gaiety was stunned by the

young woman's openness. "It's so nice to meet you," Gaiety said, taking her place on the other end of the settee. "Please sit back down and finish your tea." She refilled Elaine's cup before pouring tea for herself.

"Papa made the trip quite well, thank you. How do you know so much about us?" she asked, wondering if someone could have found out that she was Avalina Talbot and spread the news.

"Oh, don't look so concerned," Elaine said cheerfully, picking up her delicate china teacup. "When Mr. Jackson started working on this house it was natural for everyone to want to know who was going to be moving in. Your father's illness isn't a secret, is it?"

"His rheumatism? No."

"Mr. Jackson said that was the reason you were moving here where it's warmer. Of course, I understand that you've owned Lilac Hill for several years. After working on this house for the better part of six months, Mr. Jackson was bound to know a little bit of news about you and your papa. I do hope Mr. Jackson didn't tell us anything we weren't supposed to know." Keeping the smile on her lips she set her cup back on the table.

"I'm sure he didn't."

Mimi was right. Elaine had a lovely face. Her green eyes were almond shaped and her hair was a deep shade of brown. And Gaiety was struck by something else. This woman could quite possibly outtalk Mimi.

"I know I should have given you more time to get settled in your new home before I came for a visit, but the truth is, I was so excited to hear someone my age was going to be living close by that I couldn't wait. I do hope you don't mind."

Gaiety gave her a genuine smile. "Of course not. I'm pleased you came. As you can see, we have only a few things in the house so far, but I plan to finish decorating this summer."

"How wonderful." Elaine's gaze roamed over the room, checking every bare wall, every empty corner. "I'm getting married in September. I'll be furnishing my house in Savannah this summer, too. Maybe we can do some of the shopping together. I know all the best places to go." Elaine took her delicate-looking hankie out of her beaded drawstring purse and dabbed at the corner of her mouth.

"I'd like that." Gaiety picked up her tea and sipped. It was already cold, but she didn't mind. She'd made her first friend.

"I've already ordered some pieces from Boston. I'm engaged to Fredrick Williamson. We'll be married in September. My intended's cousin is giving us a party at his house Saturday night. Would you and your father like to attend?"

"A party?" Gaiety asked. "It's very nice of you to want to include us in your guest list. But surely you'll want only your closest friends and family."

"Oh, don't be silly." Elaine stuffed her handkerchief back into her purse. "That's one of the reasons I came over. Naturally, I want my party to be the first one you attend. Aston will make sure it's as big as our engagement party was."

Gaiety stiffened at the sound of that man's name. Could it be this warm and friendly woman was related to a man she'd sworn to hate and see revenge upon? "Aston?" she questioned, wanting to sound casual, but realizing she sounded soft and throaty.

"Aston Rutledge. Fredrick's cousin. Aston has been very generous to us. Fredrick and I are staying at his house on Southern Oaks this week. I'm sure you've heard of his plantation."

"Yes," Gaiety answered, and cleared her throat. "I believe he's the one who wanted to buy Lilac Hill from my father a couple of years ago."

Elaine paused. "I heard some talk about that. It has something to do with the pond, doesn't it?"

Gaiety shrugged in a noncommittal way. She could tell that Elaine knew more than she was letting on. Two could play that game. "I'm not sure about the facts, either. Papa bought the land when I was very young. He always thought we'd make it our second home. But he never could get away from his work. Now his rheumatism has forced him to do what Mama was never able to talk him into doing—giving up his work and moving south."

"Oh, well, we don't want to talk about business things, anyway, do we? Mr. Jackson told us your mother died about three years ago."

Gaiety set her cup down and took a deep breath. She didn't want to talk about dying. Too many people in her life had died. "Yes, that's right."

Lowering her lashes over her eyes for a moment, Elaine breathed deeply. "I lost my mother a few years ago, too, but—" she raised her lashes and smiled sweetly at Gaiety, "we can't change the past. Please tell me you'll come to my party."

Taken aback by her abrupt change, Gaiety had to think quickly. She didn't know that she wanted to go to a party at Aston Rutledge's house. But on second thought, maybe she did. It might be the perfect time to meet him.

"All right," she said, still a little unsure of her answer. "What time should we arrive on Saturday?"

"Oh, anytime after four. There'll be refreshments when you arrive. A buffet will be available all evening, and the dancing will start at eight. Actually, Fredrick and I were most surprised when Aston offered to give us a party."

Elaine picked up her purse and slipped the braided handle over her wrist. Gaiety knew she was getting ready to go.

"Doesn't he like parties?" she asked, wanting to know a little more about the man before Elaine left.

"Oh, heavens, yes! He loves parties." Elaine's eyes rounded with excitement. "He just doesn't believe in marriage. He was married for a short time years ago. From what I've heard, the union wasn't a very happy one. Such a shame. It ended tragically and Aston vowed to never marry again. There was a lot of gossip surrounding the marriage and his wife's death. The only thing I'm sure about is that he's never remarried. He goes to the parties and dances with all the women. Aston doesn't pick and choose, like a lot of men. He dances with the pretty ones, the fat ones, the older ones, and the married ones. Aston charms them all. But he has never courted one. Never."

That bit of information about the man surprised Gaiety. She decided to give it more thought later. Right now, she wanted to hear what Elaine had to say about Theodora's death. She wanted to know if it was different from what she'd heard twelve years ago.

"What happened to his wife?" Gaiety asked.

"Oh, she fell down the stairs, killing herself and the baby she was carrying."

Two

The sun rested low in the western sky as Lane and Gaiety rode in the covered carriage taking them the ten miles to the main house of Southern Oaks. Gaiety stared at Maine's back, but her thoughts weren't on the driver, who was as old as her father but twice as strong. She was wondering what she was going to say to Aston Rutledge when she met him.

Gaiety had dressed with care for Elaine and Fredrick's party. Of all the new dresses she'd had made for their first summer in Georgia, the light amethyst-colored gown with its heart-shaped neckline and chiffon overskirt was her favorite. She wanted to look her very best when she arrived at Southern Oaks and met Mr. Rutledge for the first time.

She wondered if he'd find any resemblance to Theodora when he looked upon her face. She didn't think so. She remembered hearing that she took after her mother, while Josh and Theodora took after their father.

Her father had agreed to go to the party at

once. She knew he always had her happiness in the front of his mind. Although he never said it, she believed he saw the party as a way for her to meet Aston and settle her feelings about him, then get it over with so she could get on with her life. He was wrong; just meeting Aston would not make his wrongdoings or her feelings disappear.

Although she'd put on a smile for her father, she was apprehensive about meeting Aston Rutledge. In truth, she didn't know what she would say to the man. She only knew that she had to see him. She had to look at the man who had destroyed her family.

Lane was quiet as the carriage moved along at a leisurely pace. There was no need to hurry. It was a beautiful day, and Gaiety had already seen an improvement in her father's health. His movements weren't as stiff as they'd been just a few weeks ago. She thanked God he wouldn't have to spend another winter in Connecticut.

Her father reached over and patted her hand. She looked up at his smiling face. His ruddy cheeks and pale blue eyes showed his Irish heritage from his mother's family. He was still a handsome man when he was all dressed up for the evening.

"What are you thinking about?" he asked.

"Nothing in particular."

"You don't expect me to believe that, do you?"

She smiled. "No. I was thinking about the party and Aston Rutledge."

"I thought as much."

"He's never remarried. Did you know that?" she asked as the carriage hit a bump, throwing them forward a little.

"I knew he hadn't as of two years ago, when his lawyer first approached me about buying Lilac Hill."

"According to Elaine, he's vowed to never take a wife again. I find that interesting."

Lane grunted and shifted in the small confines of the carriage. "Why so? He's still a young man. Not quite thirty, I've heard. He'll probably change his mind." He looked at her with a curious expression. "But what's it to you?"

"Nothing," she answered, but then immediately added, "I couldn't help but wonder why he appears to be so set against remarrying."

"Are you thinking that maybe he loved your sister so much he thinks no one could replace her?"

Gaiety scoffed at that idea. "No, Papa," she said firmly, her mouth set in a grim line. "I don't think he loved her at all. Remember, he was forced into marrying her. It's my guess he enjoys the attention of a lot of women and doesn't want to settle for just one. Why should he limit himself to one woman when he has all of them falling at his feet?"

Lane chuckled a little, his round stomach bouncing underneath his checked waistcoat. "I think you shouldn't give so much thought to what Elaine says. I'm sure she's giving the man credit for more charm than he has. Besides, it's a man's nature to want to settle down with one woman and have children to carry on his name."

"There's always an exception, Papa," she said, and turned to look out the carriage at the late afternoon sky.

"Did you and Elaine talk about anything other than Aston and his party?"

"Yes. We talked a little about decorating the house."

"Humm," was all he said.

As they rode on in silence, Gaiety's thoughts turned to her conversation with Elaine the other evening. She had just begun to get over the trauma of having been sent to the orphanage when Mrs. Conners had told her that Theodora had fallen down a flight of stairs and that she and her baby were dead. Gaiety remembered that she'd started screaming, then kicking and hitting the woman.

She wouldn't speak to anyone but Titus, who was too young to understand what had happened or her feelings about it. The only thing Gaiety understood was that everyone she loved except Titus was gone never to return. A week later she was swept up in the arms of a robust man and carried away to Connecticut. She'd vowed never to be that weak again.

Gaiety had made another vow a few months earlier, when she'd sat in the sheriff's office after her father and Josh had been killed. She vowed to make Aston Rutledge pay for Josh's and her papa's death someday. And she would.

Gaiety sighed and rested her head against the side of the bumping carriage as she and her father continued to ride in silence. She wondered if her real mother was the one who had named their house and land "Lilac Hill." It didn't sound like the kind of name a man would give a house. She tried to recall her mother, but couldn't. She'd been too young when she'd died. And she remembered very little about her real father, Dewey Talbot, and Josh and Theodora and Titus.

What would she do if one day she woke up and didn't remember them at all? What would her life have been like if her father and brother had lived? She still wasn't sure Aston hadn't been directly involved in Theodora's death. All Gaiety would think was that because of Aston Rutledge they had died. They'd all died too young.

"Look ahead of us, Gaiety. There's Southern Oaks," Lane said as he leaned forward in the carriage, pointing ahead of them.

In the distance Gaiety saw a large white house with six fluted Doric columns rising three floors. Five windows sat evenly spaced on each side of the doors. The roof was capped by chimneys and a windowed cupola. As they approached by the circular driveway Gaiety could see that the tall front double doors were open.

"Well, Gaiety, the time has come. We have

arrived at the home of Aston Rutledge. How do you feel?"

Her father's question surprised her. How did she feel to be at the house of the man she'd grown up hating? She was shocked, confused, stunned. She turned to her father. "It's strange, Papa," she said in a whispery voice. "I feel like I'm supposed to be here. It's as if this was something I had to do."

His expression turned to a stern look of disapproval. "You're not planning to tell that man you're Avalina Talbot tonight, are you?"

"Of course not, Papa." And she wasn't—not tonight.

Gaiety watched Maine help her father down. For some disturbing reason she felt as if she were destined to arrive at Southern Oaks, at this house. And she felt it even more strongly when she stepped down from the carriage, stood at the bottom of the steps, and looked up at the large house with its six massive columns.

A darkie, handsomely dressed in a crisp white shirt and black breeches, stood at the top of the steps. Soft music, gentle laughter, and various tones of murmuring voices filtered from beyond the open doors. Her father touched her elbow. Still shaken by the unexpected feeling that she was supposed to be here, she lifted her skirts and started up the steps.

"Wait," her father took her arm. "Are you going to be all right?"

Gaiety smiled. "I'm fine, Papa. I intend to meet Mr. Aston Rutledge tonight, but I also intend to enjoy the party."

He looked down into her eyes and smiled. "That's my girl. Let's go."

An older darkie with graying hair stood at the door and greeted them, taking her father's hat and her fringe-tipped wrap. He was splendidly dressed in a brown suit, starched white shirt, and brown-striped cravat.

"Mr. Rutledge had to step away from the door to take care of some business," he greeted them. "He asks that you go inside and help yourself to refreshments. The buffet will be ready at eight."

"And who might you be?" her father asked.

"Josie, sir. I been with Mr. Rutledge since the day he was born."

"You say Mr. Rutledge is taking care of business?"

"Yes, sir," the older man said.

"Well, no need to bother him. We'll meet him later."

Lane turned to Gaiety. "Are you sure you're going to be all right?" he asked again.

She placed a confident smile on her face, realizing she wasn't as nervous as she'd expected to be. "Don't be a fusspot, Papa. I'm going to be fine."

Gaiety turned and looked through the open doorway. The expanded foyer and hallway ran the length of the house to the back double doors that matched the front doors. The staircase, arched like a bridge on both upper floors, was the only thing that broke the length of the wide hallway. With a mere glance inside, the grandeur of the house was apparent.

She'd waited a long time for this meeting. For a long time she'd known that one day she would look upon Aston's face. It was crazy, she knew, but she didn't feel like she could continue her present life until she'd settled the past.

"Oh, there you are, Gaiety. I've been watching for you. And this must be your father. How do you do, Mr. Smith? I'm Elaine Harper. I'm so sorry I missed you the other afternoon. I hope you're feeling better." Elaine's gaze darted from one to the other.

"Quite well, young lady. Thank you for the invitation. We were delighted to accept."

Beautifully dressed in a gown the color of the sun, Elaine wore her hair swept up and away from her face, and it made her appear a little older than her eighteen years. She wore two large oval-cut topazes clipped to her ears and a matching necklace around her neck. A dazzling smile set firmly on her lips.

"I'm so happy you could make it. Come, let's find Fredrick. I want you to meet—oh, here he comes now."

Gaiety watched as a handsome young man dressed in a black evening jacket strode toward them. His wavy brown hair was brushed away from his face and neatly trimmed. His nose and chin were sharp, but didn't take away from his handsomeness. As she looked at him, she found herself wondering if he looked anything like his cousin, Aston Rutledge.

"Fredrick, come meet the Smiths." Elaine took hold of his hand for a moment, then let it drop. "I told you about them. They're the owners of Lilac Hill."

He smiled and shook Gaiety's father's hand. "I'm so glad you could join us." He turned to Gaiety. "How very nice to meet you, Miss Smith. You did a splendid job of charming Elaine the other day when she visited you. She hasn't stopped talking about you."

"Then we were both charmed, Mr. Williamson, and please call me Gaiety."

"And I'm Fredrick." He then turned his attention back to his fiancée. "Linda Sue was looking for you just a moment ago."

"Oh, that's perfect. Gaiety, I want you to meet Linda Sue. Come with me. I'll introduce you to everyone. All my dearest friends are here tonight."

"I'm afraid I didn't get to meet our host, Mr. Rutledge, and I was hoping to," she said, deliberately avoiding her father's eyes. She didn't want him sending her warning signals.

"You and every other eligible woman here." Elaine quickly glanced around the room. "I don't see him right now. Don't worry; you'll get to meet him. He usually tries to accommodate all the ladies and dance with each of them at least once." Elaine flashed her dazzling smile. "You'll have your turn. We'll see to it.

But remember what I told you—don't let him steal your heart."

Gaiety looked first at her father, then back to Elaine. "You can count on it."

"You know, for some reason I believe you." Elaine reached down and took hold of her hand. "Come with me."

Gaiety turned to her father, ready to decline, but he said, "You go ahead, Gaiety. I think I'd like to find something to drink. The drive over worked up a thirst."

"All right, Papa. I'll find you in a few minutes."

"No need to worry about me. I can take care of myself. You go have fun, and—" He paused and pointed a finger at her, something he usually did when he wanted to be firm. "Don't forget what we talked about."

"I won't."

As Gaiety let Elaine lead her through the crowd of beautifully dressed women and stylish men, she wished Mr. Rutledge had been at the front door to greet them. It would be all over. Now she would have to wait.

An hour later, twilight lay upon the sky and merriment lay within the walls of the house. Gaiety was tired from being dragged around from room to room by Elaine. She was sure she'd met everyone but Aston Rutledge. She found that most of the young ladies Elaine introduced her to were as talkative as Elaine and eager to ask her questions about her life in Connecticut.

Gaiety walked out on the front porch for a breath of fresh air. Elaine must have been right when she'd said all of Savannah had turned out for the party. Gaiety was sure she'd met over a hundred people. She'd already caught the eye of several young men and had promised dances to all of them. That would please her father. She hoped he was having a good time. She hadn't seen him since Elaine had taken her hand and led her away.

With the sun past the horizon a chill cloaked the air, but Gaiety wasn't ready to go back inside. Most everyone she'd met had lined up for his or her turn at the buffet. Hunger had eluded her. She needed a reprieve from the incessant questions about herself and her life in Connecticut.

During the evening she'd met Linda Sue, Jennifer, Bonnie, and Carol Ann. With each young lady, Aston's name had come up. Gaiety assumed it was because he was the most eligible man in the county. It appeared all the young ladies agreed with Elaine about Aston's vow never to marry. She was cautioned repeatedly not to set her cap for the man. They warned that he was unattainable; he'd dance and flirt and be charming, but he'd never come calling. Gaiety chuckled to herself. As if she'd want the man to call on her! She convinced herself of one thing: should Aston Rutledge ever take a wife, it would break all their hearts.

Aston was obviously very clever. A sure way to keep all the young women wanting him was not to profess too much interest in any of them. It was not only strange but unsettling, too, that with all the hostility she felt inside for Aston, she felt comfortable in his home, among his friends.

Gaiety walked to the far end of the porch and looked out over the spacious lawn. White, pink, and lavender flowers bloomed. Shades of deep purple, pale orange, and dusty browns spread across the darkening sky. She could still hear the music, the muffled laughing, the muted voices.

A movement at the center of the porch caught her attention and she glimpsed a man bounding up the stairs. He hesitated when he glanced at her, but as recognition dawned he stopped.

"We meet again," he said, and started toward her.

Gaiety found herself looking into the eyes of the man she'd met at the pond. If she'd thought him handsome in fishing clothes, he was dashing in his black evening jacket, white shirt, and gray-striped cravat. His dark eyes, high cheekbones, finely sculpted lips, and slightly rounded chin would make any woman take a second look.

Gaiety faced him directly. "I had a feeling you were more than a mere vagabond when I caught you fishing on our land."

He laughed and Gaiety found it a pleasing sound. She also found that she was still drawn to the man. That didn't bother her so much, now that she knew he was a gentleman.

"Really? You didn't act like it."

"Even though your clothes were old, they were clean, and your hair was long but neatly trimmed. You spoke like an educated man."

"You're very perceptive. Yet you threw me off your land and insisted I ask permission at the back door before returning."

"If you assume the role of a poacher, you have to be prepared to be treated like one." Gaiety was actually enjoying her banter with him. She looked into his brown eyes and knew she wanted him to enjoy her company as well. "I assume you've been invited to this party tonight and that you're not at this house the same way you fish . . . without permission."

He laughed again and Gaiety felt a smile lift the edges of her mouth. How unlike her to continue to enjoy the company of a man, especially a man she hadn't been properly introduced to.

"Well, I don't know that I was actually invited by anyone in particular, but I don't think anyone here will take me to task over it." He paused and took a step closer to her. "Unless you're up to the challenge."

Gaiety pretended to think it over, then said, "Being a guest in this house myself, I'm not at liberty to question your rights."

He bowed. "Glad to hear it, for I fear you'd throw me out, or at the very least, send me to the back door."

She wanted to hide her smile, her genuine enjoyment of being in this man's presence, but she couldn't. Her face showed it all. "I think you could depend on it."

His teasing expression changed to one of appreciation. "Might I say how lovely you look tonight? You are by far the most beautiful lady here."

"Thank you. But I fear you're trying to flatter me for some ulterior reason."

"No . . . merely telling the truth."

He definitely had her interest, and that surprised her. In Connecticut, she had rejected men far more handsome than this one. Maybe it was his teasing smile and friendly eyes that affected her so acutely.

"If you are a gentleman, why were you fishing for your supper?" she asked.

He came closer. "I enjoy the pastime of fishing. It gives me time to think."

A young man and woman walked out on the porch, looking dreamily into each other's eyes and talking softly. Gaiety pivoted and walked to the other end of the porch, away from the couple, hoping he would follow her, yet knowing he shouldn't. She heard his steps behind her and smiled to herself before turning to face him again.

"What kind of things do you think about when you're fishing?"

His gaze met hers, then lightly scanned her face, telling her he *was* attracted. "Humm." He cupped his chin thoughtfully. "If I were to go fishing tomorrow, I'd think about a beautiful woman in an amethyst-colored gown."

Gaiety's heart raced. As a defense against his magnetism, she said, "So you fish so you can think about women."

He chuckled softly. "Not all of the time, no. I enjoy eating the fish, too. May I have the pleasure of a dance later this evening?"

Her skin prickled. She was tempted to say yes, but knew that discretion dictated she say, "Absolutely not. We haven't been properly introduced. I've not the slightest idea who you are, or where you're from."

"I know all about you, Gaiety Smith." His voice remained soft and alluring as he folded his arms across his chest and leaned against the fluted Doric column. "You're from Connecticut, but now living at Lilac Hill. Your father bought the place a few years ago, but only recently had the house restored. You're not betrothed, and your mother died a few years ago. Have I been accurately informed?"

Too accurately, Gaiety thought. When Elaine had told her that everyone in Savannah already knew about her and her father, she wasn't kidding. And Gaiety wasn't so sure she liked the idea that this man knew so much about her when she didn't even know his name.

Lifting her chin ever so slightly, she said, "Since you know so much about me, who are you?"

He reached over and placed a finger against her lips. She was so stunned she couldn't move.

There was no pressure from his finger. She found it stimulating, alarming, awakening.

"You'll find out," he whispered. "If you're interested enough. Anyone here can tell you who I am. Ask."

She twisted her head away from him and scrubbed her lips with the back of her hand. How dared he touch her so freely, so intimately? How dared he not tell her his name after she'd asked him? Feeling rebuffed, she said, "I'm not interested. I find your arrogance intolerable, and I don't care who you are."

"I think you do, Miss Smith." He chuckled, then turned and walked away.

Gaiety fumed as she watched his retreating back. "And don't presume to touch me again," she called to him. He didn't turn around or acknowledge her as he disappeared into the house. She wanted to run after him and tell him what a dirty trick she thought it was for him to flirt so openly with her and leave without giving his name. But she'd caught the attention of the other couple on the porch when she'd called to him, so she remained quiet and tried to reclaim her aplomb. The nerve of the man! Just who did he think he was to treat her so? The–the no-account poacher.

He was a trespasser one minute and a dashing gentleman the next, then a rogue breaking the accepted rules of social behavior by touching her lips. Well, she wasn't going to let him take her mind off the reason she was here. She wouldn't let the–the rogue cross her mind again. And she'd bite her tongue in two before she'd ask anyone to tell her his name.

Shaking off the effects of that man, she decided she'd go inside and ask someone to point out Mr. Aston Rutledge. After all, meeting him was the reason she was here. And it was time she stopped avoiding the inevitable and found him.

But the minute Gaiety stepped back inside she found it impossible to get away from the young men who wanted to dance with her. As she danced, her gaze scanned the room, trying to pick out the man she'd come to meet. It appeared she was going to have to find Elaine again and ask her to introduce them.

As she searched the room, she saw that her father was having a good time. She'd even seen him on the dance floor a time or two. She hadn't seen him dance since her mother's death. And because of the illness that had crippled him most of the winter in Connecticut, he was not light on his feet.

She noticed something else as she danced. It was impossible to escape from the eyes of the vagabond-turned-gentleman. Whenever she caught his eyes, he would smile at her, that handsome, dashing smile that made her breath catch in her throat. He could watch her all he wanted. She wouldn't give him the satisfaction of asking about him.

A few minutes later, Gaiety was so busy watching for her father and trying to smile at the young man she was dancing with that she didn't realize her dance partner was changing. In one easy motion the young man was gone and in his place was the arrogant man from the pond. He held her and moved effortlessly about the dance floor. The man was definitely trying to make an impression on her. He was stubborn—a trait she easily recognized because it was one of her own. If she were here at the party for pleasure only, she might find herself interested enough to continue his game for as long as he wished. But she had other things on her mind.

"That was a sneaky way to get a dance with me."

"A determined man uses whatever means is at his disposal. Surely I deserve one dance."

"Why would you think that?" she asked, although she was impressed that he wanted to dance with her so badly he'd cut in front of another man. "I don't even know your name."

"I'm wounded. I thought surely you would have asked someone to tell you by now."

She looked into his eyes. He was lying. "No, you didn't. You knew I wouldn't ask."

He smiled. "True. But I had hoped I might be wrong," he said, as the music came to an end. "Shall I remain a stranger to you, then?"

"I think so," she said hesitantly, thinking that she didn't want to go home without knowing his name.

"And why is that?" he asked, as the dancers started leaving the floor.

"You presume too much. A gentleman never

would have been as forward as you've been. A gentleman wouldn't have been poaching on our land, and a–"

"A gentleman wouldn't have touched your lips with his finger or looked so deeply into your eyes. He wouldn't stand before you nameless and tell you he wanted to kiss you."

"That's right," she answered in a whispery voice, knowing she was being drawn closer to him with each word he spoke. She found herself wanting, needing to know more about him.

"So you don't believe I'm a gentleman."

"I think you are a rogue. Every town has one. A handsome, dashing man who flirts with and teases all the young ladies, making each one think she is the most beautiful woman at the par–" Her words faded away and her eyes rounded with sudden fear. Her heartbeat increased and her stomach muscles knotted. She was describing the man Elaine, Bonnie, Linda Sue, and all the others had described to her. She gasped as she looked into his handsome face, his beautiful brown eyes. It couldn't be.

"I believe you have summarized me accurately."

Gaiety wasn't sure she was breathing. A chill went up her back. The music started again.

"May I have this dance?" he asked.

"No," she whispered, unable to say more.

He smiled. "Still holding me to a proper introduction, are you? You win. Mr. Aston Rutledge–at your pleasure, Miss Gaiety Smith." He bowed again.

Her breath came so fast and in such large gulps she thought she might faint. She was speechless. She'd touched the man. She'd laughed with him, talked to him, enjoyed him. She'd actually fallen for his charm. How could she? She should have known! Why had fate drawn her to this man? Her corset was too tight, her throat too dry, her heartbeat too fast. When she'd seen him as a vagabond, she'd liked him. When she'd seen him as a rogue, she'd been intrigued by him. Now she saw him as he really was . . . the man who had destroyed her family.

Because of this handsome man her father and brother had been killed. Theodora and her baby had died, and no one knew what had happened to Titus.

"No," she whispered, as she backed away from him, bumping into someone's shoulder. "No," she said louder. Blinded by tears, by fear from her own feelings, Gaiety turned and fled into the midst of the dancers on the crowded floor.

Aston watched Gaiety disappear among the ballgowns and cutaway jackets. He wondered why she'd reacted so strongly when she'd heard his name. Perhaps he'd pushed her too far too fast. But her rejection of him proved one thing: she wouldn't allow men to be forward with her. He found himself pleased by that. He hadn't lied when he'd told her she was the most beautiful lady at the party. Her golden brown hair was swirled in a mass of curls on top of her head with a small cluster of flowers and ribbons pinned to one side. Her clear blue eyes had sparkled invitingly at him even while she'd rebuffed him.

Yes, Gaiety Smith had proved a challenge. Many women over the years had tried to ignite in him exactly the feelings that Gaiety had awakened. For the first time in his life he'd met a woman he wanted to spend time with. He supposed it was bound to happen.

Chuckling to himself, Aston headed for his study. He wasn't much of a drinker, but he found Gaiety stimulating, and a sip of brandy sounded good to him right now. He usually satisfied himself with the women at the Silver Dollar Tavern, over in the next county. And he was always careful not to go to the same woman twice in a row.

Aston closed the door of his study and strode over to the Hepplewhite sideboard that held an array of spirits in expensive decanters. After pouring himself a generous portion of fine brandy, he walked over to his flat-topped Georgian desk and sat down in his chair. He sipped the sweet, tongue-stinging liquid and let it slide down his throat.

It had been twelve years since Theodora had died, but he remembered their marriage and her death as if they'd happened yesterday. This wasn't the kind of thing a man got over quickly. His hand made a fist. He'd never be trapped by a woman again. No, Gaiety Smith was a beautiful, stimulating young woman who set his loins on fire for a taste of her. But Gaiety wasn't the kind of woman a man fooled around with, and he wasn't interested in any other kind.

A knock sounded on the door, then it opened. Fredrick peered around the trimwork. "I thought I saw you come in here. Mind if I join you?"

Surely Fredrick knew that if Aston had shut the door he wanted to be alone. But Aston liked his younger cousin and decided not to hurt his feelings. "Not at all. May I pour you one?" He held up his brandy glass.

"I wouldn't mind a sip or two," Fredrick said, and pulled on the collar of his shirt. "The party's a smash. Elaine is beside herself with happiness. Everyone seems to be having a good time and the food is delicious." Fredrick patted his stomach and smiled. "Alma does a splendid job of taking care of your house."

"I'm glad you're pleased with the party." Aston handed Fredrick a glass with an ounce of brandy swirling in the bottom of it. He was getting the feeling his cousin had a definite purpose in mind for following him into his office. He seemed nervous.

"Ah—have you met your new neighbor?"

"The Smiths? I've met the daughter—Gaiety."

"I guess there's no chance of you getting that land now, is there?"

"You know I'm more positive than that, Fred. There's always a chance."

He smiled again. "Yes, you're right, of course."

Tired of the small talk, Aston asked, "Did you want something in particular?"

"Ah—well—yes, now that you mentioned it." He took a big swallow of his drink and sucked in his breath. "There's something I wanted to mention to you." He pulled on his collar again. Sweat popped out on his forehead, his gaze shifting nervously around the room.

"Spit it out, Fredrick. What favor do you want?"

He wiped his lips with the back of his hand. "You told me last fall when I asked Elaine to marry me that if you didn't have an heir you would leave Southern Oaks to my heir."

"That hasn't changed. No need for you to worry."

"I'm not. You're a man of your word. But I've been thinking about something else. It's no secret that you don't plan to get married."

Aston sighed and finished his drink. "That hasn't changed either, Fred, so where is this conversation going?"

"Well, I thought if my heir might one day own this plantation, he should be born here and live here so that he'll grow up knowing how to take care of it properly." He took out his handkerchief and wiped the sweat from his brow.

Aston looked at him curiously. Fredrick's suggestion surprised him. "You want me to take your son and raise him here on Southern Oaks? Have you talked with Elaine about this?"

Fredrick chuckled nervously. A twitch developed in one of his eyes. "No, no, you misunderstood me. I was thinking that maybe Elaine and I should live here with you and raise our family here. The house is big enough. You could move up to the third floor to ensure your privacy."

The hair on Aston's arms prickled. "I'm not moving to the third floor," he said in a deadly calm voice.

"Oh, well, you don't have to—I—I was just thinking that it would be easier on Elaine not to have to climb so many stairs when she—has our first child." His hand trembled as he finished off the brandy.

Aston wanted to tell Fredrick that he had no intention of letting him and Elaine move into Southern Oaks, but he could see where his cousin's plan had merit. It would stand to reason that if Fred and Elaine's son inherited the plantation, it would be good for him to have lived here. But did he want his cousin living with him?

"I'll think about it," he said honestly.

"So good of you, Aston," Fredrick said, with some of the blushing color leaving his face.

"But in the meantime, I think you should continue to furnish the house in town."

Three

Gaiety sat on her bedroom windowseat, looking out at the beginning of a beautiful spring day. She'd spent the whole week thinking about the party and Aston Rutledge. After she'd spent a few minutes upstairs collecting herself, she'd gone back downstairs and found Lane. She'd told him she wanted to go home because she was tired, but she had a feeling he'd seen through the lie. He didn't press her to explain, but agreed immediately for them to leave.

When they'd arrived at home, he'd asked her if she'd met Aston. She admitted that she had, and it had shaken her more than she'd thought it would. He'd given her a hug and told her he was ready to listen whenever she wanted to talk about it. Now she had to put that promise to the test. Gaiety was ready to talk about Aston Rutledge.

A few minutes later Gaiety found her father sitting in front of his slant-front desk, a cup of tea in one hand and papers in the other.

"Papa," she called from the doorway of the small library. "Am I disturbing you?"

He glanced over at her and smiled. "Not at all. Come in. I didn't know you were up. A bit early in the morning for you, isn't it?"

"A bit," she agreed. She walked farther into the room. "I'd like to speak with you about something."

He pushed away from the desk. "Certainly. Come in and sit down."

Now that the time had come, she wondered if she could carry through with it. Yes, she had to. For her family's memory, she had to. Her revenge on Aston would be her memorial to her first family.

"What I have to say isn't easy, Papa." Her throat tightened. She should have had a cup of tea first. Maybe then her throat wouldn't feel so dry, her stomach so empty, her heart so heavy.

Lane's pale blue eyes softened. "You know you can talk to me, Gaiety."

She nodded.

Since she'd overheard the sheriff telling his deputy that Aston Rutledge had gotten Theodora pregnant, she'd known she would one day get even. That day had come.

"I know we've been close over the years, Papa, and I love you so very much." She paused and hugged him briefly.

"I know that, dear."

"That's one of the things that makes what I have to say so difficult." She took a deep breath and clasped her hands together in front of her. "I've met the man I want to marry."

Shock registered on his face. "No," he said with disbelief. "You've found someone here in Savannah? So soon!" He moved to the edge of his seat. "But we've been here little more than two weeks, Gaiety. I—I don't know what to say. Was it at the party last Saturday that you met him?"

"Yes," she said, weakening, still worried that she wouldn't be able to go through with this. She didn't want to hurt him. It was madness, but she had to do it. She was the only one left to avenge the death of her family. After meeting Aston, she knew she'd never be happy until she did. And this was the only way she could accomplish it.

"That's wonderful!" Lane's face suddenly beamed with joy. "You know I've wanted you to marry and have children for two years now." He rose from the chair and set his cup on the desk, then reached down and gave her a bear hug.

Tears threatened Gaiety's eyes as her arms circled his broad back. She'd never carry through with her plan, let alone get her father to go along with her, if he saw tears. She fought them. This was too important. She had to do it now, while she had the strength, before she weakened more.

Holding her at arms' length, Lane said, "I met several handsome, well-familied men at the party. Which one did you take a liking to?"

Gaiety shored up her courage by lifting her chin and shoulders. She took a deep breath. "I want to marry Aston Rutledge."

"What!" In an instant Lane's face turned red and his look of joy turned to anger. "Hellfire! Gaiety, what kind of fool thing are you trying to pull? What are you up to now? I've never heard of such a harebrained idea."

"Let me explain, Papa," she said calmly, trying to buffer the blow.

"No!" His fist came down hard on his desk, causing the cup to slosh the tea onto his papers. "Damnation, I won't hear one more word of this fiendish scheme of yours if it has to do with him. Nothing! Nothing you can say will make me agree to you marrying Aston Rutledge."

Gaiety flinched from the heat of his words. But holding her own, she said, "You've never refused to listen to me before, Papa."

"Well, this time I am." He jerked the tail of his waistcoat down over the waistband of his breeches. "I let you talk me into moving here when we could have moved farther south, where it's even warmer. I brought you here hoping that once you met Aston Rutledge you'd see that he's just a normal man and get on with your life. I won't listen to this." He stomped over to the window.

"Papa, why did you buy Lilac Hill?"

"For you," he said, keeping his back to her.

"If you bought it for me, then I assume you expected I might want to live here someday."

"No!" he thundered and faced her. "I paid off the mortgage and back taxes because it was all that was left of your family. It was the least I could do when we couldn't find Titus. I never expected either of us to live here."

"But why did you buy it for me?"

"Damn it! Gaiety, I just told you."

"Why, Papa?" she insisted. "The real reason."

He sighed and turned away from her. "All right, maybe ten years ago I wanted revenge on the man who'd killed your family and caused you so much heartache. But it was Aston's father, Howard, who had your papa and brother killed, not Aston. And Howard died years ago. I'm a little older and a little wiser." He snapped around. "Why would you want to marry the man you've sworn to hate?"

Gaiety took a couple of steps toward him. "I know you said that my revenge is in owning Lilac Hill. We've known all along Aston would like for it to be a part of Southern Oaks. I know he needs the pond to water his cattle when droughts dry up the other ponds."

Lane shook his head. "What has all this to do with you wanting to marry the man?"

Feeling calmer, now that he was going to listen to her, she explained, "When Elaine was here, she told me that Aston had vowed never to remarry."

"We've already talked about this."

"I know, Papa. Please let me tell this my way."

He nodded and grunted, pacing back and forth in front of the window.

"At the party, I kept hearing from all the young women I met how Aston would dance and flirt with all of them, but had never courted any of them."

His eyes widened in exasperation. "So?"

"I want to give him the one thing it appears he doesn't want–a wife."

"This is insane," he argued.

"No. I want to do this for Papa, Josh, Theodora, and Titus. He took their life away from them, now I want to take something from him—his freedom."

"You're talking like a madwoman. I'm going to call Mimi to prepare you a toddy and put you to bed."

She grabbed his arm when he started past her. "Papa, don't call her! I'm not sick or crazy. I've been thinking about this for a whole week. This wasn't an easy decision for me to make. But when I visited Papa's and Josh's gravesite last week, I knew I had to do something." Looking into his eyes, she pleaded, "Papa, how can I not do anything? The sheriff never arrested anyone for the deaths of my father and brother. They were murdered. And you know I've always believed there was more to Theodora's death than I was told. I have to do something."

"You've done something!" he exploded, shaking off her restraining hold. "We've kept this land from Rutledge. He wanted it badly,

Gaiety. He offered five times its value. That's revenge enough."

"No it's not!" she argued.

"It has to be, Gaiety—"

"Maybe it is enough for Gaiety!" she whispered desperately. "But not for Avalina Talbot. You might have changed my name, but not the person I was or the person I am. I vowed I would one day get even with Aston, and I intend to do it by seeing that he marries another Talbot woman." She felt stronger after having admitted that. "You want me to forget that he made my sister pregnant and possibly caused her death, that because of him my father and Josh were killed, and I don't know what happened to Titus. I can't do that. The law did nothing to him."

"That's because it's not a crime to get a woman pregnant," Lane injected. "And, Gaiety, he did the decent thing when he married her."

"What about Papa and Josh? Why wasn't anything done about their deaths?"

"Everyone in attendance at the wedding, including the minister, said both your pa and Josh aimed to shoot. They were killed in self-defense."

"I don't believe that."

"Wake up, Gaiety, do you think a man of the cloth would lie?"

"No, I'm not saying that, Papa—"

"Then what? Gaiety, you still have me."

She almost lost control. This was hurting

him more than she imagined. Should she rethink her plan? Could she? No, she had to go forward. "Yes. And I would do the same for you, Papa."

Lane hung his head. "You have your whole life ahead of you. Stop this madness. You'll never be happy as long as you're trying to get even with this man." He sat back down in his chair and rubbed his forehead, then his eyes.

"I can't get on with my life until I've made him pay for what he did to my family."

"You've gone too far with this plan, Gaiety."

"No, Papa, listen to me." She knelt in front of him and placed her hands on his knees. Looking up into his eyes, she said, "I want you to offer Aston Lilac Hill as a dowry. Tell him you'll sign it over to him the day we are married."

Lane was shaking his head before she finished. "Do you think I'd let you marry a man you don't even like, a man you hate, just so you can fulfill some invalid sense of justice?"

"I won't have to spend too much time with him before the wedding. We may have to go to a party or two together; other than that, I can avoid him. It's not unusual for the bride and groom of an arranged marriage not to see each other but once or twice before the wedding. After the marriage I'll move back home with you. He'll have his house and I'll have mine."

"Do you think I want you to marry a man in name only? My God, Gaiety. I want you to have a good home, and children to take care of."

"But that's not what is going to make me happy." She grabbed his hands and held them in hers. "When I think about how strong and handsome he is, when I see how full of life he is, how confident and carefree, I'm overcome with sorrow and anger. I love you, Papa. I have for many years now. But before you, I had another family. I can't turn my back on them."

"But how can you blame Aston for all that happened?"

"It was *his* fault Theodora was pregnant. If he'd married her without having to be forced at gunpoint, everything would have been different. Everything. That's what makes all this his fault."

Slowly he nodded and pulled his hands from hers. "Yes. Maybe you're right. Things would have been different if he'd simply agreed to marry the girl." He turned sad eyes upon her. "Don't ask this of me, Gaiety."

"I have to, Papa."

"When I saw your sad little face twelve years ago, I knew I had to take you and put a smile on your lips. I gave you the name 'Gaiety' because I wanted to see you laughing and smiling. Isn't it time you let go of this hatred you've been carrying around inside and got on with your life?"

"I can't, Papa. It's been with me too long. I can't just give it up, so I'm going to do something about it."

"And what will you do if in two years you decide you want children."

"I'll adopt a child the same way you adopted me. Somewhere there's a little boy like Titus who needs a home."

"What makes you so sure Aston will agree to marry you?"

She knew he'd found her attractive. She'd use that to her advantage, too, but she didn't want to tell her father that. "I'm betting he wants this land bad enough to say yes."

"And what will you do on your wedding night when Aston expects you in his bed?"

"He won't," she said confidently. "Right after the ceremony, I plan to tell him I'm Avalina Talbot."

"Mr. Smith, I was pleased when I received your note asking me to make time for you today," Aston said, as he poured three fingers of whiskey into a glass. "Naturally, I'm hoping you've decided to reconsider my offer to buy Lilac Hill."

Aston didn't like the way Lane Smith was squirming in his chair. Something was wrong with the man. He'd been surprised when he'd received the older man's message asking for an appointment. When he'd heard Smith was restoring the house, he'd little hope left of ever getting that land.

"Not exactly. But I do have something in mind." He ran a hand over his thinning hair.

"Why don't you call me Lane? And I'll call you Aston, if you don't mind?"

"I'd like that," Aston said, as he handed the man his drink.

Lane drank over half the liquor before bringing the glass down. He swirled the contents in the bottom of the glass, then finished it off. Aston was certain the man was nervous about something. He picked up the decanter and poured Lane another jigger. Could it be that Gaiety had told her father that he'd been fresh with her and he was here to reprimand Aston? When he'd realized that she'd left without saying goodbye, he'd been annoyed with himself for being so forward.

"Thank you," Lane said, as he rose from the chair and faced Aston. "I have an offer to make you. One I'm sure you'll want to consider carefully."

Intrigued, Aston sipped from his glass, noticing that the strong liquor had already reddened the older man's face. "I'm listening."

"You want our land?"

"Yes. I want your land. We've both known that for years. The question is, what do you want in exchange?" Aston managed to ask with a poker face.

"I want you to marry my daughter."

Aston tried to tell himself that he hadn't heard the man correctly, but knew he had. Now he knew why the man was so damn squirmy. Aston might have stepped over the line a little with Gaiety, but there was no harm done to her reputation. He had been approached by fathers wanting him to marry their daughters many times before. He always gave the same answer.

"Naturally, I'm flattered you asked, but I'm not interested."

"I've given this proposal quite a bit of consideration," Lane continued, as if Aston hadn't spoken. "As you can imagine, a decision like this wasn't made easily. You want the land so you can water your cattle, and I want the best possible marriage for Gaiety. You have a well-respected name, and the means to give her the style of life she's used to. I'll give you the deed to the land you want the day you marry her. It will be her dowry."

"Dowry." The word stuck on Aston's tongue as anger hit him like a fist in the stomach. Aston wanted that land badly. He would do anything for that land—except marry. His eyes turned cold and his hand tightened around his glass. "I'm not interested in getting married." Damn! "I'll buy Lilac Hill from you. No strings attached. Name your price."

Lane remained quiet.

"Name your price," Aston said again.

Straightening his back, looking a little put out that Aston had rejected his offer without even thinking about it, Lane asked, "You're unattached, aren't you?"

"I've been married," Aston said, and sipped his drink. This was none of Smith's business, but he felt obliged to explain, "My wife and the child she was carrying died. I don't have any plans to remarry. Ever."

Lane finished off his drink and set the glass on the well-polished desk. "Well, in that case, thanks for listening to me." Lane pulled on the tail of his waistcoat and started out the door.

Aston was surprised that Lane had let the subject drop so quickly. He hadn't even asked him if he wanted to consider it and let him know later. Lane was making it clear he either accepted or rejected his proposal. Aston had never liked the way Yankees did business.

He badly wanted that land. But could he marry again?

He'd been attracted to Gaiety. She was intelligent, beautiful, and spirited. He wouldn't mind taking her to bed, but he certainly didn't want to marry her. Was there any chance he could talk Lane into selling the land without benefit of marriage? And what in the hell did Gaiety think of all this? He knew Gaiety to be the kind of woman who could think for herself. And from the little gossip he'd heard, he knew Lane to be an indulgent father. He could only assume Gaiety had agreed to this proposal.

Memories of the little brown-haired boy he'd picked up at the orphanage flashed through his mind. Titus deserved to have his father's land. After all that had happened to Titus Talbot, how could he let the land slip through his fingers now? He owed it to Titus to do everything possible to get that land.

"Wait," Aston said, calling to Lane. He was sure he saw a gleam of light in the old man's eyes. "I have a proposal of my own," he continued, a plan forming as he spoke. "I don't even know Gaiety. We've only met briefly. Why don't both of you move into Southern Oaks for a few weeks and give us time to talk and get to know each other? I may be persuaded to change my mind about marriage."

"Move in here at Southern Oaks with you? We're less than ten miles apart. Why not simply court her?"

"This way we'll have more time together. It's planting season, and I'm very busy this time of year with the crops. Besides, wouldn't you want to know that Gaiety will be happy living here?"

Lane pulled on the hem of his waistcoat. "Humm. You two could spend more time together if we stayed here?"

Aston nodded.

"See each other every day. Take walks, ride together. Talk and dine together every night." A wide smile split his face. "A splendid idea."

"So you think she'll agree?" Aston asked, knowing it would give him more time to think about the proposal and enjoy the company of the beautiful woman.

Lane clasped his hands together almost joyfully. "I can tell you right now she'll love the idea of spending so much time with you."

Four

Aston had been in a hell of a mood—in a hell of a temper—since Lane Smith had left earlier in the afternoon. He poured himself a drink, then walked out on the front porch and leaned against one of the columns. He loosened his collar and cravat, letting the evening breeze whip down the front of his shirt. He wanted that land. He needed that thirty acres to give to Titus Talbot, but he hadn't planned on getting a bride to go along with it. Silently he cursed that thirty-acre farm.

The night air was cool, but Aston didn't mind. He'd been too restless to spend another minute inside. The black sky was dotted with twinkling stars and dark purple clouds. Crickets, hidden in the grass and shrubs, chirped loudly, and night frogs called to their mates.

Over the years, he'd tried to tell himself that he wasn't responsible for Titus's well-being or his inheritance. It wasn't his fault Theodora had lied. *She* was the one who'd caused the deaths of her father and brother. But because

Howard Rutledge had never seemed to have any remorse over the killings that late Sunday. afternoon, Aston had developed plenty.

Aston's thoughts went back in time to the last big argument he'd had with Theodora a couple of weeks before she'd died. Mrs. Conners, from the orphanage, had been at Southern Oaks that day. The woman wanted Theodora to change her mind about bringing Avalina and Titus to Southern Oaks to live. After several discussions with his father, Aston had finally convinced him to let them take Theodora's brother and sister but Aston couldn't get Theodora's consent. She told him she'd looked after those brats for eight years and she wasn't going to do it anymore. The life she planned for herself at Southern Oaks didn't include her siblings.

After Theodora's death, Aston talked his father into agreeing to let him take Titus away from the orphanage, since Avalina had already been adopted, but he wouldn't agree to Aston bringing the boy to Southern Oaks. Instead, he was given to a childless couple who were on their way to make a new home in Mobile, Alabama. Aston still sent them money once a month to care for Titus.

Somehow Aston felt if he could get that land for Titus his debt to the Talbots would be paid. He would have done all that he could do for the boy, all that anyone, even Titus's father and brother, could have expected.

Aston looked out into the darkness of night

and sipped the slightly sweet brandy. The night wind chilled him as it whipped through his hair. He heard occasional laughter from down in the darkies' quarters. One of the older men was singing a slow, hauntingly mellow tune, adding to Aston's feelings of restlessness.

Aston's father had been dead four years. Their relationship had been strained since the Talbot incident. And he hated to admit to himself he didn't miss his father. But he did miss having someone to talk to, to dine with, and to care about. That's why tonight he was considering Fredrick's idea of moving into Southern Oaks. And that's why he was considering Lane Smith's proposal, too.

He chuckled to himself. What made him suddenly feel so restless, so lonesome? He'd never needed anyone else around before. But he knew.

Her name was Gaiety. He remembered what he'd heard about her after Elaine and Fredrick's party. Beautiful, charming, angelic, and prim and proper. All those things were true, but he also found her outspoken, self-assured, captivating, and seductive. Aston moistened his lips and wiped the taste of brandy from the corners of his mouth. He wanted to kiss Gaiety. He wanted to feel her body pressed next to his with his arms wrapped around her.

He remembered looking into her clear blue eyes. Unlike his own, which were sometimes blue, but more often than not a shade of light green. Her lips were full, generous, and a healthy shade of dusty rose. He liked the way she challenged him with her feminine banter. And he'd liked the fact that she'd never asked anyone his name. Gaiety wasn't coy and childish in her approach to him, and that pleased him.

That day at the pond, and later, when they'd danced, she'd flirted with him like a mature woman who appreciates a man, not like a silly young girl hiding behind her fan. Damn, he'd found her stimulating both physically and intellectually.

What was he to do? He'd vowed never to marry again, a vow he had good reason to make, and one that he'd fully intended to keep. Aston continued to stare out into the darkness. If he stretched the boundaries, he could say that he was being forced into this marriage the same way he'd been forced to marry twelve years ago. But even as he thought that, he knew it wasn't true. Lane had made it clear the decision was entirely up to him. In fact, Smith was ready to accept defeat and walk out. He was the one who'd suggested they move into Southern Oaks so he could get to know Gaiety.

He finished off the brandy and wiped his lips with the back of his hand. It was time to face the truth. He wanted Gaiety in his house. He was intrigued by her. And yes, damn it, he wanted to get to know her better. If he decided he liked her well enough, he would marry her. Aston chuckled again. No, he'd already decided he liked her. If not, he never would have considered Lane's proposal, or asked them to his house. The only thing he had to decide was whether or not he wanted to marry her, or simply give Titus a section of land from Southern Oaks. There was no way in hell he would marry Gaiety just because her father wanted him to.

The only plus he could see to getting married, other than having the land for Titus, was that he'd have a beautiful woman in his bed each night. That brought its own rewards to Lane's proposal and deserved due consideration. Aston looked up at the heavens and pondered.

There were several women he could marry if he wanted only to produce an heir for Southern Oaks. Harriet Hubbard over in Chilton County had been eager to remarry since her husband had died and left her childless. And Harriet had a lot more land than the measly thirty acres of Lilac Hills. If he were honest with himself, he was tired of attending all the parties in Savannah and paying court to the latest bevy of young ladies to come of age.

He found he grew tired of visiting the whores at Madrue's place. All of her women were beautiful and professional lovers. But he found that his desire for her women had lessened over the years.

It all came down to whether or not he could break the vow he'd made to himself. Did he owe Titus that much?

Many times over the years he had wondered,

could he have done more for Titus? And because he was unable to do more than place the boy with a good family, should he break a vow he'd made to himself and see to it that Titus received what he deserved, his father's land? And did he have a choice if he were going to clear his debt to the Talbots?

"Papa, how could you have agreed to something so outlandish as spending a few weeks in *that* man's house?" Gaiety paced back and forth in front of the settee, the ruched hem of her puce-colored dress brushing the table legs as she passed.

"You want to wed *that* man, my dear. You might as well see what he's all about."

"You know that I don't intend for ours to be a real marriage." Gaiety clasped her hands together in front of her, bristling. "We'll simply decline, that's all. I told you I don't want to be in his presence any more than necessary."

"I'm afraid we can't decline." Lane walked over to the brocade-covered armchair and eased himself down, groaning lightly.

"Why?" Gaiety asked, stopping in front of him. "It seems simple enough to me. There are at least a dozen excuses we can make, all of them legitimate and more than acceptable."

Lane winced and rubbed the front of his shoulder with the heel of his hand. "He won't agree to a marriage until he's spent some time with you and gotten to know you. Besides, I'm in favor of the suggestion."

"Papa, I can't believe you'd agree! And since it's an arranged marriage, why should he want to get to know me?" Gaiety peered down at her father.

A wrinkle formed on Lane's forehead. "Damnation, girl. Have you not thought that it may have something to do with the fact he thinks you're serious about wanting to become his wife?" He didn't try to hide his irritation.

Gaiety's lips formed an O. "I think you're probably right." She pursed her lips. "But I hate the thought of *that* man thinking I *want* to marry him."

"That man has a name, and if you're planning on marrying him, you should at least learn to speak his name civilly." Lane switched and started rubbing the other arm. "Spending a few weeks in his house sounds like a wonderful idea to me. It just may help you come to your senses—the ones the good Lord gave you, not the ones that have entered your head since we arrived here."

Gaiety knew she'd upset her father, and with good reason, although she hadn't meant to. She'd begged him to do this for her, and now she was complaining to him because Aston hadn't responded the way she'd wanted him to. She had to realize that Aston Rutledge wasn't going to necessarily fall into line with every idea she had. He'd already proved to her he was a strong-willed man, one who wouldn't easily be fooled.

"I'm sorry, Papa," she said, immediately softening.

Lane remained quiet.

"You're angry with me, aren't you?" she asked.

He looked into her eyes, a serious expression masking his face. "Gaiety, I'm willing to call the whole thing off and tell Aston we've changed our minds." He reached over and placed the tips of his fingers under her chin. "I'll go tonight if you'll but give me the word."

"No, Papa." She shook her head for emphasis. "But I will try my best to convince him to change *his* mind."

"What? How?"

"I'll send him an invitation to come for dinner." She rose and brushed her skirts. "If you'll allow us some time alone, I'll speak to him about this. I'm sure I can get him to agree to marriage without having to spend weeks in his home."

Lane sighed. "Very well, if I can't talk you into changing your mind about this entire scheme, we'll send Maine with the invitation tomorrow. But Gaiety, mark my words." He pointed a finger at her. "He's not a man who is easily swayed from his position. And remember, you're the one who has so much to lose."

Gaiety sat in front of the large embroidery hoop, stitching a flower design on a pair of pillowcases for the guest bedroom. Mimi sat in the chair opposite her, hemming the bottom of a curtain panel. Lane had ridden with Maine into town and the house was quiet. Gaiety knew her father was having a difficult time adjusting to not being busy during the day. She'd promised to go fishing with him when he returned later in the afternoon. Every time she thought about fishing in that pond, she was reminded of Aston and how much she'd liked him before she'd found out who he was. She'd never met a man with such a warm and inviting sense of humor. And she couldn't remember when a man had attracted her more.

"There's no one to talk to around here, Miss Gaiety—not like in Connecticut," Mimi said, breaking into the quiet that had settled around the two. "The houses here are so far apart I could walk a hundred miles and not meet a single neighbor."

"I believe you are stretching the truth, Mimi." Gaiety didn't bother to look up from her stitching. "There's a plantation not more than ten miles from here. I think I heard there are more than forty people who live on Southern Oaks."

"A lot of good that does me. I can't walk that far to visit with their servants. Besides," she whispered and leaned closer to Gaiety. "Most of them are darkies."

Gaiety looked up and smiled at her. "You can say the word out loud, Mimi. There's nothing wrong with it."

Mimi didn't change her sullen expression. "Well, back home all I had to do was walk down the street and I would meet five or six people I knew. Or I could talk to Hazel over the fence. Maine, Jeanette, and Helen get tired of me talking to them all the time. I don't know why. I don't know who else they expect me to talk to, except you and Mr. Lane."

"I never mind you talking to me. You know that," Gaiety said, trying to make her maid feel better. Everything Mimi said was true, and Gaiety knew Mimi missed visiting with all her friends. But Gaiety didn't know what she could do about it. They wouldn't be moving back to Connecticut. And she was just as sure that Maine and Helen grew tired of listening to her all the time. However, Jeanette was more like Gaiety and would listen to Mimi as she cleaned the house.

Gaiety knotted the blue thread she'd been using to make a flower and picked up her basket to search for the right shade of green for the leaves. She caught a glimpse of Mimi's long face and felt prompted to say, "I believe in time you'll learn to like the peacefulness of living out here away from town."

"No, Miss. Not me," Mimi said quickly. "Anyway, who wants peacefulness? Not me." Mimi shook her head as a loud knock sounded on the door. She jumped up from her chair and threw her sewing on top of the cushion. Her brown eyes rounded with delight and a big smile appeared on her face.

"Oh, we have a guest, Miss Gaiety. Maybe it's Miss Elaine, come back to visit with you again. Maybe she brought her maid this time. But if not, I can talk to her driver. He seemed like a nice man last time he was here. A mite older than I'm used to, but he was nice. I'll take him into the kitchen and give him something to drink. You stay right there. I'll bring her in here and tell the driver to meet me at the kitchen door."

Gaiety laughed as Mimi hurried out the door.

Mimi still mumbled to herself as she brushed the wrinkles from her apron. She took a deep breath and threw open the front door. But instead of Miss Elaine and her driver, she saw a tall, lanky young man who looked to be a few years older than her own seventeen years. He whipped his dark gray hat off and held it in front of him. A crease circled his head where his hat left an outline of its shape on his hair.

"How do you do, Miss. I've got a message to deliver to Miss Gaiety Smith."

"Who might you be?" Mimi asked, looking him over carefully. His sandy brown hair fell to the top of his collar. He didn't wear a tie or cravat, but his clean white shirt was buttoned tight at his throat. His eyes were the color of a midsummer sky. He stood too thin and too spindly to make her swoon, but he had caught her eye.

"Hank, from Southern Oaks. Mr. Aston asked me to deliver a message."

After looking him over so thoroughly, Mimi felt flushed. "You can give me the message for Miss Gaiety. I'm her maid." She held out her hand. For a moment, he looked at her hand as if he didn't know what she was doing, so she added, "I'll take the message to her. No need for you to disturb her."

"Oh, it isn't written on paper," he said, finding his voice, still clutching his hat between nervous fingers.

Mimi frowned. "Well, tell me what is it? I can't have you bothering Miss Gaiety."

"Uh—ah, Mr. Aston would be happy to join Miss Gaiety and her father for dinner tomorrow at five o'clock in the evening."

He was tongue-tied around her, a surefire sign that he liked her. That pleased Mimi greatly. She liked him, too. And with Southern Oaks being less than a dozen miles away, she had a feeling she'd be seeing him again. Her pulse raced at the thought.

"I'll tell her." She batted her eyelashes at him a couple of times, then asked, "Would you like something to drink before you return, Mr. Hank?"

"That would be real nice. Except," he paused. "You can call me Hank."

"And I'm Mimi, Hank." She smiled prettily at him as she brushed her hair with an open palm. "Would you like a glass of water or a cup of tea?"

He kept his gaze on her face. "Water would be nice, if it's not too much trouble."

Mimi smiled and batted her lashes again. She couldn't remember the last time she had so much fun talking to a young man. "Not at all, Hank. You go around the house to the back door and wait for me there by the cook house. I'll give Miss Gaiety her message and be around to get it for you in just a minute."

She turned away, but just as quickly spun back to face him. "Hank, would you be driving Mr. Aston over here tomorrow night?"

"Oh, no Miss—Mimi," he said, his voice sounding more confident. "Mr. Aston will ride his horse over tomorrow evening. He doesn't take anyone with him unless he's going into town, and then he usually takes Josie."

Mimi swung her shoulders slightly and smiled as she asked, "And who might Josie be?"

"He's one of the slaves Mr. Aston freed four years ago, after Mr. Aston's father died. He's been at Southern Oaks all his life, I guess. He helps around the house, looks after Mr. Aston."

Mimi nodded excitedly. Hank was just packed full of information and didn't mind talking. Maybe she would learn to like it here in Georgia after all.

"You hurry around to the back of the house and wait for me there." She closed the door behind him and hurried back into the parlor to see Gaiety. She didn't fully stop as she swung by the door and said, "That's a messenger from Mr. Aston. He said Mr. Aston will be here tomorrow evening at five o'clock for dinner. I'm going to give him something to drink before I send him on his way." All of a sudden she stopped short and backed up and stood in the doorway. "It's all right, isn't it?"

"Of course," Gaiety said, then laughed as Mimi dashed away.

Hooking her needle into the material so she wouldn't drop it, Gaiety sat back in her chair thoughtfully. She was agonizing over her mixed feelings for Aston. She would have never found him attractive if she'd known who he was the first time she saw him; she was sure of that. Why had fate tricked her by letting her get interested in him before she discovered his name?

She sighed. It no longer mattered that it had happened. Those feelings had to be put aside. Gaiety had to prepare for her confrontation with Aston tomorrow night.

Gaiety brushed at her blueberry-colored dress and straightened the small bow fastened to the waistband. The skirt of the dress had a silk underskirt with folds of white lace draping over it. The long sleeves had rows of gathered lace at the cuffs. She knew the rich blue color set off her eyes and made them look darker than they actually were.

She'd heard the knock at the door and knew it was time for her to go downstairs. A quick glance in the mirror let her know her inner turmoil didn't show on her face. For that she was grateful.

After struggling and sifting through many different possibilities, she'd decided to tell Mr. Aston Rutledge it simply wasn't permissible for her to spend so much time in his house when they were not formally engaged. She would insist there should be an air of mystery and mystique to their courtship that would be lost if they spent too much time together. And there were still things to be done at Lilac Hill that she should oversee.

Deep inside herself Gaiety was troubled by what she had to do, but she wouldn't let the disquieting feelings rule her. Justice was on her side, she reminded herself, as she headed downstairs to join Aston and her father. Even though Lane didn't approve of what she was doing, she knew he would always stand by her. His support was crucial to her having the strength and courage to carry out her plan.

She swept into the parlor and saw Aston standing in front of a painting of their house in Connecticut. He stood tall, proud, and more handsome than a man of his questionable character should be. Somehow, she had to learn to deny the warm feelings that wanted to grow inside her when she found herself in Aston's presence and learn to concentrate on her goal.

Her gaze quickly darted around the room. Lane wasn't there. She would have to face Aston alone. She couldn't panic. Hadn't she asked her father to give them some time alone?

Taking a deep breath, she willed herself to remain calm inside and out. "Good evening, Mr. Rutledge. How kind of you to accept our invitation to dinner. I'm sorry if we kept you waiting very long."

He turned around. As soon as his gaze lit upon her, a smile flew to his lips. It didn't take a scholar to know that he appreciated the time she'd taken with her appearance and he was pleased to see her.

"You look absolutely stunning tonight, Gaiety. You are a very lovely young lady. Surely no color could look better on you than dark blue."

Pleased by his flattery, charmed by the appealing grin on his lips, Gaiety found her resolve weakened by the sincerity she read in his eyes. As she looked at his strongly built shoulders, wide chest, and long legs, she knew it would have been easy to return compliments. She mentally shook herself, knowing she had to regain her composure and take control.

Gaiety cleared her throat and walked farther into the room to stand before him. "Thank you. Has my father been in to offer you a drink?"

"Not yet. A young lady named Mimi showed me in here."

He took hold of her hand and carried it to his lips and kissed it. Taken aback that he'd kissed her hand when she hadn't offered it, stunned by the smoldering heat his touch sent rushing through her, Gaiety found herself stumbling over her words. "I—I apologize f-for our tardiness. What can I get for you?" She found it difficult to meet his eyes as she gently slipped his fingers out of his cupped hand. It was harder than she thought it would be to feel one way and act another.

"Nothing right now, thank you."

Keeping a pleasant smile on her face even though her stomach muscles knotted, Gaiety said, "I don't know what's keeping Papa, but I'm sure he'll be along shortly. Please sit down. Did Mimi ask if you'd like to freshen up?"

"Yes, but I'm fine. It's not a long ride over here. In fact, I've fished so many times in your pond, I'm sure my horse thinks of this place as home."

Gaiety wondered if he had reason for mentioning the pond. Did he want to remind her of that first meeting, when she'd treated him as a common poacher? Thinking of that time reminded her of how much she'd enjoyed their conversation on the front porch of his home.

Brushing those thoughts aside, she said, "While we're waiting for Papa, I would like to tell you how much we appreciate your generous offer for us to stay with you at Southern Oaks, but we couldn't possibly accept."

"Of course you can." His gaze fluttered across her eyes, down her nose and over her lips. "It's the perfect solution to getting to know each other."

"No, really. There are many things yet to be done to this house that I should personally take care of, and—"

"If I decide we should be married, nothing else need be done to this house," he said, interrupting her. "You will live at Southern Oaks." He looked directly into her eyes and smiled. "I thought a free-thinking young woman like you would want to be sure she'd be happy in her new home and, at the very least, approve of her husband."

Gaiety wanted to look away from his penetrating stare but found she couldn't. "We can have dinner together once or twice a week. That will give us ample time to get to know each other." Her voice was soft and unevenly husky.

"Not good enough. I spend most of my day at my office at the sawmill. I don't want the worry of having to ride back and forth each evening, especially this time of year, when I also have to help oversee the planting of the crops. Besides, I want to know what it's like to have you in the house, waiting for me when I come home for dinner."

Her skin prickled at his bold answer. "Next you'll be asking to know what it's like to have me in your bed before you make up your mind whether or not you want to marry me."

"If you are suggesting it, I might be interested."

Aston chuckled and Gaiety bristled. How dared he make fun of her? "*You* are the one who wants this land, Mr. Rutledge."

"And *you* are the one who wants a husband."

A blush of scarlet stained her cheeks. "I–I

do not!" She felt hot with outrage. "M—my father is arranging this marriage."

He smiled. "Then allow him to do it. Lane and I have already discussed the matter and agreed you should come. What more is there to say?"

Gaiety held firm. "But he hadn't discussed your proposal with me."

"He didn't have to. As you pointed out, marriage proposals are handled between the father and the bridegroom."

She was losing the argument by her own words. "I have objections to moving into your home."

"And I have objections to marriage, but I'm willing to give Lane's proposal consideration. Do you have reason to be afraid to live at Southern Oaks?"

His voice maintained a firmness she couldn't avoid. She swallowed hard and moistened her lips as she turned and moved away from him. "No. Of course not," she lied uneasily, not unaware of the challenge he issued.

"Good. It might be *your* home one day."

"He's right about that, Gaiety," her father said, coming up behind her. "Good evening, Aston. I trust you had a pleasant ride over." He extended his hand.

Aston shook it. "It was, Lane. It's good to see you again."

"I take it you haven't changed your mind. You'd still like for us stay with you at Southern Oaks for a time."

Aston's eyes met Gaiety's. The fine hairs on the back of her neck bristled. She wasn't through fighting this yet. There was still time to get out of residing at that man's house, but maybe she should let it rest for tonight.

"Yes." Aston answered Lane's question but kept his eyes on Gaiety. "It should prove to be a most interesting time as *we* get to know each other. And of course, my household staff will be available to see to your every need and answer any questions you might have."

It was on her tongue to protest again when she was struck by what he'd said. Perhaps she should rethink her objections. Aston's servants would be available to answer any questions she might have. Would that include questions she had about Theodora and her death? She'd always wondered exactly what had happened to make Theodora fall down the stairs.

Yes, staying at Aston's house might be just the thing to do. She could talk to his staff and find out what had really happened between Aston, Theodora, and their baby. Why hadn't she thought about that before?

A quick intake of breath and renewed determination lifted her spirits. She calmly looked at Aston. "In that case, Papa and I will be happy to accept your invitation to visit at Southern Oaks. Now if you'll excuse me, I'll check on dinner."

Gaiety saw the shocked expression on her father's face as she swept past him. No need for him to know what she had planned. She was sure he'd try to talk her out of it. If Aston wanted her to live at his house, so be it. She'd simply use the time to find out what she wanted to know.

Five

"We're going to love it here, Miss Gaiety," Mimi said, as she unpacked Gaiety's trunk and hung her dresses in the wardrobe. "I hope Jeanette and Helen don't get too miserable without us to talk to. Of course, we can visit them once or twice a week, like Mr. Lane said, if you want to. Maine won't mind driving us over to Lilac Hill."

Gaiety answered Mimi with a heavy sigh as she laid her brush and box of hairpins on the dresser. Staying at Aston's house might not be as bad as she'd first thought. They'd arrived late in the afternoon yesterday to find that Aston had been called into town on business and wouldn't return for a couple of days. She might be able to endure her time in his home if he traveled often. And if she planned everything carefully, she shouldn't have to spend too much time in his presence when he was home.

Alma, the older woman who managed the house for Aston, had met them at the door. A gentle-looking woman, she appeared to be close to Lane's age. She'd been friendly but reserved as she'd showed them to their rooms and seen to dinner. Gaiety wondered if it was just her personality, or if she was unhappy that three people were moving into the house for an undetermined amount of time. It was bound to upset the way she was used to doing things.

The housekeeper had served Gaiety and her father a beautifully prepared dinner of roasted duck, potatoes, greens, beets, and bread fresh from the oven. From Alma, Gaiety had learned that two darkies took care of the cooking and three others helped Alma take care of the three-story house which stood in the center of Southern Oaks. Josie, Aston's manservant, was one of them.

Knowing that Aston was going to be gone a couple of days helped Gaiety relax, get settled, and come to terms with the fact that she was living in the house of a man she'd sworn to hate and get even with for what he'd done twelve years ago. She never thought she'd have to live with him to do that.

It pleased her that her father seemed to be having a grand time looking over the stables and the gardens. She'd promised to go riding with him later in the day. Even Mimi was happy. The smile hadn't left her face and she hadn't stopped talking. Gaiety was sure it was because she had more people to talk to, and because a certain young man named Hank lived at Southern Oaks.

Gaiety leaned against the dresser and looked around the room. The walls were stenciled with clusters of softly colored flowers. The coverlet thrown across the bed was crocheted out of a pearl-colored yarn. It was a beautiful room, a large room. She couldn't help but wonder if this bedroom had looked like this when her sister had lived in the house. She wondered if Theodora had had her own room or if she'd shared her husband's room. An odd feeling stole over her when she thought about Aston and Theodora together, but she managed to shake it off.

Mimi continued to talk, but Gaiety wasn't listening. She walked over to the window and pushed the flower-printed drapery panel aside. She looked down upon the rose garden bathed in late afternoon sunlight. The beautiful colors of the blooms winked and twinkled up at her.

Having been at the house only twenty-four hours, she wondered if it was too soon to start asking questions about Theodora. Should she bide her time and wait for the staff to trust her, or would they assume it natural she'd want to know about Aston's first wife?

Her thoughts returned to that time so long ago when the sheriff had told her about her father and Josh. Why hadn't Theodora been there to break the news and comfort her? Why hadn't Theodora visited her and Titus at the orphanage? She'd often wondered about those things when she was younger. As she got older, it was easy to blame her sister's husband.

"Are you listening to me, Miss Gaiety?" Mimi asked, walking up behind her.

Gaiety let the panel drop and turned around to face her young maid. "I'm sorry. I didn't hear what you said. I was thinking about how beautiful it is here."

"Yes, Miss, it is. I've finished unpacking your trunks. Did you want me to do anything else before you have to dress for dinner?"

Looking around the room her gaze lighted on the rosewood dresser and highboy with its bonnet top. Everything was in order. Gaiety said, "No, I think you've done an excellent job, as always."

Mimi beamed with pleasure. "Thank you."

"Tell me, do you like your room?"

"Oh my, yes. It's right beside Alma's room, which is off the warming kitchen. It's the biggest room I've ever had, and a real soft bed, too."

"I don't think there are any small rooms in this house, Mimi," Gaiety said.

"I agree," the maid answered, then continued without a pause. "They have a lot of darkies around here during the day, but none of them stay in the house at night. They have their own little village half a mile away. Alma told me Hank is Mr. Aston's overseer's son. He has his own room in the carriage house just down the road from here."

Gaiety smiled and searched the pretty face of her maid. "I think you are quite taken with that young man."

Mimi opened her mouth to protest, but a knock on the bedroom door silenced her. "Wonder who that could be?" she asked, and hurried to see who was there.

"Papa, come in," Gaiety said, when she saw her father towering over Mimi's head as she swung the door open. "Have you had a good day?" She walked over and kissed him on the cheek.

"I have. Aston has a grand place here. I'm ready to see more of it."

Gaiety looked around the room again, a feeling of restlessness stealing over her. "You're right about this plantation being grand, Papa."

He pulled on the waistband of his trousers. "Are you ready to go for a ride? You need the practice."

That sounded like a good idea. She needed to get out of the house for a while. "Yes. I'll get my hat and gloves and meet you downstairs."

Mimi hurried toward the carriage house a short distance down the way from the cook house. She had at least an hour or two before she had to be back upstairs to help Miss Gaiety dress for dinner. Alma had told her Hank took care of the riding and carriage horses for Mr. Aston. She hoped the older woman hadn't picked up on how interested she was in Hank. He'd sent her heart a fluttering that day he'd come to Lilac Hill, and she was dying to see him again.

Even though the carriage house was basically a barn, care had been taken to see that the outside structure complemented the appearance of the main house and was beautiful to look at. Shrubs had been planted along the front of the building and around the porch.

The double doors were swung wide open so she walked inside the large, semi-dark building. The whinny of a horse signaled her arrival. She stood still for a moment and let her eyes adjust to the darkness within the room. Stalls lined the two side walls and carriages, saddles, and a wagon were lined against the back wall. Mimi wrinkled her nose. It smelled like a barn, an odorous mixture of hay, dirt, and dung.

"Hello," she called.

At one end of the back wall Mimi saw Hank walk out of a doorway. His light brown eyes rounded in surprise when he saw her. He laid the harness he held in his hand on top of the nearest carriage and started toward her. "Mimi, what are you doing down here?"

He stopped in front of her. A thick whiskey-colored substance covered his hands and leather apron and a smear of it graced his cheek.

Mimi gave him a big smile and said, "I asked Alma where you worked. I hope you don't mind?"

"No." He shook his head. His fine sandy-brown hair fell across his eyes and he brushed it away with the back of his wrist. "I was hoping to see you while you were here, but I didn't know—if you wanted to see me."

Mimi clasped her hands together behind her back, slightly swaying back and forth. "I felt the same way, but decided you wouldn't know I wanted to see you if I didn't let you know I wanted to see you." Mimi wondered if she'd said that correctly. Being this close to Hank had her heart thumping and her stomach jumping so fast she could hardly breathe.

Hank smiled, pulled a soiled rag from his apron pocket, and wiped his hands. "This is where I live. Mr. Aston fixed me up a nice place in back of the tack room. Want to see it?"

Mimi studied on his question. It wasn't that she didn't want to see his room; she did. But she knew she couldn't appear too eager or allow improper advances. "I expect I'd best not do that."

"Oh, I didn't mean—I—only wanted—I mean—" Hank's face reddened and his eyes widened as he stuttered over his words.

Mimi laughed lightly, pleased that he hadn't wanted to offend her. "I know you weren't trying to be forward. I can see you're much too nice a man for such as that."

"No, Mimi. Not to you."

"I can't stay. I've got to get back and help Miss Gaiety dress for dinner." She started slowly making her way toward the door. "I don't suppose you make it up to the house very often."

"Sometimes, when I do errands for Alma or Mr. Aston, I have to go up to the house. Like when I went over to Lilac Hill with the message for Miss Gaiety. Mr. Aston wanted to talk to me personally about what to say."

"Well, maybe you'll ask about me sometime when you're there." She stopped just outside the door.

"I will. You can be sure of it. And maybe—you'll take a walk with me some evening when you've finished work for the day."

Mimi's heart thumped loudly. "Maybe," she said, but inside she was dying to say, *How about tonight?* "But I won't be free until after Miss Gaiety goes to bed."

"I understand. I won't mind staying up late to take a walk with you."

Mimi didn't want to leave, but knew she shouldn't appear too eager see him again. From now on, he'd have to make arrangements to see her. She looked up at the tall, lanky young man and batted her eyelashes one last time before hurrying away.

Late in the afternoon Gaiety walked out on the verandah of the house and sat down on the swing that hung from the roof of the wide porch. The light blue sky was littered with puffy white clouds. The air was crisp with spring. It had been three days since Gaiety and her father had arrived at Southern Oaks and there had been no sign of Aston.

She didn't understand why, but that irritated her. She should be immensely happy he had stayed away. Instead, she found herself thinking it ungracious of him to invite them into his home and then not have the courtesy even to show up.

The days were long, and she quickly grew tired of her needlework. If she were at Lilac Hill she could be working on draperies, tablecloths, or quilts, but here at Aston's house, she could work only on the smaller items, like scarfs for dressers or collars and cuffs. She hoped Alma liked the collar she'd embroidered for her. Gaiety had noticed the woman's dresses were plain and thought she might enjoy having the detachable collar.

Gaiety gently rocked the swing, enjoying the stillness of the afternoon. Occasionally she'd hear voices or laughter from the darkies in the quarters or birds chirping in the trees surrounding the house. Aston's three dogs, Pete, Spider, and Alice, were yelping in the distance. Mimi was right: it was much quieter in the Georgia countryside than in the small town where they'd lived in Connecticut.

She enjoyed sharing dinner with her father at the long, highly polished table in the dining room. Alma and Jolly, one of her helpers, did a good job of making them feel comfortable, and the food was superb. She knew she wouldn't be feeling so peaceful if her father were not with her. Tomorrow she planned to go riding again. That should help fill the day. And what she wouldn't give to have a piano to play in the evenings. Her piano hadn't arrived from Connecticut yet. But as soon as it did, she would go over and make sure it had come to no harm.

The front door opened and Gaiety looked up to see Alma. She was carrying a rug thrown over one arm.

"Good afternoon, Miss Gaiety. I didn't know you were out here."

"Hello, Alma. I was tired of stitching and thought I'd rest for a while. It's a beautiful day." Alma took the rug to the other end of the porch and shook it fiercely. Dust particles flew into the open air, causing Alma to sneeze.

When the housekeeper had finished with the rug, Gaiety thought it might be a good time to give the woman the collar she'd made for her.

Gaiety rose and walked over to where Alma stood folding the tightly woven rug. She pulled the flower-embossed collar out of her pocket and said, "Alma, I hope you don't mind, but I made this for you. I haven't seen you wear a collar and thought you might like it."

An appreciative smile spread across the woman's face. "Oh, Miss Gaiety, this is beautiful. The colors are so bright and cheerful." She laid the rug aside and took the white collar in her hands. Carrying it close to her eyes she stared at the delicately stitched flowers on either side.

"I'm so pleased you like it."

Alma looked up at her. "I do. I was never clever with small needlework like this. Thank you."

"Let's see how it looks on you," Gaiety said.

Alma draped the wide flair of material around her neck and Gaiety stepped behind her and fastened the two buttons at the back. "There. It looks lovely."

"I can't thank you enough." Alma tucked a strand of gray hair back under her chignon and smiled graciously.

"Nonsense. I wanted to do it for you. I get tired of working on the same things all the time. And Mimi has more collars and cuffs than she can wear. Now, tell me, is there anything in the house I can do? Do you need help with the sewing, planning the menus, or keeping the household accounts? I'm very good with sums."

"Oh, no, thank you, Miss Gaiety. I have a hard time finding enough things to do for all the help we have now. Mr. Aston wouldn't want me to let you lift a finger to do any kind of work, including the account books. He said you were to relax and enjoy your time with us."

Gaiety couldn't help but wonder how *Mr.* Aston would enjoy having nothing to do but needlework. But she smiled at Alma and asked, "How long have you been here?"

"Oh my, I guess it's close to thirty years now." She reached up and fingered the embroidered flowers on the collar.

"So you were here when Aston married his first wife." Gaiety hadn't meant to ask that right now. It had just popped out as the natural response after her first question. She didn't want Alma to think she'd made the collar for her and now expected information from her.

The smile left Alma's face, and she picked up the rug. "Yes."

"I hear she died when she was very young."

"That's right. It was a tragic thing to have happened. Death always is. I was Mr. Aston's mother's maid until she died. Mr. Aston's father kept me on as the housekeeper. That was more than fifteen years ago."

Surprised at how quickly Alma had changed from friendly back to coolly reserved, Gaiety smiled warmly at her. It was apparent Alma didn't want to talk about Theodora, for she'd quickly moved the conversation back to herself. And Gaiety liked her enough to respect her wishes . . . for now. But the time would come when she would ask again and she wouldn't be so easily put off.

When it came right down to what she should do, Gaiety knew that Aston was the only person she should question about Theodora, but she didn't trust him to tell the truth. She knew her sister had fallen down the stairs, but what had made her fall?

Gaiety noticed Alma still watching her, so she said, "Then you were a young woman when you came here."

"Yes, I was. Probably not much older than your maid Mimi."

"She's seventeen."

The smile returned to Alma's face. "I was closer to twenty."

Gaiety walked back toward the swing. "Tell me, what's for dinner tonight? I'm feeling hungry."

"That shouldn't be a problem. I told Jolly to boil a chicken and drop some corn dumplings in and make a thick soup. It will be easy to serve that—" The sound of an approaching horse drew Alma's attention and she stopped. She and Gaiety stood silently and watched the rider approach.

"That's Mr. Aston," Alma said, when the man and horse came into full view, but Gaiety had already recognized the erect figure who sat so proudly in the saddle.

"I'll leave you to greet Mr. Aston and I'll go tell Jolly and Aleta to set his place."

Alma hurried away and Gaiety kept her eyes on the rider. It was odd how she had subconsciously anticipated his arrival. She'd wanted him to come, yet she'd wanted him to stay away forever. There was a tingling along her spine and a fluttering in her stomach.

From the corner of her eye she saw Hank walking toward the porch. He must have heard the horse, too. Apparently everyone got busy when Mr. Aston returned to the plantation.

Aston dismounted from the horse and threw the reins over the hitching post. He looked freshly handsome, even though Gaiety knew it was more than an hour's ride into town. He should at least look a little tired or dusty.

He handed his gloves to Hank and mounted the steps, taking off his hat as he took them two at a time. The teasing grin she'd come to know was firmly on his lips. She had to fight an overwhelming desire to be happy to see him, happy he was finally home.

"Watching for my return, Gaiety?" he asked, stopping in front of her. "Very dutiful of you. I'm impressed."

His arrogance caused her to glare at him even as she found her body responding to the sight of him. "I was not watching or waiting for you. I merely came outside for fresh air."

"In that case, Gaiety, you have excellent timing."

Unable to hold on to her temper, she asked, "Did your mother not teach you that if you invite someone to your house for a visit, you should be there to greet them when they arrive?"

He bowed and his light brown hair fell attractively across his face. "I do apologize. I asked Alma to tell you that unexpected business took me into Savannah for a few days."

"She did." Gaiety remained coolly distant in manner, refusing to be placated by his conciliatory tone or his disarming grin.

Showing he wouldn't be humbled or intimidated, Aston smiled and said, "It was extremely important to the well-being of Southern Oaks, or I surely would have been here to greet you and your father and welcome you into my home."

Imposing self-control, Gaiety held her anger in check and politely responded, "I accept your apology."

"Thank you, and I insist upon apologizing to your father personally."

"He's not here." She forced herself to remain stiff as she spoke to him, knowing it would be so easy to soften and enjoy Aston. "He rode over to Lilac Hill for the day."

"Then I'll apologize to him at dinner tonight." He walked past her but turned to face her again as he reached the door. "And, Gaiety, I think I'm going to enjoying having you in my house." He winked at her and walked inside.

Gaiety fumed. How dared he be so casual! But even as she thought that, she knew it was his friendly manner that had attracted her to him when she'd talked with him at the pond. Her hands curled into tight fists of frustration as she walked to the edge of the porch. Why couldn't Aston Rutledge have been the evil old man she'd always imagined him to be? Why did he have to be young, charming, and so very appealing to her senses?

After looking over the paperwork stacked on his desk, then changing into a fresh suit, Aston went into the parlor to pour himself a drink and wait for Gaiety and Lane to join him for dinner.

He wasn't surprised Gaiety was upset about his absence when she arrived. From the first time he saw her, he knew she was a woman who liked things done the socially accepted way. Why else would she have told him to go to the back door?

Aston chuckled to himself. He liked that about her, and it told him she would know how to manage his house and keep it orderly. She'd also proved she could hold her own with him. But more important, he believed there was a passionate woman behind those clear blue eyes. And that intrigued him more than the quick responses and spicy looks she gave him.

When he thought about it, he realized he actually wanted to pursue her. Yes, he wanted her in his home, where he could talk to her, look at her, and enjoy her.

"Oh, Aston, there you are," Lane said, as he strode hurriedly into the parlor.

Aston set down his drink and met Lane in the center of the room with outstretched hand. "Lane, I'm sorry I couldn't be here when you and Gaiety arrived. One of my buyers came into town unexpectedly and I had to talk with him about this year's crops."

Lane shook his hand. "No harm done. My daughter and I have been quite comfortable. We took advantage of the hospitality you offered and have enjoyed riding over your property and walking through your gardens."

"Glad to hear it. What can I get you to drink?"

"Your Scotch is good. A little of that would do nicely."

"Sit down. Gaiety tells me you spent today at Lilac Hill," Aston said as he poured the drink.

"Yes. I need to speak with you about that." Lane grunted as he took a seat on one of the gold-striped wing chairs. "I had a letter waiting for me when I arrived. I'm afraid I have to go to Connecticut on business. I'm not sure when I'll return. Though it shouldn't take more than two or three weeks to clear up the matter once I'm there."

The pleasant expression faded from Aston's face. He handed Lane the drink. "What? You have to leave Southern Oaks?" Aston couldn't keep the dissatisfaction out of his voice.

"Oh, yes." Lane sipped the drink, then smiled. "Just as you were called away to attend to business, so was I."

Aston felt an unusual twinge of disappointment. He didn't want Gaiety to leave his home, and that surprised him. He remembered the warm feeling that washed over him when he'd looked up and seen Gaiety standing on the porch waiting for him. All right, he thought, as something pricked his conscious. She said she wasn't waiting for him, but it had looked that way at the time. And whether or not she was watching for him when he rode up, he liked the fact that she was there.

"I realize this has happened suddenly. It's a shame that you've just arrived and we'll be leaving. But that's the way of it."

Aston felt a tightening in his jaw. He wouldn't let her go. But how could he keep her here? And when had he become so possessive of the woman? He wasn't sure he liked that. Aston eased into the chair opposite Lane, knowing he had to be careful how he handled this. "I understand that you have to go for business." He paused. "But is it necessary that Gaiety accompany you?"

Lane eyed him carefully. "Well, I've not thought about making the trip without her."

"Would you? Think about making the trip without her?"

"Well—uh—I don't know." Lane shifted in his chair. "I know you wanted to get to know her, but I—I don't think it would be appropriate for her to stay here without me."

Aston didn't understand it, but he had an overpowering need to have Gaiety with him. It was if he'd already decided she belonged to him. He took it as a challenge to keep her at Southern Oaks. He kept his voice level and smooth as he said, "Lane, I assure you I will protect Gaiety as if she were already my wife. And there shouldn't be a hint of scandal as long as Alma and her maid are here with her as chaperones."

"I don't think you know what you're asking." Lane sipped his drink.

Aston remained silent, giving her father time to think.

At last the older man said, "I don't think it's the right thing to do."

Trying to remain cool and not let his emotions get out of hand, Aston said, "Lane, you have my word as a gentleman I'll be a circumspect guardian of Gaiety. If she's to be my wife, the last thing I would do is harm her reputation. Surely you agree to that."

"Yes. But keep in mind that Gaiety didn't want to come here in the first place. I have to consider her thoughts on this suggestion."

Aston smiled. "I remember. However, I don't think she's unhappy, now that she's here."

Gaiety's father seemed to be studying the matter a few moments, so Aston remained quiet. He couldn't explain why he was so bent on her staying. Maybe it was just that she intrigued him, and maybe it was more than that.

Finally, Lane said, "I'll agree to it on one condition."

"Name it."

"You'll have to have an answer for me by the time I return. Yes or no to marrying Gaiety. It will be a week's travel to and from Connecticut, two or three weeks there. You must be ready to give me your decision."

The message in the older man's eyes told Aston there'd be no compromise on this point. In five to six weeks he had to have an answer as to whether or not he'd marry Gaiety. "You have my word," Aston said, knowing that the question he had to answer wasn't whether or not he wanted to marry Gaiety. He'd be a fool not to. The question was, did he want to marry?

Lane finished his drink, then looked at Aston. "I'll talk to Gaiety after dinner."

"Papa, come in," Gaiety said, as she removed the silver and pearl earrings she'd worn to dinner. She laid them on the dresser and faced her father. She was certain she would get a lecture from him about taking Aston to task over his ideas concerning the expansion of the railroad.

Lane turned to the maid. "I'd like to speak to Gaiety alone, Mimi."

"Yes, sir," she said. "I'll wait down the hall for you, Miss Gaiety. Call me when you're ready to change."

"Thank you." Gaiety closed the door behind Mimi. She didn't like the expression on her father's face. He wouldn't ask to speak to her alone if he didn't plan to reprimand her.

"I'm sorry, Papa. I know I must have embarrassed you tonight by speaking my mind, but that man gets my temper hot. To think, he agrees to laying railroad westward before—"

"Gaiety, that's not why I came in here."

"Oh. What is it, Papa?" she asked, walking over to join him in front of the window.

"Today I received disturbing news." He ran a hand over his thinning hair.

"What? Come sit down and tell me." She led him over to her slipper chair and knelt in front of him as he lowered himself into it.

"Maine gave me a letter that was delivered to Lilac Hill after we left." He reached into his pocket and handed it to her. "No need for you to take time to read it now. It's from the wife of the man who bought the ironworks from me. It seems he died suddenly a week after we left."

"Oh, Papa, what a terrible thing to have happened. He was a nice man." She slipped the letter in her pocket to read later, as her father had suggested.

Lane nodded. "For sure. It's a downright shame." He held his shoulder and rotated it a couple of times as if trying to loosen the joint. "Their only son is twelve, and not old enough to take over the running of the business. She asks if I can possibly come back and help until she can get her affairs in order and find a competent manager."

"I don't want you to have to make that long trip back to Connecticut, Papa. Surely you can write to her and recommend someone to her."

He looked into Gaiety's eyes. "I'm not sure I can. She's not looking for someone who can work the iron. She's looking for a manager she can trust to keep the workers going as well as balance the account books until her son is old enough to take over the business.

"But, Papa that's her problem now, not yours. That long, bumpy trip is hard on you.

And it's still cold in Connecticut. I know you've felt better since we've been here."

"All you say is true, Gaiety. But you know how difficult it was for me to give up that business. I can't let her turn it over to just anyone. Not when she's asked for my help. I feel I have to go. Besides, it's April now. It will be much warmer than when we left."

Gaiety immediately had mixed feelings about going to Connecticut. In a way, it was a godsend. She was having trouble keeping her mind on the reason she was at Southern Oaks. But on the other hand, she saw all her plans crumpling in front of her. Everything was in motion for her to exact her revenge on Aston. Now she would have to put it off until they could return. He might not be so accommodating when she returned, but she couldn't refuse her father. He was right to want to help the woman. She knew how much he'd given up when he'd sold his company to move south. If he wanted to go, they would.

She took hold of his hand and smiled, happy that she could do something to please him. "You're right, of course. We'll pack tonight and be ready to leave at first light tomorrow. There's no need to wait."

Lane gave her a half smile. "No, dear." He touched her cheek with the palm of his hand and gave it a couple of pats. "You won't be going with me."

Stunned for a moment she said, "Papa, I—I don't understand what you mean."

"I've agreed you should stay here at Southern Oaks with Aston as your guardian while I'm away."

"What? That man my guardian! Papa, how could you? I loathe the idea." She was too shocked to move. "I don't want to stay here without you."

He pursed his lips and nodded slowly. "It's like this. I've gone along with you on this outlandish scheme. Now, you'll have to go along with me on this. You'll be staying."

Gaiety swallowed hard. It was seldom her father took such a firm stand with her. She moistened her lips and stepped away from him. "All right, Papa."

"I don't need you to go with me. In fact, I may only be there two or three weeks at most. You see, girl, just as you know how important it is for me to go back to Connecticut and help Olivia Taylor, I know how important it is for you to stay here and settle this hatred you have in your heart. The sooner you get this revenge out of your system, the sooner you'll get on with the life I've always intended you have. You know, I don't like seeing you this way."

Gaiety's heart saddened. "Oh, Papa, I know what this is doing to you, and I'm so very sorry. But I don't have a choice."

"Yes, you do."

She lowered her lashes over her eyes. "Not one I can live with."

"I know. That's why you have to stay here

and settle this madness you have inside you once and for all."

"But I don't want you traveling alone."

"Who says I'll be alone? Maine will be with me. And the coldest days of spring will be gone by the time I get there next week. Jeanette and Helen can manage Lilac Hill quite well on their own. You might want to send Mimi over once or twice a week to see if they need any supplies. And you will be adequately chaperoned with Mimi and Alma in the house."

Gaiety wondered if she should tell her father she couldn't go through this without his strength, but knew he'd see it as a weakness. She took a deep breath and shored up her courage.

"You're right. I'll have Mimi to look after me, and Maine will take care of you. Do what you can for this woman and the company, but hurry home, Papa. You know I need you."

"Yes." He patted her cheek again. "I know how much you need me, and that is the only thing that will worry me while I'm gone."

Six

Two days after her father left, Gaiety worked on her embroidery in the brightly lit sunroom and remembered the previous evening with Aston. She'd been very cool and distant toward him during dinner, answering only the questions he asked. After dessert, when he'd asked her to join him for coffee in the parlor, she'd insisted Mimi stay with them. It was easier for her to keep her guard up with Aston when others were around. When they were alone together, she found herself softening toward him. That would never do.

She was glad Aston hadn't questioned her about her life in Connecticut. If it was at all possible, she didn't want him to know she'd been adopted until they were married and she told him she was Avalina Talbot. Always at the back of her mind was a small voice that told her to drop the entire idea, but she'd remember her father, Josh's young face, and Theodora with pale brown hair and sky blue eyes. How could she live with herself if she didn't do something? The perfect revenge would be coercing Aston into marrying. The perfect justice would be that Aston marry another Talbot woman.

"Hello?" someone called from the front of the house, startling Gaiety from her thoughts. "Is anyone home?" the man asked.

Gaiety didn't recognize the male voice. She knew that Aston had left the house right after breakfast. She waited in her chair for a moment, thinking Mimi or Alma would take care of the gentleman. Then she remembered Alma and Mimi were up in the attic looking for a larger embroidery hoop for her, so Gaiety left the needle in the material and walked into the hallway, wondering who felt comfortable enough to enter the house without knocking or being properly announced by Josie, Alma, or one of the servants.

A tall, well-dressed young man stepped out of the parlor as she approached the front of the house. "Oh, Fredrick, good afternoon." She smiled pleasantly at him and started toward him.

His dark brown eyes registered his shock at seeing her. He was clearly taken aback. "Gaiety, what a surprise, but so nice to see you again. How are you?"

"Very well. And you?"

"Good." He took hold of her hand and politely kissed it. "You look fresh as a flower in morning sunshine in that yellow dress. It's so becoming." He hung his hat on the hat tree in the corner of the foyer.

He was filled with flattery. Gaiety had discovered early in her teens that most men were. "It's good to see you again. How is Elaine? I enjoyed her so much. And the party was simply grand."

"She's very well. Thank you for asking. I'll be spending the weekend with her at her father's house in town."

"Do tell her that I hope I'll be seeing her again soon."

"I'll be sure to." He looked down the hallway, then back to Gaiety. He scratched the back of his head as if confused about something. "Is Aston here?" he asked, his dark brown eyes looking into hers.

"Not right now. I assume he's about the normal things he usually does each day. Alma said I shouldn't expect him back before dinner. Alma and Mimi are up in the attic. I'll call Josie to get you something to drink."

Fredrick rubbed his chin thoughtfully. "No thanks, but I will be staying for dinner and a bed for the night, if Aston doesn't mind."

"Oh, I'm sure he won't," she replied, clasping her hands together and holding them in front of her skirt. "You are his cousin, after all."

"It's a shame you came over for a visit and Aston isn't here to entertain you." He smiled a little sheepishly and slipped his hands into the pocket of his wide-striped trousers.

Gaiety laughed lightly as she tried to figure out if Fredrick was being friendly or sarcastic. "Oh, I don't mind. You see, I'm staying here at Southern Oaks for a few weeks. I don't expect him to entertain me."

"Really?" Again he was unable to hide his surprise. He wrinkled his forehead, drawing his tapered eyebrows together as the full weight of her words registered on him.

"Yes." Keeping the smile on her face, Gaiety hesitated. Should she tell him the real reason she was at Southern Oaks was so Aston could look her over and decide whether or not he wanted to accept her father's offer of marriage for land? No. It was none of his concern. He was Aston's cousin and she'd leave it up to Aston to tell the young man whatever he wished, be it truth or lie.

"I find that surprising. You just moved here. Is there trouble at your house?"

Fredrick took his hands out of his pockets and folded his arms across his chest. Gaiety was sure he was getting ready to question her at length, on exactly what was going on between the two of them. His curiosity almost jumped out at her.

Gaiety deliberately started walking back toward the sunroom. "Oh, no. Everything is fine at Lilac Hill. And it's not so surprising I'm here," she answered. "My father had to return to Connecticut on an unexpected business matter and arranged for me to stay here under Aston's guardianship while he's away." That was close to the whole truth and as much as she intended to say.

"That strikes me a bit odd." He scratched the back of his head again and a baffled expression crossed his face.

She paused just inside the doorway. "I don't see why," she said, intentionally misreading his remark. "I'm perfectly chaperoned here with my maid and Alma." Then, remembering Aston's cool remark, she added, "And I'm quite sure Aston's reputation isn't in any danger from me."

"Ah—no, I'm—sure you are both well chaperoned. Yes," he stuttered, as they stepped into the sunroom. "I only meant that Aston doesn't usually—" He paused. "Well, I think I'll ride over the property a bit and see if I can find Aston. I—I'll see you for dinner."

"I'm happy you'll be joining us," she answered.

Gaiety watched Fredrick nod, then hurry out. Her visit to Southern Oaks had clearly disturbed Aston's cousin and Gaiety wondered why.

Aston couldn't fault Gaiety on her manners, her charm, her appearance. If he wanted a wife, she'd be perfect. She almost had Fredrick eating out of her hand, she was so pleasing throughout dinner and dessert. Aston even found himself falling under her spell and wishing he were alone with her so he wouldn't have to share her intellect and beauty with his cousin.

But the minute coffee was finished, Gaiety excused herself to her room as any proper young woman would have, leaving the men to enjoy a brandy or smoke if they wished.

Aston poured a small amount of aged port into two glasses and walked out on the verandah to join Fredrick. He'd been surprised to arrive home late in the afternoon and find his cousin waiting for him at the stables. The spring breeze was cool but gentle, soothing him immediately. The crickets, frogs, night birds, and other sounds welcomed him into their world.

Fredrick leaned against one of the columns, smoke from his pipe swirling about his head. Aston had never developed a taste for tobacco but found the scent of a freshly lit pipe pleasant enough. A clearly defined half moon hung high in the starry night sky and shone down on the porch with a pale light. He found himself wishing Gaiety was the person waiting for him on the porch.

He handed Fredrick a glass, then walked over to one of the high-backed rockers and sat down, content to enjoy his drink, the night, and thoughts of the intriguing, lovely young lady upstairs.

"It's a bit unusual for you to have a young woman staying at your house, isn't it?"

Aston cut his eyes around to Fredrick. He wasn't in the mood for conversation, and with short answers Fredrick might get the hint. "No."

Fredrick had been too forward as of late. Aston had always liked his cousin, but he was pushing his luck recently. He wasn't about to get into a discussion about his personal life with him.

"Well, I don't believe that you ever have before." Fredrick paused. "In fact, with the way you feel about women, I'm downright surprised you'd let one spend the night in your house."

Aston couldn't let that challenge go unanswered, no matter how much he wanted to be alone with his thoughts. "What kind of remark is that, Fredrick? You make it sound as if I hate women when just the opposite is true. I find most women very enjoyable company. Can't imagine what I did to make you think otherwise."

Fredrick blew smoke into the air and it curled around his head before the night wind took it away. He propped one foot on the white pillar behind him and sipped his drink again. "Well, you have to admit, you've never spent a lot of time with a woman of standing. Never courted one."

"So?" Aston didn't intend to make this easy for Fredrick. If his younger cousin was so eager to know about his business, Aston intended to make him sweat out each question.

"It's a bit unnerving, is all." Fredrick cleared his throat and sipped his port.

"Why?"

"Well, you did say that you'd never get close

enough to a woman again so she could say you were the father of her baby or trap you into marriage."

That was true, and the whole damn county knew it. He'd made the mistake of telling a pushy father that at a party when he was twenty. From the day he was born to Howard Rutledge, the owner of Southern Oaks, he'd been the most eligible male in town. Theodora Talbot had known that, too. His place in the community hadn't changed after Theodora's death. As soon as the proper mourning time had passed, the fathers of the county had come calling with proposals of marriage to their daughters. And that hadn't changed. The proof lay in one of his beds upstairs.

"That's a tiring subject, Fredrick, and it's none of your business. Besides, I doubt Gaiety is going to accuse me of ruining her reputation. You saw her tonight. She refuses to be left alone in my presence for even a moment. And since her father left, her maid sleeps on a cot in her room. I don't think I have to fear Gaiety. I'm merely looking after her while her father is away."

"Well, surely you must agree I have cause to be concerned." He walked closer to where Aston was sitting. "You've promised Southern Oaks to my son."

"*If* I don't have a son of my own, Fredrick. That's always been the case."

"I've never had cause to worry about that until now. In fact, the reason I stopped by today was that I wanted to talk with you again about the possibility of Elaine and me moving in here with you after our marriage."

Aston sat up straight, alarmed by his cousin's words. He'd had the two of them with him the week before the party, and that was all he could handle.

"She's healthy," Fredrick continued. "She should bear me a son within a year of our wedding."

Rising from the chair, Aston said, "Elaine may do that, but I don't think moving in here will work. I like my privacy."

"Privacy? With Gaiety here? Surely you—"

"Don't question me on what I do, Fredrick," Aston interrupted, in a tone meant to let the young man know he'd gone too far. He stood before him and met Fredrick's reluctant gaze.

His eyelashes fluttered uncontrollably, his lips paled a little, and there was a noticeable twitch in a muscle that ran just beneath his jawline. "I—I'm just trying to see that you don't go back on your word."

Aston took a step closer and backed Fredrick against a column. "Don't threaten me, Cousin. My word to you I'll keep. If *I* don't have an heir upon my death, I'll leave Southern Oaks to your son. That hasn't changed. Don't give me reason to regret my decision or to change my mind."

"I—I won't." His voice was unsteady as he continued. "I only thought it would help if Elaine and I lived here. That way, the future heir could grow up here on the plantation. Right from the start he'd know his place in life."

Broadly, Fredrick's idea had merit, but it didn't make Aston like it any better. "We'll talk about that possibility when you have a son." Aston started to let it go at that, but realized he couldn't, so he added, "And if *I* don't."

"All right. Agreed." Fredrick stood quietly a moment longer. He knocked the tobacco out of his pipe, then mumbled something about being tired and that he was going to bed. After a hastily said goodnight, Fredrick excused himself and went inside.

Aston finished his drink and thought about Fredrick's suggestion. And the more he thought about it, the more he was certain he didn't want his cousin and his little wife making Southern Oaks their home. Just maybe he was going to have to renounce the vow he'd made many years ago and marry and have a son.

Sleep had eluded her, so Gaiety lay in her bed, reading a book by low candlelight. Mimi lay soundly asleep on her cot over by the window. Gaiety had been so nervous at dinner trying to be charming to Aston and Fredrick that she'd hardly eaten a thing. The growl in her empty stomach told her she wouldn't find peace until she found nourishment.

The house had been quiet for more than an hour, so she felt sure everyone was in bed asleep. It should be safe for her to go downstairs and see if Alma had left anything to eat in the warming room. Careful not to make any noise, she stepped into her slippers and put on her long-sleeved cotton robe, belting it at the waist with a gold-braided sash. She picked up the candle to light her way and quietly opened the door.

In one hand she held the candle and in the other she held up the hem of her robe and nightdress as she made her way down the stairs. The house was darker in the hallway where there were no windows to let in shafts of moonlight. She took her time and made her way through the elaborately decorated dining room and into the warming room. She was thankful the door leading into Alma's room was shut tight. Gaiety didn't want to awaken her.

After setting the candle on the counter, she found a pone of bread under a napkin and milk in a bucket covered by a piece of cheesecloth. Not bothering to skim the cream, she dipped the ladle into the milk and filled a cup. She took the candle and her fare over to the small worktable in the center of the room and sat down to enjoy her meal.

The milk was tepid but rich with cream, the bread cold but fresh. Feeling comfortable, she pulled out another chair and propped her feet up in the seat. The relaxed position caused her robe and gown to rise to her knees and expose her legs. She leaned back, content to enjoy the late night supper.

A few minutes later, after popping the last bite of bread into her mouth, she reached for her milk again and from the corner of her eye realized there was a faint light shining in the doorway. Startled, she jumped, jerking her feet to the floor. She hadn't heard a sound. She turned to see Aston lounging against the door-frame, shirtless and holding a candlestick.

"Hungry?" he asked, grinning. "Comfy, are you?"

Gaiety scrambled to make sure her legs were covered and to sit up straight. Why hadn't she heard him approach? With nervous fingers she threw her long hair over her shoulders and fiddled with the front of her robe to make sure it was closed properly.

That Aston had caught her in such a relaxed state didn't bother her so much. That he was amused by it did. She didn't think it funny. He'd almost scared the life out of her. She bit back the angry retort she wanted to make and said, "I'm sorry if I awakened you. I tried not to make any noise."

"I'm a light sleeper."

"I'll have to remember that," she said tightly.

"Mind if I join you?" He walked over to the table and sat down in the chair that had held her feet. He set his candle on the table and the extra light cast shimmers on his bare chest and made his softly-golden-colored skin gleam.

"It's not acceptable for you to join me. We're

not properly dressed, and there is no one else present," she said, clutching her robe together at the throat, trying her best not to look at those rippling muscles in his chest and arms, but knowing she was losing. She wanted to study him at leisure. She wanted to touch him.

"I'll try not to let you ruin my reputation. Besides, I'm not going to tell anyone we met down here, are you?"

His smile was so pleasing, his presence so enticing, it drove her to distraction. Of course not, she thought, but she managed only to shake her head.

Aston grinned again. "I'm not surprised you're hungry. You didn't eat much tonight at dinner. I hope I don't make you nervous."

"Don't be silly," she said, regaining some of her aplomb. "Of course not," she lied and let her hands fall to her lap, willing herself to hold them still. "I wasn't hungry at dinner."

"Maybe I should tell Alma to always leave a little something more than bread in case you make a habit of getting up in the middle of the night to eat."

He was still teasing her, but it wasn't bothering her so much anymore. In fact, she probably wouldn't mind talking to him for a few minutes if she were not dressed in her nightclothes and he without a shirt.

"That's not necessary. Milk and bread are fine."

He picked up her cup and drank from it.

"The milk is rich. You didn't separate the cream."

Astonished that he'd be so bold as to drink from her cup, she remained silent and looked into his eyes. Against her will, she was very much aware that he was a man and she a woman. By the softness she saw in his expression, he was aware of that, too. She shook her head, not to answer his question but to clear the fog of intimacy that surrounded them. He stirred feelings inside her that she wanted to keep hidden, untouched. She had set out to deceive and manipulate this man, she couldn't become enamored of him. But the way his gaze stole over her eyes, down her cheeks, and across her lips had her breath growing short and her heart rate at an all-time high.

Why did she take pleasure in watching the way candlelight made his skin gleam in the yellow light, delight in the way it cast sparkles of glimmers on his hair and in his green eyes? Why did she like the way his eyes spoke to her, the way his words sounded in her ears? Why did her whole being come alive with the promise of discovery whenever he was near?

Aston set the cup down and leaned toward her. "I'm going to kiss you, Gaiety," he whispered, as his face came closer to hers.

"No, I should be going up." She rose so fast she knocked the table and rattled the cup.

"Wait," Aston said, trying to grasp her arm as she rushed by him. "Gaiety, wait," he said again as loudly as he dared, knowing Alma's room was beyond the back wall. Gaiety managed to elude him and fled through the doorway.

Aston opened his fist and let his hand drop to his side. *Damn, she was a tempting woman.* He had stood in the doorway and watched her a couple of minutes before she'd realized he was there. He'd noticed her shapely legs, well-toned muscles, and cute slippered feet immediately, and it had caused an instant reaction in his lower body. Her golden brown hair fell across her shoulders and shimmered invitingly down her back, making him want to catch it and fill his hands with its softness. How innocent, how carefree she'd looked sitting so confidently casual, enjoying her late-night supper.

Her eyes had snapped at him when he'd asked her if she were comfy, and her lips had tempted him with their fullness and their dusty rose color. *Damn, she was a beautifully tempting woman.*

He picked up her cup and drank the milk again. He let its thickness, its richness, linger on his tongue before he swallowed. Yes, the cream was the best part. Gaiety had been right not to mix it with the milk.

Aston returned the cup to the table and rubbed his eyes with his thumb and forefinger as he pondered. Gaiety had all the qualities he liked in a woman. She was smart, beautiful and clever. She teased him. She challenged him. She opposed him. She wasn't moonstruck over him. And he actually felt comfortable with her.

He remembered when she'd thought he was a poacher and told him to be sure to go to the back door. He remembered the defiant young woman who'd insisted he introduce himself before she would accept a dance with him. He approved of her wanting to make sure she was properly chaperoned.

All of a sudden he realized he liked Gaiety. He liked the fact that she didn't let him kiss her the first time he tried.

Not only did he like her, damn it, he *wanted* to kiss her, and not just because his lower body was telling him to kiss her. He wanted to kiss her because there was a need inside him to feel her lips upon his. This realization gave him reason to think. He kissed women as a prelude to making them feel good before he entered them. He'd never really thought about wanting to kiss a woman because of who she was and because of the feelings she stirred inside him. But he'd wanted to kiss Gaiety for the pleasure he expected it to give him.

Aston looked down at the cup. Maybe it was time to reconsider, forget, heal, and start over. Maybe it was time to trust a woman again. Maybe it was time to let a woman into his heart. And just maybe—Gaiety Smith was that woman.

Seven

"It's time to get up, Miss Gaiety." Mimi pulled back the sheet and plumped Gaiety's pillows. "We've got a big day planned for us. It's going to be wonderful, and I can hardly wait for it to get started. I've got your tea and biscuits right here."

Gaiety brushed her hair away from her face as she sat up in bed and leaned sleepily against her pillows, her head throbbing from lack of sleep. Thinking about her late-night encounter with Aston had kept her awake until daylight loomed on the horizon. She felt as if she'd just gone to sleep when Mimi called to her. Most of the time it was a blessing and a pleasure to have a maid as chipper and pleasant as Mimi in the mornings, but at times like this it was a curse.

Mimi yanked back the drapery panel, spilling fresh morning sunshine into the room. There was the slightest bit of a chill to the early morning air. Gaiety shielded her eyes with her hands, wondering how Mimi could think another day filled with sewing, embroidery, and reading was going to make for a wonderful day. She didn't even have a piano to play in the evenings, as she'd had in Connecticut. With luck, her piano would have arrived at Lilac Hill by the time she'd returned to live there with her father.

"It's beautiful outside. Just listen to those birds chirping and singing," Mimi told her, as she looked out the window. "I've already been up more than an hour. Everybody else in the house has, too. You're the only one sleeping late this morning."

Maybe she was the only one who'd spent the night thinking about a man, revenge, and justice. Gaiety rubbed her eyes with her fingertips. No, she wasn't going to start that all over again. It didn't matter that Aston appeared to be different now from the young man who'd gotten Theodora pregnant and had destroyed her family. He'd never paid for what he'd done, and Gaiety was the only one left who cared enough to see justice done.

Mimi said something again about looking forward to the day, so Gaiety answered in a grumbling tone, "Mimi, I hardly think we have a big or a wonderful day ahead of us."

"Oh, yes, Miss," the maid said, pushing up the last shade as she twisted around to face her. "Mr. Aston told Alma that she wouldn't have to prepare dinner tonight because he would be taking you on a picnic late this afternoon. He said for her to have a basket ready when he returned from his office down at the sawmill."

"A picnic?" Gaiety straightened her nightgown about her shoulders as Mimi set a tray across her lap.

"Yes." Mimi's eyes were wide with joy. "And you know what, Miss?"

Gaiety was afraid to ask but did. "No, what?"

"I'll be going along."

Thank goodness, Gaiety thought. Obviously, Aston was serious when he said he wanted to spend time with her and get to know her before he decided whether or not he wanted to marry her. That meant she had to measure up to Aston's expectations, and she wasn't sure she liked that. She didn't like the warm and tender feelings he created in her, either. But how could she avoid spending time with him when she was the one who wanted to marry him?

"Alma told me that you'll be riding in a carriage with Mr. Aston and I'll be in a carriage right behind you. And guess what?"

Gaiety shook her throbbing head. "No, Mimi, just tell me. I don't want to guess."

A smile stretched across the maid's lips, her dark eyes sparkled, and a blush stained her cheeks. "Josie will be driving your carriage, and Hank will be driving mine." Mimi clasped her hands together in front of her. "I can hardly wait. I came back upstairs and put on my best dress." Mimi held out her arms and twirled around for Gaiety's inspection. "What do you think?"

How could she continue to be in a grumblesome mood with Mimi in the room? Gaiety smiled, laughed as she brushed her hair away from her face. "I think you're the prettiest, brightest young maid in this county. And young Hank better watch out or you'll have him hooked around your little finger."

Mimi joined Gaiety's laughter, beaming with confidence and pleasure.

"You just be careful around him. Don't let him take advantage of you."

"I'll be careful, Miss," she said, and turned toward Gaiety's wardrobe. "Now, while you have your tea and biscuits, I'm going to look at your dresses. Maybe a lightweight cotton with a wrap would be just right for today. It might get warm with all that sunshine."

Gaiety looked down at the tray set before her and saw two plain teacakes, a small dish of cooked apples, a small pot of tea, and a glass of milk. Gaiety blinked. Mimi had never put milk on her breakfast tray. A tightening formed in her stomach. Somehow, she knew Aston was responsible for the milk, and that he was trying to send her a message. But what? And why did the thought of it bring all her senses to life?

"Mimi?"

"Yes, Miss?"

"Why is there milk on my tray?"

Mimi whirled to face her. "Oh, I told Alma you wouldn't like that. If you wanted milk on your tray you'd have told me long before now, but she said Mr. Aston insisted you were to have a glass of milk each morning and for her to make sure it was thick with cream. Imagine that. I didn't take him to be a curious fellow." Mimi left the wardrobe and took a couple of steps toward Gaiety. "I don't know for sure, but it's my guess that Mr. Aston thinks you're on the puny side and thinks to fatten you."

Gaiety nodded and poured steaming tea into her cup. Alma probably assumed the same thing, Gaiety thought, but she knew the real meaning behind the milk; Aston wanted her to remember that he'd wanted to kiss her last night and she'd run away. Gaiety felt a tightening in her chest. The thought of him kissing her was heady, threatening.

"We need to pick out just the right dress for today. Maybe that buttercup-colored dress with all the little flowers on it and the bonnet to match. What do you think?"

A strange feeling of unease swept over Gaiety as she realized what Aston intended with the picnic and the milk. He was ready to pursue her. Ordinarily she would have been elated that a man whose company she enjoyed wanted to chase her, court her, but not this man. She had to remember Aston as the young man who caused the destruction of her family, not as the interesting, intriguing, confident man he was today.

"Did you hear me, Miss Gaiety? Do you want to try on the yellow dress, or should we go with the poppy-colored one?"

Gaiety realized she hadn't been listening to

Mimi. "Yes, that will be fine. Whatever you decide on will be fine." She picked up her cup and sipped the tea.

Later that afternoon Gaiety found herself sitting shoulder-to-shoulder, leg-to-leg with Aston in an open carriage heading for a grassy knoll about fifteen minutes away from the main house. When she realized how near she was to him, she became rigid and leaned toward one side of the carriage.

It had never occurred to Gaiety to think about how close she would be to Aston during the carriage ride. When he'd spoken to her a few moments ago his breath had fanned her cheek. He smelled of shaving soap, and she could feel the heat emanating from his body. She hadn't been prepared for the thrill she felt in her breast at being so near to him.

She'd been too busy spending the morning with Mimi fussing over what she was to wear and Alma worrying about what to put in the picnic basket to think about the possibility of being so close to Aston that she could actually feel him. It was an awakening experience.

Just as Mimi had said, Josie drove her and Aston, and Mimi followed in the carriage driven by Hank. Gaiety tried to concentrate on the gently rolling landscape with woodlands in the distance, rather than on the effect his nearness had on her.

"Why are you so nervous?" Aston asked, about five minutes into the ride.

She faced him. "I'm not," she lied with a half smile on her lips.

He grinned appealingly. The look in his eyes challenged her answer. "If not nervous, at the very least tense. I see it in the way you're sitting. You're stiff as a poker and rigid as a tree trunk."

Gaiety knew there was no need to deny it further, although she didn't intend to tell him the whole truth. "I'm not used to traveling alone with a gentleman." That was no lie and easier to say.

He chuckled lightly. "You needn't worry I'll try anything with your maid not twenty yards behind us. I may want to kiss you, Gaiety, but I'm not going to." He paused. "Not right now, anyway."

Her breath caught and held in her throat at the mention of a kiss. She'd hoped after she'd rebuffed him last night he wouldn't suggest such a thing again. The very thought should be a violation to the memories of her family, but somehow she wasn't insulted as she should have been. She was interested. That realization shook her.

"Relax, Gaiety. You're so strained you're going to have sore muscles tomorrow."

He was so serious-sounding that Gaiety had to laugh, and that made her relax a little, as he'd intended. But she wouldn't forget his reference to a kiss and how it had made her feel inside when he'd said it. His eyes were such a light green they were luminescent. He kept his gaze on her face so long she felt she had to say something.

"I'm not afraid you'll try anything, really. And sitting beside you doesn't make me nervous, it makes me—careful. There's a difference."

Aston smiled. "Agreed. And I like the fact you're careful."

Gaiety accepted his compliment with a mere nod, but inside she glowed from the praise. Aston was right: she had to learn how to relax around him, if her plan was going to work. She looked over Josie's broad back as he handled the reins. The horse plodded along at a leisurely pace. Gaiety breathed in the fresh air. The late-afternoon sunshine warmed the perfect spring day with a mild temperature. The smell of a freshly plowed field was in the air.

Her gaze searched the landscape. She tried hard not to like, not to be interested in the man sitting beside her. This wouldn't be happening, she told herself, if Aston would simply have agreed to the marriage and let the engagement follow accepted rules. But no, he had to have her in his home. In his life.

"What are you thinking?" he asked. "I saw you tense again."

"You have to admit that all this is a bit odd." She said aloud what she was thinking.

"What? That we're going on a picnic?"

"No, no." She shook her head and the ribbon of her poppy colored bonnet grazed her cheek. "The whole thing—that I'm here for you to look me over and decide whether or not you want to marry me. And that I stayed here rather than traveled back to Connecticut with my father."

He seemed to think about her statement for a moment, then asked, "But don't you want to look me over, too? Or is it possible you've already done that?"

Guilt assailed her and she looked away, not wanting him to read anything that might show in her eyes. He was looking at her for a possible wife. She was after him for vengeance.

"Actually, Gaiety, while you're father is away, it might be a good time for us to discuss this marriage he's proposed between the two of us."

Gaiety refused to look at him. No, it wasn't a good time to discuss it. In fact, she didn't want to discuss it at all. She was deceiving him. And even though it was necessary, she found she didn't want to be reminded of it. She didn't want Aston to make her lose sight of her goal to marry him, then tell him she was Theodora's sister. Gaiety swallowed hard. She refused to let his appealing ways and charming personality sway her from her mission. The sooner she could get him to marry her, the sooner she would have her revenge and get on with her life.

Willing her pulse to stay under control, she turned to him and asked, "Is there something you'd like to know about me?"

"I guess one thing I want to know is why a beautiful woman like you isn't already married."

"I've never found anyone I wanted to marry, and my father has never forced the issue." That was easy enough to say because it was the truth.

"Is your father forcing the issue now?"

His question demanded the truth. She knew how he would take what she was about to say, but it had to be said. "I'm not being forced to marry you."

Slowly, a pleasing grin spread across his lips. "That's good to know. I haven't—" The carriage lurched and Josie pulled on the reins, bringing the two horses to a halt.

"How 'bout here, Mr. Aston? Does this spot look all right to you?"

Aston took his gaze off Gaiety's face and looked around. "This will be fine, Josie. After we get out, you can tie up over by that tree."

"Tell me, do you ride?" Aston asked, as he jumped down from the carriage and reached for Gaiety.

"I ride, but not very well," she answered as she rose. Aston's hands slid around her waist. His touch was warm, exacting. It sent her heartbeat racing. She looked down and her gaze met his clear green eyes. They were happy eyes, not the eyes of a man who'd destroyed a family. Could he have changed so much?

Aston smiled at her. "I thought you might enjoy riding over the plantation with me one day. Why don't you start riding every morning and afternoon for an hour or so? You'll be a good rider within a couple of weeks."

Her feet settled on the ground, but she felt as if she were standing on air. Aston didn't turn her loose immediately. His fingers spread across her back and his thumbs caressed her midriff. His touch was strangely comforting, and that bothered her. Their eyes met again for a brief moment before she stepped away from him.

"I can have Hank help you. He's good with horses."

Gaiety knew at once that would make Mimi happy. And it would help her fill the days with more than sewing and reading. She was pleased Aston had suggested it. It appeared he wanted her to enjoy herself while she was staying in his home. There was so much to like about Aston Rutledge.

"That would be nice. I think I'd enjoy learning to be a better rider."

Mimi hurried over and started spreading a blanket while Gaiety looked around at the lush greenery the landscape had to offer. Down in the valley she saw the main house, the carriage house, the cook house, and the stables. Beyond those buildings she could see the rooftops of the darkies' homes lined in rows.

After the blanket was in place and the picnic basket on top of it, Mimi, Josie, and Hank moved a short distance away from Aston and spread their own picnic.

Gaiety sat down, settled her skirts around her

feet, and loosened the ribbons of her bonnet. She let the bonnet fall to the back of her neck. Wisps of hair fell from her chignon, framing her face. She opened the basket as Aston sat down opposite her. From inside the basket she pulled a flask, a loaf of bread, cheese, chicken, and balls of crushed apple, cinnamon, and sugar. Aston quietly watched her as she filled the plates. In the distance she heard the muted voices of the others, although her back was to them.

She deliberately kept from looking into his eyes as she gave Aston his plate. She found too many things to like about him already and didn't want to get caught up in the romantic atmosphere surrounding them. She'd come to Aston's home to complete a mission and already she was losing sight of that goal.

"We were talking about you, me, and the marriage proposal when we stopped. Do you think you'd be content married to me?" He took a bite out of the chicken leg.

She had trouble swallowing the cheese in her mouth. Clearing her throat, she said, "I think 'satisfied' might be a better word."

"So if your father and I come to an agreement, you won't be unhappy?"

She looked into his eyes. She owed him that much. "No. If we marry, I won't be unhappy." Even as she said the words she doubted their truth.

They ate in silence for a few minutes. Gaiety

listened to the friendly chatter and laughter that came from Mimi, Hank, and Josie.

"Do you have any questions you'd like to ask me? You could find yourself married to me one day."

That last statement caught her attention, and she looked up from her plate. She felt as if her skin heated, and her stomach rejected the thought of more food. Yes, she had some questions for him about Theodora. She needed some answers to how and why her sister had fallen down those stairs. But would he answer them? "You were married once. Tell me about your wife," she said.

Gaiety was astonished by the rapid change in Aston's expression. The smile left his lips and they paled. She wasn't certain what she saw in his face. Was it pain, or regret? Aston swallowed, wiped his mouth with his napkin, and pushed his plate aside. It was clear that the mention of his marriage disturbed him greatly. Why after twelve years did it bother him so? What did he know that she didn't?

"There's nothing to tell you." Aston's words were clipped as he pulled the stopper on the flask and filled a glass with red wine.

Gaiety surely didn't believe that. There were so many details she didn't know. "How long were you married?" she asked.

"Less than three months." He stretched his legs and crossed his feet as he looked down on the valley below while he took a slow drink of the wine. Now he was the one rigid as a poker.

She waited a few moments to see if he'd offer her any information. He remained quiet.

"I heard she was with child when she died." Her voice was hardly more than a whisper. She became oblivious to her surroundings. This wasn't any easier for her than it appeared to be for him, but Aston didn't know that. He couldn't know the pain that was in her heart. The pain she hoped would ease when her plan was complete. "Is that correct?"

"Yes." He took another swallow, still refusing to look at her, refusing to expound on his answer.

She saw that his hand gripped the glass so tightly his knuckles whitened. Again she was struck by the amount of pain she sensed within him. But why? "I believe it's only natural that I be curious about your first wife. And you did ask if I had any questions."

At that he turned back and faced her. Their eyes met. "You're right, of course." He finished off his drink and wiped his lips with the back of his hand. His expression was pensive, reflective. "Her name was Theodora. She was fifteen and I was seventeen when we married. She was already pregnant. I turned eighteen the day she fell down the stairs, killing herself and her baby."

Gaiety squeezed her eyes shut as she envisioned Theodora tumbling headlong, her skirts swirling about her. "Were you with her when she fell?" she asked.

He shook his head. "No. Do you have any more questions?"

Yes, her heart screamed. She wanted to know if anyone else was with her sister when she fell. She wanted to know if Theodora knew she'd lost the baby. She wanted to know if her sister suffered before she died, or if it was quick and painless the way Josh and her pa died. But she couldn't ask those questions. Aston would want to know why such details were important to her.

Instead she took a deep breath and asked, "Did you love her?"

"No." His voice carried no emotion.

"Did she love you?"

"No. We married because she was pregnant, and for no other reason."

Instinctively she believed him. He looked into her eyes and for a moment she felt the need to comfort him. She could see he was hurting. She wanted to move over beside him and wrap her arms around his back and hold him close so they could share their pain. These feelings astonished her, confused her. She wanted to deny them. How could she feel this when he was the one who had destroyed her family?

"Gaiety, you may hear a lot of gossip about my marriage. Some of it might even be true. It's not something I like to talk about, maybe you can tell. But I can assure you, even after all these years, Savannah is still abuzz about it."

"I've heard some of it." Her voice was still whispery. "I wanted to hear your side."

He took a deep breath. "Now you have. It was a marriage that should never have taken place. There's no reason for me to go into it any further. It was a marriage that never should have taken place." He rose. "Come on, let's go for a walk." He reached for her hand.

Gaiety allowed him to help her rise and they started walking toward a stand of trees. He had admitted he didn't love Theodora and that she didn't love him. That gave her much to think about. But why would Theodora have allowed him to touch her and get her pregnant if she didn't love him? There were still things that didn't make sense, things she wanted answers to. But Gaiety knew she couldn't ask too many questions at one time without arousing his suspicions about why she wanted to know so much. And she had to remember she didn't want him asking her any questions about her past. Her ruse would have to be carried out until they were married.

A nagging thought wouldn't leave her as they walked in silence. For the first time since she'd come up with the plan to get even with Aston, she was having doubts about it, about him. And that worried her. The horror of it all was, she found that she really liked Aston Rutledge, but she couldn't let that keep her from avenging her family's death.

Eight

While Mimi unbuttoned the bodice of Gaiety's dress, she pondered over the past two weeks in Aston's house. Since the picnic with Aston, Gaiety had become more aware of him as the intriguing man she was attracted to the first two times they'd met. She seldom saw him during the day, but in the evenings, while they had dinner, he kept the conversation going with talk of happenings on the plantation and gossip he'd heard from the people of Savannah.

Through these conversations, she learned that during the course of each day he checked on the fieldhands, the sawmill, and the livestock, and kept up with the account books for all his business ventures. Occasionally he would mention something that happened specifically to him. He always asked about her day, but rarely did he question her about her past. She found that she appreciated and respected the way he handled their time together in the evenings.

Gaiety was happier, now that part of her day

was devoted to her learning to be a better rider. Hank had taken Aston's words to heart and was also teaching her and Mimi how to post and take low jumps. Gaiety especially enjoyed the late afternoon rides, when the sun hung low in the sky and painted twilight with a coppery glow.

Many times over the past few days Gaiety had thought about the conversation she'd had with Aston the day of the picnic. He'd confirmed the story she'd heard in the sheriff's office before she and Titus were taken to the orphanage: that Aston and Theodora had married because she was pregnant. But Aston had failed to mention that he was forced to marry Theodora at gunpoint and that her father and brother were killed because of it. She also found herself wondering if he'd told the truth about not being home when Theodora had fallen down the stairs. She had a nagging feeling there was more to that story than anyone had ever told her. Aston had settled one thing that had plagued her since her arrival at Southern Oaks: he and Theodora hadn't been in love.

Gaiety had also concluded that while it was quite possible that Theodora had accidentally fallen down the stairs, she still wasn't totally convinced that there hadn't been a contributing reason. It wasn't that she thought that Aston or anyone else in the house had deliberately pushed Theodora, but she could have been arguing with someone or running from someone or something could have caused her to fall.

She'd questioned Jolly and Aleta, the darkies who helped Alma in the house, and discovered that neither of them had been working at Southern Oaks when Theodora had lived there. They had been no help whatsoever. She'd also tried to question Josie. It didn't take her long to realize somebody had taught him to answer "I don't know" to every question about Aston's past. And even though she'd tried to question Alma again, she had avoided the subject with ease.

A thought Gaiety had been considering crossed her mind as she tied the ribbons on the front of her nightgown. "Mimi, how well have you gotten to know Alma and Hank?" she asked, as she pulled out the covered stool to her dresser and sat down.

Mimi turned from hanging Gaiety's dress in the wardrobe. "As if we've been friends for years. It took Alma a couple of days to warm up to me, but she's real friendly now. We're going to get along like kittens. Don't you worry about that, Miss. If you decide you want to marry Mr. Aston, we'll get along just fine here."

She picked up the petticoats and hung them in the free-standing closet while she continued to talk. "Me and Hank don't talk as much. Sometimes, like this afternoon, when you told me I could go see him for a few minutes, we just sat there and looked into each other's eyes, smiling. We don't have to talk. It just makes me feel good to be near him."

Her maid's last statement caused a pang of envy in Gaiety. How wonderful it must be to know that someone could make you feel good just by being near—and that you made them feel good, too. She looked at her reflection in the mirror. Even though she fought it, even though it pained her to admit it, she knew that she felt good whenever Aston was near.

"I'd like you to do me a favor, Mimi." Gaiety hesitated. She hated to use Mimi's friendship with the household staff to further her own desires, but she had to know more about Theodora's life in this house, and she wasn't getting very far on her own.

"Yes, Miss?" Mimi looked at her.

Gaiety rose and took a couple of steps toward her. "Will you see if you can find out anything about Aston's first wife?"

Mimi's almond-shaped eyes rounded considerably. "Like what, Miss? I already know they weren't married for very long and that she wasn't accepted by his family."

Gaiety knew that much. She was good enough for him that he could take his pleasure with her, but not good enough for him to make her his bride. She'd gleaned that much information from the sheriff twelve years ago. Gaiety clenched her fists at the thought of Aston feeling that way about her sister. She wanted to turn that fist on herself when she thought of how much she enjoyed Aston's company. How could she betray her family that way? How could she live with herself if she let the soft feelings for Aston continue to grow? She had to work harder to counter his enchanting attractiveness.

She cleared her throat. "Oh, things like what she did during the day, which rooms were hers. I'd like to know if there's anything that belonged to her still in the house. And—anything you can find out about her death, I'd like to know."

By the expression on her maid's face, Gaiety knew that Mimi was considering whether or not to question her mistress about this further. Finally Mimi said, "You want to know all this, but you don't want anyone to know you want to know. Is that why you're asking me to see if I can find out these things?"

It took her a while, but Mimi figured it out without Gaiety having to come right out and ask her to pry for information. She had to find some ammunition to fight her growing attraction to Aston. "Yes. I'd rather it not get back to Aston that I'm interested in his first marriage."

"I understand. I'll be careful how I ask questions." Mimi put a finger to her lips and pondered. "I don't suppose Hank would know much. He's only been at Southern Oaks for three years, but he may have heard talk."

Gaiety looked into Mimi's eyes. "I've heard talk. But I want to know what happened from someone who was here at the time."

"Leave it to me." Mimi smiled. "I'll see if I can find out what you want to know."

Gaiety nodded and went back to the dresser to take her hair down. She hoped her father would return soon so he could demand an answer from Aston. She couldn't stay in his house much longer. She found him too appealing, too charming. She was too comfortable with him. In the evenings she looked forward to dinnertime, when she would see him, and that had to stop. She couldn't be swayed from her mission.

She found herself wanting to believe he'd had nothing to do with her father's and Josh's death. Nothing to do with Theodora's and her baby's death. For the first time in twelve years she found herself wanting to think about the future and forget about the past. That would never do. She had to deny the man Aston was today and remember the young man who'd taken advantage of her sister, then refused to take responsibility for his actions. She owed it to her family to avenge their deaths.

Gaiety reached for her hairbrush. Her father had to return soon.

Aston walked in the front door of the house and hung his hat on the coat tree in the corner. Every time he thought about it, he was amused that Gaiety had told him to go to the back door of her home. Right from the start he'd liked her assertive attitude. As he looked down the long hallway, he was struck by how quiet the house was. That puzzled him. Since Gaiety and her maid had arrived, the house seemed to be as lively as he remembered it being when he was a young boy and his father and his mother were alive. He walked into the parlor thinking he'd find Gaiety working on her embroidery. She wasn't there. Neither was her maid. A small shiver of apprehension crept up his back but he shrugged it off and dismissed the feeling. What could be wrong?

It occurred to him Gaiety might be in the dining room, checking on dinner, so he glanced in there. He walked through the warming room, the library, and the drawing room. There was no use in going upstairs to look. Gaiety wasn't in the house. He didn't know how he knew, but he did. He could feel her absence. But where was she, and why had she gone? Finally he went to the bottom of the stairs and called to Alma. Within a moment or two she appeared around the corner.

"Yes, Mr. Aston?"

"Where is Gaiety?" His tone sounded like an accusation, and he didn't mean for it to.

"Oh, she went over to her home at Lilac Hill," she said, as she started down the stairs. "She left right before noontime. She received word this morning that her piano had arrived, and she was so excited, she prepared to go over there immediately."

An unexpected feeling of relief settled over Aston. For a brief moment all he'd been able to think was that she was gone and she wouldn't be coming back.

He cleared his throat of the unexpected rush of emotion that shook him. "Yes, I knew she was looking forward to her piano arriving. Did she ask to hold dinner until she returned?"

"Oh, no, sir," Alma said, stopping in front of him and folding her hands together at her waist. "She told me she planned to stay the night at Lilac Hill and return tomorrow afternoon. I tried to get her to let Josie or Hank go with them, but she wouldn't hear of it. She said she didn't need to be looked after as if she were a young girl."

"What?" Aston tensed. "Surely you're not telling me Josie let them go alone in the carriage?"

Alma paled, a worried expression wrinkled her forehead, and her gaze searched Aston's face. "No, sir." She shook her head. "I mean yes, sir, they went alone, but they didn't take the carriage. They rode their horses."

"Horses? Damn! Gaiety has been riding only a couple of weeks. I can't believe Hank let them leave the plantation on horseback." Aston strode over to the door and plucked his hat off the tree.

"She said it was only ten or so miles away. And I don't want to be out of line, but I've seen them ride. They're both very good riders, Mr. Aston."

"That's not the point," he argued. "They needed an escort. Where the hell are Josie and

Hank?" he muttered irritably. "They should have known better than to let the women go alone. Josie should have insisted one of them go along." Aston was furious. He was overreacting, but powerless to stop himself. He wouldn't rest until he knew that they'd made it safely to the house. "I wouldn't care if it was only five or six miles to Lilac Hill. Those women don't know enough about the area to go riding off on their own. They may be halfway across the state by now." Aston actually doubted that, but it made him feel better to say it. Gaiety probably had no problem finding Lilac Hill, and he was sure she had no problem putting Josie in his place when he wanted to go with her.

Alma probably thought he'd taken leave of his senses, but he knew what the real reason was. He'd come to care for Gaiety. That surprised him, and he wasn't sure he wanted to believe it. Aston opened the front door, but Alma's soft voice halted him.

"What about dinner, Mr. Aston? Should I hold it for you?"

"No. Just prepare a plate and leave it in the warming room. I don't know what time I'll be back. No need for you to wait up for me. I'm going to ride over to Lilac Hill and make sure they made it without any trouble." He was sure Alma could see through his excuse. The fact was, he wanted Gaiety at Southern Oaks, not at Lilac Hill.

"Yes, sir," she answered in a shaky voice.

Late-afternoon shadows fell across the path to the Smith house as Aston's horse cantered toward Lilac Hill. He decided to take a shortcut through the woods surrounding the pond where he'd first seen Gaiety.

He knew that piano was important to Gaiety, but until now he hadn't known how important. Hell, if she wanted a piano that badly, he'd see about getting her one for Southern Oaks. He often listened to women play when he attended dinner parties in Savannah. He appreciated the music and found it a pleasant way to spend the evening. He wouldn't mind hearing Gaiety play the piano after dinner. He wouldn't mind at all. Aston chuckled to himself as he rode. It surprised him how easily Gaiety had fit into his life and how quickly he was ready to give her anything she wanted, how his temper flared when he thought about her leaving Southern Oaks.

It was odd the way Aston had known immediately that Gaiety wasn't in the house when he got home. The only way he could explain it to himself was that he felt her absence. He wanted to make sure she'd arrived at Lilac Hill safely, but also, deep inside himself, he felt a driving need to pick her up and take her back home with him, where she belonged. This escapade had made him realize he didn't want her to leave Southern Oaks, and because of that he had to consider the possibility of her living there as his wife. That stunned and excited him.

Aston enjoyed her being there in the evenings when he returned from his office at the sawmill. He had been looking forward to riding with her in the stillness of early mornings when the dew glistened on the grass and sparkled with sunshine. He actually liked the idea of chasing her and courting her. He was comfortable with her, and—he wanted to hold her and kiss her. He wanted to know if her lips pressed against his would make him feel the way he believed it would. He wanted to make love to her. At last he could freely admit to himself that he was seriously considering accepting her father's proposal.

And why shouldn't he? Why should he hold himself to a vow he'd made as a young man, a vow that had come about because of a lie that had destroyed an entire family? Should he let events of the past deprive him of happiness today? Over the years he'd learned to live with what had happened twelve years ago. But, damn it he still felt somehow responsible for Dewey and Josh Talbot's deaths, even though there was no way he could have prevented them. But Theodora and her death was another matter. Justice had its own way of getting even.

His horse stopped. Aston realized he'd become so caught up in his thoughts of the past that he'd tightened his hold on the reins. He took his hat off and wiped his forehead with the back of his hand. He wondered if he'd ever be able to think of Theodora without tensing.

Maybe a woman like Gaiety could make him forget.

He placed his hat back on his head and looked around. In the distance he saw the pond and the figure of a woman sitting on a large rock, watching the still water. Aston urged his horse forward at a walk until he was close enough to see that the woman was Gaiety. The gelding she'd ridden from Southern Oaks stood tied to a tree a short distance away. Mimi was nowhere in sight. Obviously Gaiety made a habit of going to the pond alone. He thought about hurrying over and admonishing her for taking off to Lilac Hill without an escort, but he knew he didn't want to fight with her. He was in the mood to love her.

That thought brought him up short. He pulled his horse to a stop once again and watched her. Her father had trusted Gaiety to his care, and he'd see she came to no harm. Especially from himself. He intended to kiss her, but he'd make sure nothing more happened.

Gaiety was a beautiful woman of social standing. Because of her father's position in life, the women of Savannah would have no trouble accepting her as a part of their society. And unless he wanted Fredrick's son to inherit the plantation, he needed an heir for Southern Oaks. But the main thing he had to be certain of was that he wanted Gaiety for his wife.

He was easily more attracted to her than he'd been to any other woman. If he was going to marry in order to have an heir, it might as well be to someone who stirred his blood as much as Gaiety did. A smile spread across his face. He pressed his knees into the horse's flanks, urging him forward. Aston knew he wouldn't marry Gaiety just to have an heir. There would have to be more in their relationship than that for him to agree to marriage. And he was fairly certain there was.

It was a warm afternoon for the last week in April, and Gaiety had taken off her shoes and stockings and lifted her dress to just above her knees as she sat on a small boulder overlooking the still waters of the pond. As soon as she'd arrived at Lilac Hill she'd played her piano, entertaining Mimi, Helen, and Jeanette for over two hours. It had been wonderful. Toward the end of her playing, she'd drifted into softer melodies which put her in a mellow mood. She decided she wanted to ride down to the pond and reminisce about her childhood.

Gaiety had shaken Mimi's and Jeanette's attempts to accompany her, and she was glad she had. She needed this time alone to reestablish that fast-fading link with her first family. She needed to feed that hunger for revenge that had been with her for so many years. She desperately needed to reconnect with the past and shore up her determination to carry through with her plan.

Closing her eyes, Gaiety lifted her face toward the sky. The sun had slipped behind the horizon and the first threads of twilight lay on the evening sky. Sounds from frogs and crickets and occasional splashes in the water drifted past and into the trees behind her. The air was still.

She cleared her mind of the present and took herself back in time to when she was a young girl and known by the name Avalina Talbot.

Gaiety saw herself as a little girl playing in the shallow water of the pond with Josh, Theodora, and baby Titus. She saw smiling faces, heard laughter, felt the coolness of the water on her face. She saw her family at the dinner table with heads bowed, her pa asking the Lord's blessing on the food. She saw them dressed for church in their Sunday clothes: Josh with his hair slicked down across his forehead, her father wearing a wrinkled jacket and crumpled bow tie.

But Gaiety's mind also showed her things she didn't want to see. She saw Theodora locking her and Titus in the house and leaving them alone most of the day while Josh and her father worked in the fields. She saw Josh and Theodora screaming at each other. Then she saw Titus with his long brown hair, but he had no face. He was at the orphanage, sitting on the floor, his arms outstretched toward her, his chubby baby fingers beckoning her. She heard him crying, but she couldn't see his face. What did he look like? She couldn't remember. She heard him calling her name, but it was the wrong name. He knew her as Avalina. Why wasn't he calling her Avalina? Why was he calling for Gaiety?

"Gaiety. Gaiety!"

With a jerk Gaiety's eyes popped open. The shadow of a man fell across her face. She jumped up, knocking into someone. Startled, she let out a small scream. A hand closed around her arm and she was pulled against a hard chest. Fear made her fight, made her breathless.

"Gaiety, it's me, Aston."

She stopped struggling and turned in the circle of arms that held her. Aston's face was so very close to hers. Her chest heaved, her pulse raced, her heart hammered. His arms tightened around her.

"Everything's all right. I'm sorry. I didn't mean to frighten you. I thought you heard my horse approaching."

"I—I think I was asleep. I must have been dreaming." Inside she trembled. Her forearms rested on his chest, her hands were close enough to cup his face and let her fingers slide across his cheeks over his jawline and down her neck. She centered her gaze on his lips. She didn't want to look into his telling green eyes.

"Are you all right now?"

She swallowed hard and nodded.

His arms tightened around her and he pulled her closer. "Gaiety." He whispered her name softly.

As if with a will of their own, her lashes lifted and her gaze met his. In that moment, she knew he was going to kiss her, and she didn't want to stop him. Her lips parted for a feeble protest, but all they found was the warmth of his lips covering hers. He kissed her so softly, so briefly, so sweetly, it might have been fatherly but for the way he held her, the way he looked at her, the way it made a rush of excitement spiral through her, then collect in her lower abdomen.

The kiss left a lingering moment of stillness as they looked at each other. He lowered his lips and kissed her again, adding more pressure, more motion into it this time. She was aware of his hands on her back, his arms clutching her to him. He gently moved his lips back and forth over hers, teaching her how to kiss. It seemed natural when she slipped her hands up his chest, over the crest of his shoulders to clasp her fingers together at his nape. Her movement allowed him greater freedom to bring her breasts up tight against his chest.

Gaiety felt his strength, his warmth, his passion within the circle of his arms. She heard his sighing breaths turn into short, shallow breathing. She tasted the sweetness of his tongue, his mouth. The scent of shaving soap favored her nose with its aroma. The pressure of his lips increased upon hers and she met his ardor with a surprising fervency of her own.

A loud splash in the pond startled Gaiety and broke them apart. She stepped away from Aston and covered her mouth with her hand, astonished, appalled by her behavior. She moistened her lips and found the taste of Aston. She wiped her palm down her lips and chin.

"We shouldn't have done that," she murmured in an outraged voice, trying to calm her breathing. Gaiety couldn't believe she'd let him kiss her, and worse, that she'd actually participated in it, wanted it, enjoyed it. How could she? She was betraying her sister, her family. She wanted to cover her face and run away from this violation she'd committed.

A grin slid across Aston's face. "Perhaps, but remember, Gaiety, the worst thing your father could make us do for kissing is get married. He already wants that to happen, so even, if he heard, I don't think he'll mind."

He was teasing her again, and she didn't want to be susceptible to his charm. She didn't want to be captivated by him. "It wasn't proper for you to kiss me that way. And I'm sure Papa wouldn't approve of your taking advantage of me." She was angry at herself, but decided to take it out on him. She whipped up her shoes and stockings and plopped back down on the small boulder. She needed a couple of minutes to collect herself.

"I didn't take advantage of you," Aston argued good-naturedly. "You wanted that kiss as much as I did. I felt it in your response."

"That's ridiculous. I did no such thing. Now, if you don't mind, I'd like to put on my stockings."

With the grin still in place on his handsome face, Aston turned around and placed his back before her. "Deny it all you want. Kisses don't lie, Gaiety."

That might be true, but she'd never admit it. She had to get him off the subject of that kiss. The sooner they stopped talking about it, the sooner she could forget about it. "Why are you here?" she asked, as she slipped a stocking over her foot. "Fishing again?"

Aston laughed. "After the scathing reprimand I received from you last time? Not a chance."

"Then what are you doing here at the pond? I'm going to assume you're not here simply to spy on me."

"No. When Alma told me you had ridden over here alone, I wanted to come and make sure for myself that you'd come to no harm."

"I wasn't alone. Mimi was with me."

"Not a valid point. There was no escort with you. Your father left you in my care. I was taking a shortcut around the pond to your house and happened to see you sitting on the rock."

Gaiety stepped into her shoes and tied them. "As you can see, I'm safe. There was no need for you to worry. Mimi and I have become good riders." Keeping her distance, she walked around to face him. "You've done your duty, so you can leave now."

He folded his arms across his chest. His eyes questioned her. "Just like that. I can leave. He smiled and slowly shook his head. "Not before

I see the piano. Not before I hear you play it. It would be a shame to have ridden all this way and not seen or heard you play the piano."

Gaiety cringed inside. She was hoping to hurry him on his way. She needed time to think about the disturbing sensations his kiss caused within her. She needed some time to come to terms with her feelings. If she didn't do something soon, she was in danger of losing sight of her plan for revenge.

"Very well," she said grudgingly.

Aston helped her onto the side saddle, then mounted his horse. They rode back to the house in silence. Once inside, Gaiety sent Mimi out to tend to her horse, since Maine had gone to Connecticut with her father.

Gaiety led Aston into the drawing room where the piano sat in the far corner. The cherrywood cabinet, stained a rich mahogany, glowed in the late evening light. A twin pedestal silver candelabra sat in the middle of the front lid.

"It's a beautiful piece of furniture," he said, running his hand over the highly polished wood.

"It's more than just a piece of furniture. It was a special gift from my mother." Gaiety had always considered Mary Smith to be her mother. She was only four when her real mother died and Gaiety didn't remember her at all.

"Excuse me, Miss Gaiety," Jeanette said from the doorway.

"Yes?"

"I was wondering if I should set a place for the gentleman at the dinner table."

Gaiety hesitated. It would be terribly rude not to ask Aston to stay. She wanted to say no, but instead she put a smile on her face and turned to Aston and asked, "Would you like to join me for dinner?"

He returned the smile. "I'd be delighted."

Nine

Late in the afternoon a week later, Gaiety sat in the drawing room, stitching a sampler to hang in the hallway at Lilac Hill while she pondered her encounter with Aston down by the pond. She hadn't been able to forget about it. It plagued her. She couldn't figure out why she'd been so receptive to his kisses, why she'd enjoyed them so much, why she'd participated with such fervor when he was a man she'd sworn to hate.

Her only salvation from complete humiliation with herself and her actions was in remembering the gossip she'd heard from the young ladies at Elaine and Fredrick's party. Aston obviously had the same effect on most of the women in the county.

She wouldn't have a problem keeping her distance from him if he were merely charming. She'd rejected advances of charming young men for years now. No, he was also interesting, intriguing, pleasing. Something more than she'd felt with any other young man she had spent time with. And she knew the time had come for her to do something about it. She couldn't endure a repeat of that afternoon. So far, Aston hadn't tried to kiss her again; in fact, he'd seen to it that they hadn't been alone together. Even on the mornings they'd gone riding together, Mimi was always along.

Closing her eyes, Gaiety breathed deeply and wondered. Why had she liked the way Aston's lips felt against hers? Why did she even now relish remembering the wonderful sensations of being in his arms, held closely to his chest, breathing in the scent of him and sighing with contentment? She had to deny those tender feelings and reestablish her vow to make Aston pay.

With eyes still closed, Gaiety laid her head against the back of the chair and allowed her thoughts to drift back over her conversation with Mimi last night as the maid helped her undress for bed.

"I've been asking around about Mr. Aston's first wife, just like you said. Josie was the only darkie who worked in the house, and he doesn't know anything." She paused. "Did you know Mr. Aston freed his slaves when his father died?"

Gaiety nodded.

"Some of them left, you know. Anyway, Jolene doesn't speak too kindly of Mr. Aston's wife, Miss."

"What do you mean?" Gaiety asked, recognizing the woman Jolene as the head cook.

"Jolene says no one liked her and no one was unhappy when she died."

Gaiety winced as a pain struck deep in her heart. She quickly soothed it with anger. What a horrible thing for the cook to have said about her sister. "That's kind of a broad statement, isn't it? What about her husband?" Gaiety asked in a husky voice. "Surely he was sorry she died."

"I don't know, Miss. Jolene said she whined and complained a lot, even though everyone tried their best to take care of her, her being with child. Jolene said she lay in the bed most of the day, eating sweet bread and drinking tea. When she came downstairs, she tried to order everyone around, including Mr. Aston and his papa. They couldn't do anything right for her. She even threw her dinner plate at Mr. Aston one night and broke the mirror above the fireplace in the dining room."

Naturally, they'd say those things about her sister, Gaiety thought. Untrue things. And she didn't want to hear them. Theodora had her faults, just like everyone else. But it was unfair of that woman to speak so unkindly of her.

"Did—did you find out if they kept anything that belonged to her?" she asked in a soft voice.

Mimi gave her a doubtful look. "Not that Jolene knows about. And you don't have to worry, Miss. Mr. Aston didn't have anything to do with that poor girl's death. Jolene said he'd gone to town to get Miss Theodora a strand of pearls. She'd told him that every rich woman needed pearls hanging around her neck and she didn't have any. Mr. Aston buried her with them."

Gaiety's eyes popped open and she immediately leaned forward and picked up her needle. Her hands were shaking. She didn't know why she wanted to relive her discussion with Mimi. All it did was upset her. If Theodora was demanding, she must have had good reason. She probably didn't understand how the household was managed, and Aston probably didn't try to help her adjust to her new life. Gaiety was more determined than ever to see that Aston Rutledge married her. She'd make him pay for all the horrible things that had been said about her sister.

Hearing horses approaching the front of the house, Gaiety put her sewing aside and rose from the chair. She hadn't been able to concentrate anyway. It was probably one of the darkies, but just in case they had a guest, she went to the window to look out. She needed something to get Aston off her mind. She brushed the sheer drapery panel away from the window and saw a small carriage pulling up in front of the hitching rail on the far side of the house. Maine was driving. Gaiety squealed with delight and headed for the front door. After five weeks of being away, her father was home.

She threw open the door, picked up her skirts, and hurried down the steps. One of Aston's dogs came dashing from around the back of the house and joined her, yelping as he ran beside her.

"Papa!" she called. "Papa!"

With Maine's help, Lane stepped down from the carriage and faced his daughter with a wide smile. "How's my girl?" he asked, throwing his arms open wide.

"Happy to see you. Papa, I'm so glad you're back!" Gaiety flung her arms around his neck and hugged him soundly. She felt relief and joy as she placed a kiss on his cheek and hugged him again, beaming with happiness. "I've missed you, Papa."

"I've missed you too, Gaiety."

"Are you feeling all right? Did the weather make your rheumatism worse?"

"I'm fine, dear. You know I'm always better in the spring and fall when the weather is neither too hot nor too cold. All in all, it was a pleasant trip." He patted her cheek affectionately. "Have you been well?"

"Very," she said with a smile, feeling that everything was going to be all right, now that her father was home. "Except for missing you." She turned to Maine. "Thanks for taking such good care of Papa."

Maine grinned shyly and swept his hat off his head. "Mr. Lane and me travel good together. We sort of look after each other."

"What I need right now is to stretch my legs after that long ride," Lane said. "Take a walk with me, Gaiety, so I can hear what you've been up to since I've been gone."

"I'd love to, Papa. Maine, you go on inside and tell Alma and Mimi that Papa has arrived and to make sure his room is ready."

"Yes, Miss Gaiety." He turned to Lane. "Should I go on over to Lilac Hill tonight?" he asked.

"I don't see why not. I know Jeanette would like to see you. Aston has plenty of help, should I need anything. Just leave my baggage upstairs. I'm sure Alma will have someone take care of it for me."

Gaiety hooked her arm through her father's. Maine put his hat back on his head and started taking the luggage out of the carriage. She could tell that her father's first few steps were stiff as a new colt learning how to stand.

"How are things in Connecticut, Papa? Were you able to help Mrs. Taylor find a manager?"

"I think we found her a good man, an honest man, I'm sure. Only time will tell if he's an acceptable manager of the ironworks. She promised to keep me informed on how things are going with him. I told her I'd visit her again in July or August, before the weather turns cold. I rather think she liked that idea."

"Papa," Gaiety said in a surprised tone of voice. "Did you two take a liking to each other?" she asked, as they slowly made their way to the flower garden on the west side of the house.

Lane patted her hand as they walked. "Hush that nonsense, daughter. Her husband's not been dead three months." They took a few more steps before Lane continued. "However, Olivia Taylor is an easy woman to get along with. Agreeable to a fault."

Gaiety noticed the warmth with which her father said the woman's name, and a funny feeling swept over her. Maybe it was just that Olivia was such a beautifully flowing name. "Is she pretty?"

"That she is. Her son is twelve, and she has three younger daughters, golden-haired beauties all of them. Now, tell me, how are things coming along with you, Gaiety?"

"Doing well. My piano arrived last week, and Mimi and I went over and spent the day at Lilac Hill. It was quite enjoyable." Again her mind replayed Aston's kiss, and she tried to brush it aside.

"Good," he said as they continued along the slate walkway that meandered through the pink azaleas. "And what about Aston? Have you made any decisions concerning him?"

He asked the question so casually he could have been inquiring about dinner. But Gaiety was ready with her response. "These past few weeks have made me sure of one thing, Papa. I want to marry Aston. And I want to marry him as soon as possible."

Lane stopped and bent to pat the dog standing beside him. Birds chirped in the trees and voices from the darkies drifted up from their quarters and the distant fields. Lane looked up to the sky as if hoping to find an answer, or at least the strength to deal with this.

He turned back to Gaiety, shifting his weight from one leg to the other. "I was hoping a few weeks in his house would make you come to your senses. I was hoping you'd give up this foolish idea of marrying him for revenge. I guess I was wrong."

Her eyes stung as she saw the helplessness in her father's features. She loved Lane Smith. She was pleased to be his daughter. But she couldn't forget that she'd had a father before Lane. And because of Dewey Talbot's and the rest of her family's untimely death, she had to cause Lane pain. She only hoped that when it was all over, he would forgive her.

Gaiety looked out over the garden. Blue, pink, white, and yellow flowers blurred before her in the midst of their greenery. "It's not foolish to me, Papa," she said, then cut her eyes back around to him. Should she try to explain to him again how she felt about her first family? No, she decided. He would never understand she felt duty-bound to carry through with her plan.

Shoring up her strength, Gaiety lifted her shoulders. "In fact, I'm more committed than ever to see that Aston pays for what he did." Her words and tone sounded strong. They had to in order to convince Lane Smith that she had to see this through.

"What his *father's men* did," Lane reminded, pointing a finger at her.

"No." She shook her head, refusing to let Aston off the hook. "His father's men didn't get Theodora pregnant. Aston did, and that's what started all that happened afterward."

Lane shook his head and walked a few steps away from her. Gaiety followed him and looked up at her father with a plea in her eyes. Fearful of her changing feelings for Aston, she asked, "Will you speak to him tonight after dinner, Papa? I don't want this to drag on any longer. Tell him you need an answer. I want him to say yes, but if his answer is no, I'd like to go back to Lilac Hill as soon as possible."

A light sparkled in Lane's eyes. "If he says no, you'll come back to Lilac Hill with me and forget all about this scheme of revenge?"

Gaiety gave him a smile that didn't hide her sorrow. She felt like she was betraying her family because she found Aston's embrace warm, enticing, and exciting. She had to strengthen her resolve to make Aston pay. "Not quite. If he won't marry me, I'll have to go back home and think of something else to do."

He let out a heavy sigh. "Gaiety—" Lane looked at his daughter. "All right, dear. I'll speak to him."

Aston held the door open for Lane Smith, then followed him out onto the front porch. Gaiety's father had asked to speak to him after dinner, so he poured them a brandy and suggested they have it outside. The late evening's air had lost its crispness as spring flourished and summer's humid night wind loomed ahead.

This talk wasn't unexpected. Lane had made that clear before he'd left for Connecticut. Aston remained relaxed and friendly. He knew Lane wanted to be assured his daughter's reputation hadn't been harmed while he was away. Gaiety remained pure, but not without some physical and mental anguish on Aston's part. He'd been aching inside with desire to hold her and kiss her again. During the day he'd found himself thinking about her when he should have been concentrating on his work. He'd been writing up new contracts with his dealers to ship his cotton up north, but Gaiety had been on his mind.

It was a hell of a thing to him. He didn't understand his developing feelings for this woman. He needed and enjoyed his romps with the women at Madrue's, but he couldn't ever remember wanting to just sit and look at any one of them the way he wanted to look at Gaiety in the evening, after dinner. He'd find himself studying the fullness of her bottom lip, the rounded arch of her shoulders, the beauty of her fingers as she sewed. And when he was at Lilac Hill, he'd been enraptured by her skill at the piano, her poise. Her graceful movements as she played the melody had him hard with desire.

What was it about her that made her different, that made him react differently to her? But he knew the answer: it was everything about her. He hadn't found one thing about her that he didn't like.

Lane leaned a shoulder against one of the columns by the steps and sipped his brandy while he waited for Aston to shut the door and join him. A three-quarter moon cast a hazy light on the porch and scattered the purple night. Aston walked over and leaned a hip against the column opposite Lane.

They stood quietly for a minute or two. Aston wasn't going to make it easy on Lane by starting the conversation. He would wait and let the man have his say.

Finally Lane said, "I know that I asked that you have a decision for me upon my return." He paused and sighed heavily. "While I was away, I had time to think about the proposal I put to you. I went over all your objections. I've considered my own feelings, and Gaiety's, too. As I told you from the beginning, my main concern is what's best for her. You know that I considered you as a husband for her because of your well-respected name and your position in the county."

Aston nodded, not quite sure the conversation was going where he expected it to.

"I've decided I'll just wait until Gaiety finds a man she wants to marry and have children with. I'm withdrawing my proposal. Considering your doubts about marriage in the first place, I'm sure you're glad to hear this."

Stunned, Aston wasn't sure he was glad to hear it. In fact, he was sure he wasn't. "You're withdrawing your proposal?" he asked, giving himself time to take in the shock.

"As of right now. Of course, we'll make plans to go back to Lilac Hill tomorrow."

Aston straightened and walked a step closer to Lane. His hand tightened on his glass. He didn't want Gaiety to go back to Lilac Hill. "Wait a minute." Rubbing his forehead, Aston tried to think clearly. "I don't understand. Why have you changed your mind?"

"It's simple. I no longer think marrying you is what's best for my daughter."

Aston was speechless for a moment. He'd never expected Lane to withdraw his proposal. He couldn't. Aston wouldn't let him. His first instinct was to say, "Hell, no!" but he had to consider what Lane was actually saying. Calmly, he asked, "Have you reason to change your mind about me? Perhaps someone has influenced you against me?"

"Not at all." Lane groaned a little as he shifted his weight. "It wasn't right for me to ask you to marry Gaiety in exchange for land."

"There's never anything wrong with asking," Aston found himself saying. "Besides, these kinds of marriage deals are agreed upon all the time." It hit Aston that he didn't want this man telling him he couldn't marry Gaiety. Aston shook his head to clear his thoughts. What was wrong with him? Six weeks ago he was telling himself that he wouldn't let Lane coerce him into marrying his daughter. Now he realized he wanted to marry Gaiety, and not for the land, not because Lane wanted a respectable match for her, but because he enjoyed her, he desired her, he wanted to take care of her and make her a part of his life and his home. The possibility he might be falling in love with Gaiety struck Aston with such force his hand trembled. After all these years, could it be so? He knew he couldn't entertain the thought of any other man kissing Gaiety the way he had when they were at the pond.

No, Gaiety had to be his. And he didn't mind fighting for her.

"I can't let you have the land," Lane was saying, as Aston gave his attention back to him. "That farm means more to Gaiety than you'll ever know. But if there's another drought, just come to me about watering your livestock. We should be able to work something out."

"Wait, you haven't heard what I have to say about all this." Aston set his glass on a nearby table and raked his hair away from his face. "I don't accept your withdrawal. I want to marry Gaiety."

"My word!" Lane's eyes rounded and widened, his mouth fell open. He moved away from the column and deeper into the shadows of the porch. "What?" he asked. "I don't understand. Since Gaiety and I arrived in this county, I've heard how you vowed before a roomful of people that you'd never marry again. Gaiety's heard it, too."

Somehow, Aston had known those words would come back to haunt him one day. He thought for a moment. Did he want to tell this man that he wanted to marry Gaiety because she was charming and beautiful, intelligent and assertive, warm and enjoyable? Should he tell her father that her kisses had been so sweet and tempting he ached to hold her, kiss her, and love her? Was he ready to admit that he was falling in love with Gaiety? No.

He pushed all those thoughts aside and said, "I know what you're talking about. It's unfortunate that some things never die and gossip is one of them. I was young and foolish at the time I made that vow. And until now I've never had reason to question it. I fully intended to keep it. But I find that because of Gaiety, I've changed my mind."

"How so?"

Aston wouldn't reveal much of his inner thinking to this man. "Surely I don't have to tell you how Gaiety can charm a man's heart."

"You *want* to marry Gaiety?" Lane tapped his forehead with the palm of his hand. "I'd hoped Gaiety would be softened by her exposure to you, but I didn't think you'd fall victim to her because of your attitude toward marriage."

Aston heard astonishment in Lane's voice, saw it in his action. Aston had astonished himself. He'd been prepared to let Lane talk him into marrying Gaiety. It had never occurred to him that he might have to talk Lane into carrying through with his promise of her hand.

Lane shook his head as he rubbed his shoulder and mumbled to himself before speaking aloud. "There are a lot of things I can't go into. Just take my word for it . . . it's best that a marriage between you and Gaiety not be made."

A tightening formed in Aston's stomach. Now that he'd decided he wanted Gaiety, he wouldn't let her father take her away from him. "I intend to marry Gaiety," he said again, only more strongly. "I won't let you take back your proposal."

Lane squinted as if trying to figure out something, or to comprehend. "Is there no way I can persuade you that my proposal was a bad idea?"

"None. If you won't agree to the marriage, I'll be forced to speak directly to Gaiety."

Lane shook his head again. "No need for that. Sounds to me like you're going into this with your eyes wide open. You get what you want and Gaiety gets what she wants." Lane put his drink to his lips and finished it off. "I've done all I can do. It appears you both want this marriage."

"Then we can draw up the papers?"

Nodding Lane said, "I suggest we not wait the proper engagement time. I'd like to get this over with as soon as possible. The only people Gaiety and I will have in attendance is our staff, provided you don't mind. Gaiety treats them like family."

"Of course. And I don't have a problem with a hasty marriage, but I feel we should speak to Gaiety about it. She may not want to forgo the engagement parties and a proper wedding."

A sardonic laugh rumbled from Lane's chest. "Take my word for it. She won't have any objections."

Ten

Gaiety's throat ached. Her stomach cramped nervously as she started down the stairs on her father's arm. The time had come. She was jittery inside, her leg muscles were jumpy, her joints felt unhinged.

It had taken exactly two weeks to get her bridal gown finished and all the preparations made for the wedding. When Mimi had helped her slip the gown over her head and she'd seen herself dressed in the ivory-colored silk covered with lace, pearls, and tiny white satin rosebuds, she worried that she wouldn't be able to go through with this deception.

She'd twirled away from the mirror, forcing herself not to think about Aston and what this marriage would do to him. But she couldn't help wondering if it would be easier for him to accept if he knew she had doubts about carrying through with her plan.

But in the end, she settled that in her mind, realizing she had to think about her family. Right from the beginning, she'd been doing this for them. If she kept that fact uppermost in her mind, she'd make it through the wedding. Her feelings for Aston couldn't come into this. Even if she had loved Aston, she would still have to do this to him. Her duty, her integrity, her very soul demanded that she seek revenge and justice.

Gaiety stopped her father at the bottom of the stairs. She had to catch her breath. She could hardly breathe.

Her father squeezed her arm and asked, "Are you all right?"

She tried to swallow the lump in her throat as she faced him, but couldn't. Her mouth was too dry. "I'm fine, Papa." She managed a smile and they started forward again.

A few steps down the hallway they rounded the doorway and entered the ballroom. Aston stood at the end of the room, splendidly dressed in a black evening suit, white shirt, and black-and-gray-striped cravat. He was enormously handsome, beguiling. Her heartbeat increased, her stomach muscles knotted painfully, as the weight of what she had to do made her physically ill.

I can't go through with this.

You have to.

I can't do it to him!

He's responsible for the deaths of your family.

He was young and foolish.

So were Theodora and Josh.

Does he deserve this for what happened twelve years ago?

Yes.

Gaiety warred with her inner feelings as she slowly walked toward Aston.

From her peripheral vision she saw the guests; men and women looking at her, smiling. At the back of the room she spied Mimi, Jeanette, and Maine, beaming with pleasure. Farther down front she saw Elaine, smiling from ear to ear, and Fredrick, frowning at her as if she'd done something he didn't like. Thankful for the veil she wore, Gaiety squeezed her eyes shut for a moment and allowed her father to lead her the rest of the way, hoping it would make the last few steps easier to take.

When she realized she'd stopped, she found herself standing beside Aston. She felt light-headed, sick. Her father placed her left hand inside Aston's and gave her a final pat. Aston wrapped her hand with both of his, fitting it snugly. The warmth his flesh offered traveled up her arm and quickly covered her like a sheet of silk.

The minister started the ceremony. Gaiety became as a wooden doll, standing stiffly, listening, answering when she was supposed to, but not feeling anything.

As the ceremony continued, in her mind's eye she saw her papa in his white shirt with his hair all slicked back, ready for church, and Josh with his bright blue eyes laughing as he threw her over his shoulders. The last time she remembered seeing Theodora, she was climbing in the wagon with Josh, wearing her best dress and carrying a bundle of clothing. She saw Titus, too—the little boy who no longer had a face. How could she have forgotten what he looked like? How could she?

Gaiety renewed her strength. Aston had never been punished, never felt the pain she had, never suffered as she had. He got away free and continued with his life. She knew she'd have to leave his house, his life, forever, once she made her announcement, and that troubled her.

"Ladies and gentlemen, I present to you Mr. and Mrs. Aston Rutledge. After he kisses his bride, please give them your congratulations and best wishes for a long and happy life together. Aston, you may kiss your wife."

This was it. Her plan had to be carried out now or forever forgotten. She'd never find the courage at a later date. Aston lifted her veil. Gaiety looked into his eyes. They were trusting, happy. She wanted to hurt him and she didn't. Her courage faltered. He reached down to kiss her on the lips, but Gaiety turned her cheek to him. As his lips grazed the soft skin of her cheek she whispered huskily, "My real name is Avalina Talbot. I'm Theodora's sister."

He stiffened immediately. His hands closed around her upper arms like bands of iron. She felt his body tighten so stiff she thought he'd break in two. Slowly he leaned away from her. His gaze drilled into hers, searching for an answer to her outrageous statement. "What did you say?" His voice was less than a whisper, not much more than a mere brush of the air.

"I'm Theodora's sister," she answered softly, before she could talk herself out of denying the truth of her words. "The family you destroyed was mine. Ask my adoptive father. He'll tell you I'm not lying."

Aston's eyes still denied what she said. Shock, pain, and disbelief filled their depths. His lips paled, his lashes fluttered. Hurt and devastation flitted across his face before he managed to mask it all behind a growl of anger that quickly turned to rage. She expected all those things from Aston, but where was her victory?

At that moment, Gaiety realized that her father was right: there was no glory in revenge, no honor in deceit, and no victory in claiming an eye for an eye. Only she was the loser. She no longer had a goal, a desire, a driving force. She realized that what had kept her from going crazy when she realized she'd lost Titus and the rest of her family was the thought that she'd one day get even with Aston Rutledge. Now she had, but the horrors of all the past misdeeds hadn't been erased because she'd gotten even. She'd only added to their number.

Gaiety turned to leave, but Aston quickly jerked her back to face him. Suddenly someone threw their arms around her neck. Aston was pushed aside as Elaine, Linda Sue, and other young ladies crowded around Gaiety bubbling with laughter and chatter. Gaiety felt cold.

Aston lost his breath for a few seconds, so unexpected and devastating was the shock of her words. Even now, he wanted to deny the truth of what she claimed. His heart felt as if it might explode in his chest. As he tried to contain his anger, his darker emotions, Gaiety was pulled from his grasp by the well-wishers. Hands clapped him on the back and pumped his arm, and he was bombarded with congratulations. Over the heads of his friends, Aston saw Lane walking out of the ballroom. He tensed. He couldn't let him get away.

As nicely as he could, Aston shook off the offending handshakes and hearty wishes and made his way through the crowd toward Lane's receding back.

He reached the man just outside the ballroom and touched his arm. Lane turned and faced him. Breathless, Aston asked, "Is it true?"

Lane's face reddened, sorrow shadowed his eyes. "I tried to stop you from marrying her."

Aston trembled. His hands made fists. "Damn it!" His voice remained dangerously low. "You tell me straight, with a yes or a no. Is she your daughter, Gaiety Smith, or is she Avalina Talbot?"

Without a blink of his eyes Lane said, "She's both."

Aston wanted to put his fist through a wall, through Lane's face. He wanted to hurt someone. He wanted to hurt himself to ease the pain caused by the woman he'd just married.

He had actually thought she was starting to care for him. They'd lied to him, used him, duped him. How was he going to live with this? How was he going to live with the knowledge that he'd married Theodora's sister?

"She's not a bad person, Aston," Lane said with all sincerity. "You have to understand what she—"

"You're a goddamned liar."

Aston turned to stomp away, but Lane grabbed his arm and held him. Lane's eyes hardened. "If you hurt her, I'll kill you."

Aston chuckled bitterly, dangerously, revengefully. He jerked his arm out of Lane's grasp and pivoted away. He headed back into the ballroom, hell-bent on getting to Gaiety. He wanted to put his hands around her neck and scare the hell out of her. He wanted to do something to get rid of the anger, the hurt, the devastation he was feeling over Gaiety's deceit. Why had he decided to trust a woman? He knew better.

He pushed his way through the small crowd and made his way to where Gaiety stood in the swarm of excited women. She looked beautifully pale. His heart constricted. He'd wanted to trust her. Damn it! He'd wanted to love her. He passed by Josie and stopped him. "Get the music started and keep it going. Make sure everyone has plenty to drink."

"What's wrong, Mr. Aston? You don't look so good," the old man said.

"Don't worry about me. Just do what I said."

He walked up to Gaiety and slipped his arm around her waist. She was clearly surprised by the sweet smile on his lips.

"I'd like to see you for a few minutes, my love," he said softly.

"Well—I—"

"We can talk anytime. Go ahead and be with your husband," Elaine said to Gaiety, before turning her attention to Aston. "Everyone is still in shock that you've actually gotten married. You fooled us all with your protests of marriage. I want you to know I'm taking full responsibility for bringing you two together."

Aston gave her a falsely sweet smile. "No, dear cousin-to-be. I happen to know that Gaiety set her cap for me before she came to town. I'll return her shortly," he said to those surrounding her. He smiled at Elaine and the two other ladies. "You don't mind, do you ladies? I thought not."

With his hand well placed on the small of her back, Aston ushered Gaiety forward. He skillfully mastered their way through the crowd, allowing them to be stopped only twice. He smiled and talked his way past everyone, deftly leading Gaiety up the stairs and to his room. Once inside, he shut the door and locked it. Only then did he realize that Gaiety hadn't protested. She allowed herself to be led as easily as a lamb to the slaughter.

He leaned against the door and looked at his bride, his wife, his enemy. She still held her bouquet, her veil still streamed down her back.

Her eyes were wide with fear, and at that moment she was more beautiful than he'd ever seen her. He felt as if a knife twisted in his gut, pouring his blood from his veins. He wanted to love her. He wanted to hate her. He wanted to love her. He wanted to hurt her. God help him, he wanted to love her.

Quickly he advanced on her. "You bitch!"

Gaiety stood fast. "I know."

"You lied to me!"

"Yes."

"You deceived me!"

"I know."

When he stopped, they stood nose to nose. She hadn't flinched. That surprised him. Damn it! He wanted to hurt her the way he hurt. Yes, God damn it, God help him, he wanted to hit her, too, but knew he couldn't. Would he feel better if he could? Would the pain go away, or would it live with him forever, as Theodora's lies had? He hadn't hated Theodora enough to want to hurt her, but he was so consumed with rage for what Gaiety had done that he had to do something.

In a sudden rush of burning passion, he grabbed her by the shoulders and pushed her across the room and up against the wall. She made a small whimpering sound, but Aston paid it no mind as he rammed the heel of his palm into the plastered wall beside her. Pain splintered up his arm. Gaiety made a low sound in her throat. Aston groaned from the pain in his hand. He pressed his body against

Gaiety's and lay his forehead against the wall beside her. Each heavy breath took in the softly sweet smell of Gaiety. He felt her chest moving beneath his, her breathing as erratic as his own.

He rested his body against hers, trying to calm himself. Aston had had no feelings for Theodora when they married, but he had started to care for Gaiety. Did that explain why he felt as if his world had just collapsed around him?

"Why?" he finally managed to ask, ignoring the pain in his hand, the pain in his heart.

"You are responsible for my father's and brother's deaths."

"No," he denied, raising his head to look at her.

Her eyes glistened accusingly. "Yes. Because of you, my whole family was destroyed."

He hurt. He hurt more than he ever had. And the worst of it was that it mattered to him what Gaiety thought about him, what she felt about him. He'd thought she was beginning to like him. Hell! He thought she might one day love him.

"My father's men killed your father and brother." The horror of that day so long ago flashed across his mind.

"You admit that, yet no one was ever punished for their deaths." She pushed against his chest, and he let her move away from him.

She was wrong; he *had* been punished. He was forced to marry a girl he didn't know, forced to be a witness to her death. The calm of knowing he was blameless settled over him. He could think clearly for the first time since she'd made her damning revelation. In this he knew he was right! "They aimed their rifles first. It was self-defense."

"I heard those lies from the sheriff when I was eight years old. I didn't believe them then. I don't believe them now."

"That's your right. But why marry me?"

"When Papa and I moved here, I kept hearing the one thing you didn't want, the one thing you'd vowed not to have, was a wife. The only way I could think to make you pay for the deaths of my family was to give you the one thing you didn't want. I persuaded Papa to make the proposal of marriage to you."

He nodded, thinking more clearly, reading more into her words than she was actually saying. If all she'd wanted was to see him married, she wouldn't have had to reveal who she was. Late afternoon shadows fell softly on the room. Toe-tapping music drifted up from below, as did sounds of talking and laughter. Aston stared at Gaiety. He was having a difficult time with his emotions. Inside, a voice was telling him to hate her, but looking at her, he knew he couldn't.

Finally he said, "You succeeded. I'm your husband." He folded his arms across his chest. "Tell me, what do you plan to do with me now that you have me?"

"Ah—I—" Momentarily flustered, she cleared her throat and started over. "From the beginning I planned to leave you right after the ceremony. I still plan to do that. Papa and I will be going back to Lilac Hill."

Anger surged within Aston, but he hid it behind a gentle chuckle. Even though he admired the courage it took for her to pull off such a scheme, he could in no way appreciate what she'd done. He took a step toward her. "You think so? Think again. I own Lilac Hill now. It's part of your dowry. Remember the papers your father handed me before the ceremony?" The look in her eyes told him she had forgotten about that, and it gave him a moment's satisfaction.

"Fine, you can have it," she said, a nervous edge to her voice. "We don't need it. Papa and I will buy another place."

"Lane is free to live wherever he chooses, but you, dear *wife,* will live here with me. You can forget about any other plans you had. I've just changed them."

"You can't do that. Papa—"

"Papa just gave you to me," he said firmly. "You're my wife, and I intend to see that you live here with me. You may have made a mockery out of our marriage, but I won't allow you to shame me in front of my friends. You'll live here with me on Southern Oaks for the rest of your life, Gaiety." He sneered. "Or do you prefer the name Avalina?"

Ignoring his question, she lifted her chin a little higher and said, "You can't make me live here as a prisoner. My father won't allow it."

"He can't stop it. He no longer has control over you. I do."

Gaiety advanced on him, her silk skirts swishing about her legs. "Don't do this to me," she said softly. "I lost everything because of your careless treatment of my sister. I lost Papa, Josh, Theodora, and Titus."

Titus. Did she think Titus was dead? Aston's thoughts whirled. *Of course!* She had no way of knowing that he'd taken Titus from the orphanage. Avalina had already been adopted when Aston went there to get them after Theodora's death. "What about Titus?"

Dark fringed lids dropped to hide her eyes and she lowered her head a little. "I don't know what happened to him." Her voice was husky with emotion. She gripped the skirt of her gown in her hands and bunched the silk. "He was only four the last time I saw him. There was some kind of mixup at the orphanage when Lane and Mary adopted me. When I kept calling for my brother, Papa asked Mrs. Conners about him and she told him about Josh's death. She never mentioned Titus. We think she was afraid Papa wouldn't take me if he knew I had a brother living at the orphanage, too. By the time Lane and Mary figured out that I had two brothers—Josh, who'd been killed, and Titus, who was very much alive—the orphanage had burned and all of its records. We couldn't find out any information about Titus."

She looked up at him with sadness in her

eyes. "I can't remember what he looks like. They're all fading from memory, and it's all your fault."

Aston saw her sadness, felt it. Slowly he became aware of a shocking realization: she was hurting, too. He saw a glimpse of what had driven her to deceive him. He had an overwhelming need to comfort Gaiety for the loss of her family. He'd always felt bad about Josh and Dewey's deaths. Always.

His emotions, his feelings for Gaiety were spiraling out of control. She'd deceived him! How could he feel sorry for her? How could he want to take her in his arms and comfort he? No, he wouldn't allow those feelings. His manhood wouldn't allow him to pass up the chance for his own revenge. She'd gone through hell, but so had he. It would salve his ego to know he'd gotten even with the little hell-kitten standing before him. He'd have the last laugh.

"I want my wedding night, Gaiety," he said without prelude.

Stunned, she could only mouth the word "no."

He looked at her. Her golden brown hair swirled into a mass of curls on top of her head. Her eyes glistened. Her lips were a tempting shade of dusty rose. Yes, he would do it. He would make love to her, and to get even with her, he'd make sure she enjoyed every minute of it.

"Yes, I do, but I plan to give you something in return."

She backed away from him. "What are you talking about? What will you give me? My freedom?"

"No." He shook his head. "You'll never have that. I'll give you your brother. I know where Titus is."

Gaiety gasped.

"It's true. I was the one who took him out of the orphanage and saw to it that he had a home. It appears we both had our little secrets."

"No, you're lying." Gaiety came alive with prospect. Her eyes grew wide with shock. She rushed Aston and took hold of his lapels with trembling fingers.

He circled her wrists with his hands and held her tightly. He looked directly into her eyes. "I'm not."

"My brother is alive?" She was breathless, faint. She was afraid to believe him—and afraid not to. "You know where Titus is? Tell me!"

Aston held firm. "Not until I get my wedding might."

"No!" she cried, losing all control at the thought that this man knew where Titus was and wouldn't tell her. She pulled out of his hold and struck out at him, her fist coming down hard on his chin.

Aston grabbed hold of her wrist again. "Stop, Gaiety. I don't want to hurt you." He shoved her up against the bed, bending her backward. She kicked his legs. She squirmed, trying to free herself.

"Tell me where he is!" she demanded in a tremulous voice. "All these years I've wondered what happened to him. I deserve to know."

"You're in no position to demand anything, wife. You've had your revenge. Now I'll take mine."

"You got my sister pregnant, then you didn't want to marry her. You deserved what I did to you."

All those old emotions of bitterness sprung forth. His hands tightened around her wrists. Holding his teeth shut, he said, "The baby Theodora carried wasn't mine."

"You lie," she spat out, her chest heaving beneath the awkward position he held her.

"No!" he denied vehemently, pushing her harder, arching her over the bed. "Your sister was the one who lied. She lied because she knew my father was the wealthiest man in the county, and she was looking to better her station in life. I don't know who got her pregnant, but it wasn't me."

"You're lying," she declared again, her chest heaving with uneasy breaths. Her gaze darted across his face. She trembled.

"I'm not. Damn it! after all these years, why would I lie about this? I've nothing to gain or to lose at this point. The baby was not mine. I never touched Theodora before we married, or after." His anger grew hot again. He let go of her wrists and quickly circled Gaiety in his arms, lowering his head until their noses were touching. "I've been married twice now and never had a wedding night. If you want to know where your little brother is, Gaiety, you will have to give me a wedding night."

"Never!" She hissed the word.

Aston smiled and said, "Surely after two wives I deserve at least one wedding night."

"I won't do it," she said but her voice was losing its edge. "You have no ri—"

He jerked her chest up tight against his. "I have every right. The wedding vows you just spoke gave me the right, should I choose to force you. But I don't think I'll have to." Aston turned her loose so quickly she fell onto the bed.

"This isn't fair," she whispered.

His stare was bold. "Don't talk to me about fair." He walked over, picked up her bouquet, and stuffed it back in her hands. "I suggest you put a smile on your face and join me downstairs. We have guests waiting for our reappearance."

Aston raked his fingers through his hair as he hurried down the stairs. He was hot. His stomach muscles were jerking. He felt like he'd been beaten. From the joyous sounds coming from the ballroom, it appeared no one had any idea what was going on between him and Gaiety. He was thankful for that. All he wanted to do right now was slip into the library and have a drink. He needed some time alone to think over everything that had been said.

"In a bit of a hurry to get your bride upstairs, aren't you, Aston?" Fredrick said, as he met Aston in the hallway.

Damn. The last thing he wanted was to have to deal with Fredrick. He might as well forget about the time alone. If he stayed away from the party much longer, the guests would get restless.

"Gaiety was looking a little pale from all the excitement. I took her upstairs so we could have a few minutes alone together." That wasn't exactly a lie.

"Really, then it's true?" Fredrick asked, following him into the ballroom.

"What?" he asked mechanically, looking over the roomful of people, dancing, talking, drinking, and laughing.

"Talk is that Gaiety is in the family way and that's the reason you had to get married so fast."

The absurdity of that made Aston's laugh genuine. He clapped Fredrick on the back. Josie passed by with a tray of filled glasses, so Aston reached for one. "That couldn't be further from the truth, dear cousin."

"Why else would you forgo all the parties and attention of an engagement? Does history repeat itself?"

Aston was tempted to take his anger out on Fredrick, but managed to stop himself. "Gaiety and I preferred it this way, Fred."

Fredrick smirked. "Well, time will tell."

Aston knew Fredrick was miffed by his marriage, and with what he considered good reason. The trouble was, Fredrick didn't know how close he was to still having his son inherit Southern Oaks.

He clapped Fredrick on the back again. "I'm sure you're right. Excuse me, I see someone I should speak to."

Gaiety left her wedding bouquet on Aston's bed and made her way back to the party. After speaking with several people including Mimi and Jeanette, she asked Josie about her father. He told her he was sitting in the garden.

Dusk lay on the sky with glorious colors as Gaiety made her way to the garden. Her thoughts were still reeling from what she'd done to Aston, hearing that Titus was alive and what Aston demanded in return. She desperately wanted some time alone to think, but that would have to wait.

"Papa," she called, coming up behind him.

He turned and looked at her with a weary expression. "I have something to tell you, Papa."

"Gaiety, if you're happy, let me hear it. Tell me all that's in your heart. But if you want to complain that things haven't turned out the way you wanted, I don't want to know. I can't help you; I've done all I can do for you. All I ever wanted for you was a smile on your face and in your eyes to match the name I gave you. I wanted you to be happy. If you're not, I don't want to hear it, for I can do no more for you."

"Look at me, Papa," she said with a trembling smile on her lips. "There is happiness in my face. Look. Can you see it?"

He cupped her chin and looked down into her eyes. "Yes. Did it work, Gaiety? Have you finally rid yourself of the hatred you've carried for so many years?"

She smiled again. She laughed. She rose and hugged him. "Oh, it's so much more than that. Papa, Aston knows where Titus is."

"What?"

She took a seat beside him, her wedding dress billowing around her. "Yes. It's true. He told me he took Titus from the orphanage after Theodora died and placed him with a family. Just think, Papa—if I hadn't told Aston who I am, I might never have known that Titus is alive."

"My God, where is he?" Lane asked excitedly.

Gaiety moistened her lips. "That I don't know yet."

"Why?" Lane looked confused. "Why would he tell you he knows where Titus is but not tell you where?"

Hating to say what had to be said, Gaiety rose. "He wants something in return."

"What could he possibly want? He has the land. I've already signed it over to him."

"He wants a wedding night."

Lane rose and took hold of her upper arms. "Gaiety, I—"

"Papa, it's all right. Don't worry about me." She swallowed hard. "I'll do anything to find Titus."

"Something isn't right," Mimi said to Hank, as they stood out on the back porch listening to the music coming from inside the house.

"What do you mean?"

"Miss Gaiety isn't herself. I know she was worried about Mr. Aston and his first wife's death. I told you she wanted to know all about that woman, so I found out what I could for her. Maybe that's why she's acting so strange. Maybe it's his first wife's death that's bothering her."

"No reason for it to. Mr. Aston didn't have anything to do with that girl's death. My pa is the one who went for the doctor after she fell down the stairs. I remember Pa coming home saying she was driving everyone crazy with her demands. No one could please her, not even Mr. Aston, and he tried hard. She wanted new dresses, so he brought a dressmaker out to Southern Oaks especially for her."

"That's what I heard from Jolene, too. Truth is, I'm not sure she was ready to marry Mr. Aston. I think they should have had a proper engagement. It would have given her more time to get to know him."

"Sometimes you don't need a lot of time to

get to know someone. Besides, Miss Gaiety couldn't have married a finer man."

Hank slipped his arm around Mimi and she felt a little thrill in her stomach. He took hold of her right arm and led her into a dance step. He didn't have a practiced movement, but she followed him. Mimi felt like she was floating on air. The music played, the stars shone in the sky, and she was dancing with Hank. She couldn't have been happier.

"And the best thing about Miss Gaiety marrying Mr. Aston is that you'll be living here. I'm glad about that. I didn't want you to go back to Lilac Hill."

She smiled up at him. The music stopped and Hank turned her loose. "Me either, but I better go inside now. Miss Gaiety might start looking for me."

"Mimi, will you meet me out here tonight after Miss Gaiety goes to Mr. Aston's room? She won't need you."

A feeling of excitement and fear came over her. "I don't know, Hank. Miss Gaiety doesn't mind me seeing you during the day, but I don't think she'd want me to meet you late at night."

"We won't do anything but talk," he promised. "I want to spend some time with you when we don't have to hurry."

It seemed as if Mimi's heart melted when she looked into his eyes. "I'll try," she whispered.

"I'll be waiting over by the cook house for you."

Mimi smiled.

Eleven

It was with reluctance and a bit of fear that Gaiety dressed for bed that evening. Somehow she'd managed to get through most of the wedding party. She'd even managed to keep a smile on her face when she danced with Aston and answered what seemed like a thousand questions from Elaine. All the while, at the back of her mind was the joy she'd felt at hearing that Titus was alive. Nothing else could have made her stay a minute longer at Aston's house. Nothing could have lifted her spirits to such heights.

Now she knew why she'd had that all-consuming desire to make Aston pay. It must have been fate leading her in the direction that would take her to Titus. But before Aston would give her brother back to her, she had to get through the rest of the evening. Fate had been kind and cruel to her at the same time.

Gaiety put on a long-sleeved nightgown made from a soft cotton lawn. Three rows of ruffles adorned the neckline and hemline, with matching ruffles at the cuffs. Against Mimi's suggestion, she'd kept her drawers and chemise on under the nightgown. Her robe lay across the foot of Aston's bed. The beautiful wedding gown now lay across the slipper chair.

The gold and brown wide-striped coverlet had been folded back revealing fresh-pressed cream-colored sheets, soft as satin, glowing in the yellow light from the oil lamp beside the bed. Plump pillows lay invitingly against the bedframe. Swallowing hard, Gaiety turned away from the bed, sat down on the stool in front of the dresser, and allowed Mimi to take the pins out of her hair. She had expected to spend her wedding night alone. Now that she had prepared physically to spend the night in Aston's bed, she had to prepare mentally for what was to come.

"I'll never again see anything as pretty as you walking down that aisle to meet Mr. Aston," Mimi said, putting the pins in a small china dish. "When he lifted that veil and kissed you, I had tears in my eyes."

Gaiety remained quiet and let Mimi talk. She had to admit that she felt guilty about what she'd had to do to Aston.

"I was so happy for you. He's a handsome man. You don't want me to braid it tonight, do you, Miss?" Mimi asked, as she combed out Gaiety's shiny golden brown chignon.

"A braid with a ribbon at the end will be fine, Mimi," Gaiety answered, trying not to show how nervous she was at the thought of being alone with Aston.

He had been extremely angry with her, but she had to admit he had good reason. She'd deceived him. But in the end he'd had the last laugh. Tonight, she had to be his wife.

Every time Gaiety thought about the possibility of seeing Titus again after all these years her heart soared with happiness, with gratitude to Aston for taking him out of the orphanage and placing him in a home. Aston? She didn't know exactly how to deal with her ambivalent feelings toward him.

Mimi continued to talk as she braided. Gaiety heard her voice, but not her words. She was too caught up in her own thoughts. She'd never allowed herself to imagine there would be a wedding night. But here she was in Aston's room, dressed for bed and waiting for him.

It wasn't that she found him repulsive; she didn't. In fact, it would be better if she did. Then she could tell herself she'd hate every minute of being with him. She realized what bothered her more was the fact that Aston was forcing her to do this in exchange for her brother. And that's what would get her through the night. In the end, she would find out where Titus was living and go and get him. The Talbot family would be reunited.

A knock sounded on the door, then it opened. Gaiety stiffened. Aston stepped inside, still fully dressed in his wedding clothes. Gaiety's chest tightened; her throat felt dry. Josie walked in behind Aston, carrying a small silver tray with a crystal decanter and two wineglasses on top. He set down the tray.

"That will be all, Josie. You can go to bed now." He looked at her maid. "You, too, Mimi. If Gaiety needs anything further, I'll get it for her."

Not expecting to be ordered around by Aston, Mimi looked at Gaiety's reflection in the mirror to see if her mistress was going to dispute the order. Gaiety took a deep breath and nodded for Mimi to go. The maid and Josie said their goodnights and left the room. From here on out, Gaiety would be on her own.

Aston strode confidently to the tray and poured a small amount of brandy in each glass, then walked over to the dresser and handed a glass to Gaiety. She continued to watch him through the mirror as she took it from him, making sure their fingers didn't touch.

He lifted his glass and said, "To you, Gaiety. Drink it. It will make tonight much easier for you."

For a moment she wondered if he wanted her to be frightened of him. In a way she was. He might force this night on her, but she wouldn't make it easy for him. She followed his suggestion and sipped the strong mulberry-colored liquid. It burned her tongue and throat and landed heavily in her empty stomach, seeming to boil inside her. She'd been unable to eat any of the wedding feast. The drink warmed her immediately, sending a rush of heat to her face and neck. She took another sip. Although it left a sting in her mouth, it had a soothing effect she found comforting.

Aston stared at her in the mirror and she him as he set his drink down and took off his jacket and cravat, throwing them on top of her discarded wedding gown. She continued to watch him as he slowly unfastened his waistcoat and shrugged out of it. He picked up his drink and sipped it before starting on the buttons of his shirt. She sat as if mesmerized as his deft fingers worked down the shirt, parting it slightly, showing curly dark brown chest hair. She noticed his hands. They were strong looking, attractive, hands with nimble fingers and neatly trimmed nails.

Was the drink making her so hot, or was it Aston's deliberately sensual movements? When the shirt was unbuttoned to his waist, Gaiety looked away and sipped her brandy. She would have never thought herself brazen enough to watch a man undress. Her husband, true. But a husband she'd expected to have in name only.

She chanced another peek at him and saw he had a hint of a smile on his beautifully full lips. She sensed he was hoping to shock her, to intimidate her, to get a reaction out of her.

Gaiety set her glass on the dresser and rose to face Aston. She wouldn't let him get the best of her, no matter what went on in the marriage bed. She'd find a way to cope and keep her dignity intact. Looking into his eyes, she said,

"Can we just get this evening over with? Do you have to be so slow in disrobing?"

He laughed so softly Gaiety found it pleasing, seductive when it should have kindled anger. The desirous expression in his eyes was so intense her body heated. Her gaze lingered on his. He slowly pulled his shirt from his trousers and off his arms, leaving it to find its way to the floor. His shoulders and arms were muscular, wide. The defined planes of his chest rose and fell with his breathing. It looked as if the fine film of dark brown curly hair had been neatly arranged across his chest and down his rippled abdomen.

"No, dearest wife," he spoke huskily. "We're going to do this right. I've been waiting for this night for a long time. I don't plan to rush our lovemaking."

Gaiety tried to swallow, but found her throat too dry. She tingled when she should be tensing. She wanted to forgive and forget, but she had to remember and punish the man she'd hated for so long. How could she accept with relish the wondrous feelings that sang through her body with this man's mere presence, his expression, his laugh, his promise of what was to come?

Suddenly she was afraid, but not of Aston: her own feelings frightened her. She'd hated him for good reason. Why was she pushing that aside for the traitorous feelings of desire twisting inside her, attacking her heart and her good sense? Why was she standing before this half-dressed man, wanting to hate him but knowing those negative feelings were dissolving second by second? Could she say to herself that she was only going through with this night for Titus when she knew she'd been drawn to Aston the first time she saw him?

"Are you nervous?" he asked in a low, whispery voice.

"Yes," she managed to say.

"I don't want you to be. I'm not going to hurt you. You do know that, don't you? I want you to enjoy every minute of our night together."

"How can I enjoy sharing a bed with a man I don't even like?" Her words sounded more reluctant than she felt. Even if she couldn't lie to herself, she didn't intend to let Aston know her true feelings and desires.

"I'll show you. You don't have to like me to enjoy my bed."

Her eyes followed his hands to his trousers, and he started unbuttoning them. "You must be mad even to suggest such a thing," she answered, her voice more wobbly than she'd have liked it to be. "I could never enjoy sleeping with you."

Aston grinned invitingly. "Gaiety, we will do a lot of things this night, but sleep is not one of them. So don't worry about sleeping with me. You won't have to." He took an agonizingly slow step toward her. "I don't intend to let you leave me until the sun breaks on the horizon."

He kept his gaze on her face as he slid his

breeches down his legs and stepped out of them. His long underwear rode low on his hips, hugging his body, failing to conceal the revealing bulge at the junction of his muscular thighs. Excitement rushed through her so potently that Gaiety guiltily snapped her attention back to his face.

Her breath became shallow. She had to force her gaze not to travel the length of his body and settle her mind about his physique. "You're vile," she whispered softly, and knew as soon as the words were spoken that her voice sounded more accepting than appalled.

He chuckled lightly. "You say that now, but I wonder what you'll be saying once the night is half over."

"Why do you even want to touch me after what I did to you?" she asked, not fully understanding his reasons for wanting this night with her.

"Revenge. You've had yours. Now it's my turn."

Aston walked over to her and touched her cheek with his palm, letting his fingertips rest gently below her eye. In order to salvage her dignity, Gaiety squeezed her eyes shut and turned her face away from his. After all these years of hating him, there seemed no way to accept her growing sexual feelings toward him without destroying a part of herself, a part of her past.

"I hate you," she whispered, as much for herself as for him. She thought she felt his hand tremble on her cheek, but the movement was so slight she wasn't sure.

"I know." His voice was husky. He untied the ribbon that held her hair in a braid and let it fall to the floor. With both his hands he combed through the plait and freed her hair. "But tonight, that doesn't matter. I'm going to show you that you don't have to love me or even like me to enjoy my touch. I'm going to make you a woman."

His words heated her so, she felt singed. She turned her face farther to the side, hoping to escape the pressure of his hand on her cheek.

"You need not shrink from my touch, Gaiety. I know you don't find me repulsive. I remember our embrace by the pond. I know what your lips taste like, what you feel like in my arms, how you respond to me." He let his hands glide across her shoulders to her back. He slipped his hand around her waist and brought her abdomen up against his. His lips touched her cheek.

For her sanity, for integrity, for desire to win this battle, she said, "Please don't do this to me, Aston."

"I love the way you say my name, Gaiety," he whispered. "Do you like the way I say your name?"

"No," she lied, trying to deny the feelings of hunger curling inside her.

Aston chuckled huskily, as if he knew she was lying, and Gaiety stood quietly, spellbound by his touch. He kissed her cheeks, her eyes, her nose, but not her lips. Those he left wanting his touch.

He continued to kiss her cheek, letting his lips touch her soft skin ever so slightly. "Soften, Gaiety. Bend. I don't want to hurt you, but my honor demands this." He moved his lips up and down her cheek, over her jawbone, down her neck, and across to the soft skin behind her ear. "Give me until daybreak," he whispered.

Gaiety's lashes fluttered upward. Was he asking or demanding her concurrence? She couldn't tell. And at that moment, she didn't know that it mattered. She only knew that his body was warm, hard, against hers. His lips left feathery, moist tickles across her skin that tightened her chest, hardened her nipples, and contracted her stomach. Her lips ached to feel his touch on hers, but he ignored them repeatedly.

Even though her body was telling her to accept what he was offering and enjoy it, still she had to fight him. She reminded herself that he was forcing her to do this before he'd tell her about Titus, and she couldn't allow herself to participate.

Aston's attentions were slow and unhurried. Gaiety remained rigid, denying the womanly part of her that cried out to be awakened until Aston settled his lips upon hers. He kissed her tentatively at first. He slipped his arms around her waist. She heard his intake of breath as her own shortened. His arms encircled her back, pressing their bodies together. She didn't want to get caught up in the sensual web he was weaving, but she was. She didn't want to remember all the things she'd found to like about him, but she did. She didn't want to enjoy his kiss or his touch, but she did.

He was so gentle, so caring, that Gaiety forgot her vow to resist him and slowly yielded to the tenderness she sensed within him. Intensely aware of what she was doing and why, she pushed aside all thoughts of the past and slipped her arms around his shoulders. His hands ran up and down her back, warming her, thrilling her. One of his hands slipped around her chest and caressed her breast through her nightgown. Her response was immediate, powerful, yielding. Her desire to know and enjoy his touch won out over her need to remain passive. How could she when she felt so alive?

With the skill of a practiced man he reached down and lifted the hem of her nightgown and pulled it over her head, then tossed it aside. "Damn. Gaiety, you have clothes on under your nightgown?"

He looked at her thigh-length sleeveless chemise and her drawers that ended below her knee. Aston suddenly grinned. "I always liked the fact that you're so damn proper." He hooked his arm beneath her knees and lifted her off the floor and laid her on the bed.

Aston rose up over her and looked down into her eyes but didn't speak. Gaiety sensed he wanted to say something, but for some reason decided to remain quiet. His gaze left her face, traveling down to her breasts, lingering there.

"Aren't you going to turn down the lamp?" she asked, feeling suddenly bashful as he looked at her.

"No. There will be no secrets between us tonight. Nothing hidden," he whispered, before claiming her lips with a fierce kiss that demanded she participate.

Aston made short work of getting rid of her underwear and his, too. At first she tried to hide her breasts with her hands, but Aston gently lowered her arms and whispered, "You're beautiful. Don't hide your body from me. I want to look at you."

The pressure of Aston's body lying over hers, his hands searching, caressing, outlining her body, sent thrill after shivering thrill washing through her. She spread her hands over his shoulders and back, impassioned by freedom. His skin was firmly textured, rousing instincts she didn't know she possessed. She let her hands play in the velvety softness of his chest hair.

Aston shifted his body over hers and nudged her legs apart with his knee. Gaiety accepted his weight, accepted the shocking arousal of his lower body fitting so snugly against hers, stripping the last vestiges of self-consciousness away, liberating her.

Abdomen to abdomen he placed his belly against hers and buried his face in the soft curve between her neck and shoulder. He inhaled deeply, trying to calm his wildly beating heart, slow his pulse, and avoid the onrush of the climax that threatened.

Even though she'd deceived him, betrayed him, duped him, he still wanted her, needed her. How could he not want her? She was so untouched, yet willing to accept him, he longed to make her his. He wanted to believe he was punishing her, getting even with her, getting back at her for her deception, but how could what he was doing be considered chastisement? How could the way she responded to him be merely acquiescence?

He brushed his lips across her shoulders. The clean scent of her skin was much more tantalizing than the heavy odor of sweet perfume. He found her desirable. There'd been no doubt about that from the first time he met her. Earlier in the evening he'd thought he hated her. He desperately wanted to, but he didn't. It was merely anger. How could he hate such a courageous, resourceful woman? He couldn't. He admired her, but he didn't trust her. Never in his life had he wanted to hate and love a woman at the same time.

Aston shut his eyes and closed his mind to all those troubling thoughts. Right now the only important thing was to bring the woman beneath him and himself to satisfactory fulfillment. Any other thought would have to wait until tomorrow.

He raised his head and gently kissed her on the lips. Her response pleased him, renewed his desire, his excitement, his hunger. With parted lips he softly kissed her cheeks, her eyes, her nose, then traced the length of her neck from her jawbone to her collarbone with moist little kisses.

Carefully, so as not to frighten her, he laid his hand over her breast and felt it, caressed it, shaped it with his palm and fingers, loving the feel of the bit of weight it afforded him. Heat built in the pit of his stomach, in the valley between his legs. He allowed his lips to slip lower down her chest, over the rise of slightly salty-tasting flesh, until they reached the nipple of her breast. He opened his mouth and closed the erect tip into the warm cavern. Sucking gently, he savored the taste of her, the feel of her. When he sensed she was ready, he pressed his manhood against Gaiety's womanhood. The palms of her hands squeezed and kneaded the muscles in his back, his neck, and over the plane of his shoulders, then low on his hips.

Gaiety moved gently, slowly beneath him. A soft moan of pleasure escaped her lips. Her breasts rose up to meet his ardent attention. He had no doubts that she wanted him. Aston's passion surged. He lifted himself slightly and pressed into her. Gaiety winced, pushed against his chest, shifted beneath him, and tried to pull away. Aston remained firm, constant, forceful while touching, stroking, and moving until Gaiety eased into his rhythm and demanded her fulfillment. Aston obliged, then sought his own release.

Breathless but not sated, replete but not content, Aston rolled onto his back, placing Gaiety on top of him. He spoke her name softly. Slowly her head came up, framed by tangles of golden brown hair falling straight to brush the tips of her breasts. Her eyes were filled with wonder, surprise. Her fresh-kissed lips were slightly parted, her cheeks and neck tinted with the blush of passion. His gaze feasted upon her. She was more beautiful than he'd ever seen her. She was his. How could she not be? She was the first woman he'd been with who hadn't been with countless other men. He desired her more than any other woman. He trembled with wanting. How could he let her go? But after what she'd done, how could he keep her? How could he trust her?

Still poised above him, his body firmly planted inside hers, Gaiety made a small, sensual sound as her hips began gently to rock back and forth. All controversial thoughts were pushed to the back of her mind.

"Gaiety," he whispered softly.

Aston ran a hand down Gaiety's side, over her hip, across her outer thigh, moving gently toward her inner thigh. She watched his expression and a feeling of tenderness washed over her. She wanted to give back to him the wonderful feeling he'd awakened in her.

The muscles of her abdomen contracted and quivered beneath his gentle touch. She felt strength in his body, honor in his soul. She didn't feel violated, punished, or used. She felt equal, and that was a glorifying experience.

Their eyes met.

Aston reached up and brushed her hair away from her shoulder to her back, exposing the fullness of her breast to his view. "Did I hurt you?" he asked.

"No."

"How do you feel?"

How could she tell him she felt victorious, liberated? Would he understand those feelings? Would he condone them? "I've experienced a lot of different things tonight," she answered in a husky voice.

"Me, too. You're not frightened, are you?" he asked.

"No."

"Are you angry?"

"No." And she wasn't. How could she be angry with Aston for showing her what passed between a husband and wife?

"Disappointed?" A bit of a grin lifted one corner of his mouth.

"No." She hesitated, then asked, "Are you?"

Aston placed his hands on her hips and pressed her upon him. "Hell no!" he whispered passionately, then raised his head and caught her nipple in his mouth and suckled hungrily.

Gaiety cupped Aston's head to her breasts with her hands. A warmth of tenderness took hold inside her. She realized she truly wanted to please him. With a moan of anticipation, she moved her hips from side to side, up and down, all around. Eager for him, for his acceptance of what she offered, she wanted to give pleasure as well as receive it.

Aston slipped his hands round the back of her neck and pulled her face down to his. "How do you feel now?" he asked in a low, seductive voice.

"Hot. Wonderful. Wanting."

"Damn, yes!"

He kissed the tip of her breast, the lobe of her ear, her forehead. Where his lips led him, he kissed. He was hungry for her and didn't mind if it showed.

Gaiety felt his every touch as her body came to life under his masterful strokes, the swipe of his tongue, the brush of his lips. She relished the feel of his hands on her, his gaze on her, his breath on her. Waves of pleasure radiated from her, cloaking her with fingers of satisfaction, and pierced through her, making her moan softly with wanton desire.

His hand traced the line of her shoulder and down her arm. His every touch was exhilarating. She kissed his neck, his shoulders, his chest, and moved tantalizingly slowly against him. She placed her palm against his slightly beard-roughened cheek and let the coarseness tickle her palm, excite her. They rocked, pumped, kissed, and caressed until sexual release found them. Then, not allowing her any escape, they started all over again.

Aston kissed her slowly, as if they had all the time in the world. And they did have all night. He'd already promised her that.

Twelve

Lit all night, the oil lamp flickered and burned low. Pillows had been pushed off the bed and lay in disarray about the floor. Underwear had been shamelessly discarded and scattered around the room. The black of Aston's wedding jacket lay starkly against the white of Gaiety's wedding gown. Daylight shone through the parted drapery panels like a beacon, warning that the night was over. Darkness had passed. Tomorrow had arrived.

Gaiety lay on her back, eyes open, staring up at the shadowed ceiling. Aston lay on his stomach, eyes closed, his arm thrown protectively over her waist. A rumpled sheet twined about them. They had not wasted one minute of the night. Now, in the early light of morning, she rested, wondered, worried, planned.

She'd never expected it, the tenderness that welled up inside her when she thought of what happened between her and Aston during the night. Gaiety wondered how she had become so enraptured by his touch that she'd denied her inner feelings and betrayed her family. She wanted to cry out and ask why her time with him had been so exciting, so acceptable. Why was Aston's touch so important to her that even now, in the bright light of day, she yearned for it yet again? She'd tried to deny him and the feelings he created in her. But in the end she had given in to his lovemaking just as he'd promised her she would.

Her eyes stared sightlessly at the ceiling. She never expected her time with him to feel so good, so life-altering. She never wanted it to. But he'd demanded only one night. She had to remember he'd made his feelings clear. He'd wanted only one thing from her: a wedding night. Now the light of day had chased it away. She had to swallow those conflicting feelings and treat Aston as if they'd never had this time together and pretend she didn't want more. He would never know that she believed if they had met under different circumstances she could have loved him, and that she would like to put the past behind her and trust him.

Gaiety groaned inwardly. She could ponder all she wanted, but it wasn't going to change the fact that she wasn't ashamed that she'd experienced pleasure at Aston's hands. But that she was contemplating the thought of more of the same was unforgivable. She had to do something before she reached for Aston and begged him to pull her into his arms once more.

Very carefully she rolled out from under the

sheet and his arm and scooted off the bed. The hardwood floor was cold to her feet and had a sobering effect. She pushed a pillow aside and picked up her nightgown and slipped it over her head. She needed a good dose of perspective.

"Gaiety."

She cringed. She'd hoped to leave the room before Aston awakened. Facing him, she took a deep breath and said, "I thought you were asleep."

He rose on one elbow. The sheet covered only the lower half of his body. Seeing his wide expanse of chest caused her heartbeat to speed up. She wanted to lie with him again and run her hands up and over his handsome body. One muscular, hairy leg had found its way out from under the cover and peeked at her.

His gaze searched her face, then settled on her eyes. "I was until you left the bed." He paused as if waiting for her to say something. When she remained quiet, he asked, "You're going back to your room?"

Of course that's what was expected of her, now that their night together was over. The romance of the night had vanished. She swallowed hard, denying the emptiness that threatened to consume her, wishing with all her heart things could have been different between them. She wanted to be his wife, but the very thought of that made her feel like a traitor to her family's memory.

"I thought I'd like to visit Theodora's grave," she said, making a hasty decision.

Something that looked like pain flashed across his face so briefly she might have imagined it, had it not been so heart-wrenching to witness.

"I'll take you," he said, and threw the sheet back and tumbled from the bed.

"No—I—I'd rather go alone. I know where it is," she answered, feeling suddenly nervous, shy. Somehow, this seemed like the right time to go. It might help her regain control of her feelings where Aston was concerned and keep her from softening too much.

Aston stood on the opposite side of the bed, holding the tail of the sheet in front of him. "It's too far for you to walk. I won't go up to the gravesite with you. I'll only drive you to the hill where they're buried. You'll have all the time you need."

They? Gaiety felt the lump in her throat grow. How easy it was for her to forget about Theodora's baby. All of a sudden she felt calmer than she had just minutes ago, and she asked, "Her baby—was it a boy or girl?"

The bed still between them, his gaze never left her face. His expression was one of disappointing resignation. "I don't know. She died before—" He stopped, moistened his lips, and looked away from her. "The baby was never born."

Feeling stronger she asked, "And Titus, where is he?"

Aston took a deep breath. "A long way from here. I'll have to take you there."

She squeezed her eyes shut. It was too much to hope her brother was only a few hours away. She cleared her throat. "No. I'm sure I can find him on my own."

His gaze never left her face. It heated her and brought back the memories of last night, even though she wanted to forget them.

"You probably could, but it's several days' journey. I'll take you. Just as I'll take you to your sister's grave." He reached over and pulled on the cord by his bed. "Go to your room, Gaiety. I'll have Josie bring you wash water and tea. As for going to see Titus, I should be free to leave by the end of the week. You should make plans to be gone for at least a month."

"A month? How far away did you send him."

"Far enough he wouldn't be reminded of what happened to his family." In a gesture of anger Aston threw the sheet to the bed, standing naked before her. "I'll wait for you downstairs."

Feeling she was being rudely dismissed, but unable to protest to a startlingly attractive nude man, Gaiety nodded and hurried out the door.

A bath and a lecture to herself made Gaiety feel much better as she waited in her room for her father to join her. She'd decided that she'd allowed, even gladly participated in, her wedding night, but today she had to be a different woman, even though, she would never forget last night.

Mimi had seemed much happier than usual as she helped Gaiety to dress. She bubbled over with joy as she talked about love and marriage. Finally, unable to take any more of her happiness Gaiety sent the maid for her father while she had tea and biscuits. She wanted to talk to him before she met Aston downstairs.

A knock on her door signaled Lane's arrival, and Gaiety rose from the slipper chair to meet him.

"How are you this morning, dear?" Lane asked, as he walked into the room and closed the door behind him.

Gaiety stood in the center of the room, her amber-colored dress billowing around her. A soft smile spread her lips. "I'm fine, Papa."

Lane placed a finger under his chin and looked her over carefully before taking a stance in front of her. He folded his arms across his chest and harrumphed. "You look better than I imagined you would. No bruises, I see. No puffy eyes or dark circles. Your color is good. I see I had no cause for concern."

"Papa, what are you talking about?" She eyed him. "Stop teasing me."

"I'm not teasing. I didn't sleep a wink last night for fear I wouldn't hear if you screamed or called for me."

Gaiety managed a laugh that sounded more

like a grunt. If only her father knew. "No, Papa. Aston didn't hurt me."

"I really didn't think he would. I'd never have let you go into his room if I'd thought that."

Gaiety considered his comment. "I guess all along I knew there would be some kind of retribution for my actions. But I'm not going to think about that anymore." She gave him a small smile again. "I'm just so happy that all this is going to lead me to Titus. I feel vindicated for my deception. I feel it was my destiny to come here and find my way to Titus. Surely it was all worth regaining my brother."

"You paid the price. Only you know its worth."

He held out his arms to her and Gaiety went into the strong embrace of her father. She was no longer his little girl. She was his grown daughter—a married woman with desires she couldn't share with anyone.

Stepping away from him, she said, "I'm going to meet Aston downstairs in a few moments. I want to visit Theodora's grave."

Lane nodded agreeably. "I know you've wanted to. Maybe it's best you get it behind you. What about Titus? When can we go get him?"

Her father's words thrilled her, reminded her that she was going to be reunited with her brother. Tears of joy threatened, but she held them at bay. "Aston won't tell me where he is. He insists on taking me there." She folded her hands in front of her skirt. "All he'll tell me is that it's a long journey and that I should be prepared to be gone at least a month. He said he'll be ready to go by week's end."

"Damnation!" Lane exclaimed, releasing some of his frustration at last. "How far away is the boy? It's no wonder we couldn't find him."

"Don't get upset, Papa," she said, calming him. "It won't make Aston change his mind about not telling." A deep feeling of gladness covered her. "I'm just going to take one day at a time. I'm going to try to be thankful that I'll see Titus when this is all over. As you know I've had a lot of bad feelings for Aston for many years. I'm learning to deal with those, and with new feelings about Aston."

"New feelings?" He wrinkled his forehead, drawing his eyebrows together.

She felt as if her heart swelled in her chest. "I'm grateful to him, Papa, for taking Titus out of the orphanage and finding him a home. If not for that, Titus might have been one of the children who died in the fire."

"I agree. But I do have to wonder why he waited so long to go to the orphanage." He threw his hands up in a helpless gesture. "But that's no longer important. We'll prepare to go right away."

She took hold of his arm. "No, Papa. I don't want you to go. You just came back from that long trip to Connecticut. I know the stagecoach ride is hard on you."

"It doesn't matter. I want to be there for you."

"I have no fear that Aston will take very good care of me. I'll be fine. He's my husband," she said softly, trying to sound much stronger than she felt. "I'll be all right. But I'm going to ask Aston if I can go back to Lilac Hill with you and live there until it's time to go."

Lane eyed her warily. "Is there something you're not telling me, daughter?"

How could she tell her father she didn't trust herself around Aston? "No. I don't think Aston will mind. I know he's very unhappy about what I did to him. In fact, he'll probably be glad to get me out of his house. You don't mind, do you?"

"Me? Heavens no! But, Gaiety, Lilac Hill is no longer ours. I signed it over to Aston as your dowry. He may not let us stay there."

Gaiety pursed her lips. Her father was right. She lifted her chin. "Well, we'll try it, and if he doesn't want us to live there, I guess he'll tell us. If that happens, we'll take rooms in town. How does that sound?" She kept the smile on her face and did her best to sound positive and chipper.

Lane chuckled lightly as he rubbed the joint of his shoulder. "It sounds like you never give up when you want something."

A thought crossed her mind as Lane laughed: what would happen if she decided she wanted to continue to be Aston's wife in every sense of the word? Aghast at such an idea, she mentally shook herself. What a horrible thought. What was wrong with her, letting such a thing even enter her mind? She wasn't sure her actions portrayed her inner feelings any longer. She couldn't deny that she felt drawn to him, but she didn't have to give in to those feelings. After last night, she wasn't sure she could trust herself to be rational where he was concerned. She needed to get away from Aston Rutledge.

Gaiety turned somber. "A lot has happened. I want to spend some time playing the piano, walking down to the pond. I need some time alone."

Lane patted her cheek. "Let me know, if he doesn't agree. I'll speak to him. Aston and I get along fairly well, you know."

"Yes, I know."

Aston waited by the carriage for Gaiety. The gray clouds that had moved in to cover the blue sky and sunlight matched his mood. He'd kicked the toe of his boot into the ground a couple of times as he tried to figure out what was wrong with him? Had he gone soft where women were concerned? Had he gone completely daft? Hadn't what Theodora had done to him taught him anything? He'd been duped twice now. Last night, as he lay in bed with Gaiety, he felt that he was willing to forget the whole thing. Now, in the light of day, he didn't think he could.

Remembering each soft sigh, each gentle caress, each passionate kiss they shared reminded him of how his plan had backfired on him. He'd hoped to punish her for her deceit. But if what they'd shared last night was punishment, he didn't want to think about what heaven with her must be like.

"What a hell of a mess I've gotten into," he muttered to himself.

What a woman!

"She deceived me."

She went after what she wanted. You.

"She lied about everything," he mumbled to the little voice inside him.

Doesn't matter.

"The hell it doesn't."

Think of the outcome. She's in your bed, isn't she?

"Only for one night."

You can change that.

Aston spun away from the carriage and rubbed his eyes as if they hurt. With no sleep, he was tired. He wasn't thinking clearly. He leaned against the hitching rail and looked up into the sky. It was the color of pewter, with puffs of charcoal-colored rainclouds lingering in the distance. It promised to be a stormy day.

He forced himself to get his mind off Gaiety and think about what had to be done today. If he was going to leave for Mobile at the end of the week, he had to make travel arrangements and work lists for all his workers. He made a mental note of things he didn't want to forget to take care of before they left.

But before he realized it, his thoughts were back on Gaiety. The thing he found hard to forgive was that he'd trusted her. She was so charming, how could he have known she was Theodora's sister? She didn't look anything like Theodora, not that he'd spent a lot of time looking at his first wife. Theodora was usually scowling because things weren't going her way. He'd seen Gaiety angry, but never bitter, as Theodora had always seemed to be. How could the two of them be so different, in their nature, their looks, their disposition, in the way they behaved? Theodora was a whore by age fourteen, Gaiety still a virgin at nineteen. And the one thing they seemed to have in common, the strength of determination to get what they wanted, was what he'd originally admired in Gaiety. And even though it was for different reasons, they'd both picked him as the means to accomplish their goals.

Gaiety was a woman of rare strength. He admired her support of her convictions. Until yesterday, he was beginning to think he could love her. He'd wanted to love her. But her deceit had changed all that and ignited a storm of violent emotions in him. He wanted to hate her, to be cruel to her, and hurt her the way he'd been hurt. He'd hoped to do that last night, but when he kissed her and she returned the kiss, he knew he couldn't hate her, he couldn't hurt her. But could he love her? How could he leave himself vulnerable to something that strong, something that could hurt him that deeply? That would leave him open to her scorn?

And he wouldn't beg her to believe him about his relationship with Theodora. And he'd never tell her the whole truth about her sister. He couldn't be that unkind to her.

Aston would have to live with the fact that she blamed him for everything. Theodora, the deaths of Josh and her father. Would she always hate him because of a past he was unable to circumvent, a past that had haunted him for years? Had she no inkling that he had begun to care for her? It was difficult for him to accept what he was feeling for her—feelings he never intended, never wanted to have for any woman. And now it was especially hard on him knowing he had wanted Theodora's sister.

But when he thought of last night he knew it didn't matter who she was, Gaiety Smith or Avalina Talbot, he wanted her again. He appreciated her need to deny the way he made her feel. The important thing was that she finally relaxed and let him love her and openly gave back to him. He knew he didn't want to live the rest of his life without having Gaiety in his bed again and again. Never had a woman stirred him so violently or satisfied him so completely that he ached for more of her. And he had to ask himself if she'd made love to him without feeling anything for him except the satisfaction he gave her body?

A soft breeze stirred his hair and thoughts of Gaiety stirred his sexual desire as he leaned against the rail and looked up at the dark expanse of sky. He longed for her soft touch again. He longed to hold her. Had it been unfair of him to demand his wedding night? No. His honor wouldn't have accepted anything less.

For years he'd sworn not to marry. Now he was married to a woman who said she hated him. But he had to admit she stirred him as no other woman had. He'd never married her if that hadn't been the case. And he needed to decide just exactly what he planned to do about that now and what he planned to do about Gaiety after he'd taken her to her brother. Even though he didn't trust her, could he live without her?

He heard the front door open and he turned around. Mimi and Gaiety stepped out on the front porch. Her bonnet and shawl were in place and in her hands she held a bunch of flowers. Aston knew she must have chosen a bouquet from the wedding flowers scattered about the house. As he watched her, he knew there was no doubt about it. She pleased him as no other woman had. The depth of her loyalty was unquestionable, her fortitude and courage admirable. He couldn't think of one other woman he knew who had the strength of conviction to do what she did.

Aston walked back over to the carriage and waited for her to approach before he lifted a small tin box off the seat. Gaiety stopped in front of him but didn't look into his eyes. He knew this wasn't easy for her and didn't mind her avoidance. He couldn't condone what she'd done to him, but he did understand her feelings. She'd lost her family.

He extended the box toward her. "This contains what I kept of Theodora's things. I expected to give them to Titus one day, but I think maybe you'd like to have them."

Gaiety looked up at him with those beautiful blue eyes and his heart lurched. Suddenly he was nervous. He was on edge. He wanted to deny the softness he felt for this woman.

She hugged the box to her chest. "Oh, thank you, Aston," she whispered. "I had wondered if you'd kept anything. And—and thank you for taking Titus out of the orphanage."

He nodded once. He wanted her to believe him when he told her that he'd never touched Theodora. But he wouldn't beg her. And he was right to decide not to tell her the truth about her sister. No one wants to believe anything bad about the dead.

Continuing to look at him, she asked, "Was Theodora in a lot of pain? Did she suffer long?"

Why couldn't the day have cooperated and at least given her sunshine? "No." He lied without effort. There was no need for her to know.

Her eyes were glassy with unshed tears. "You

said she didn't have the baby. Did she know? Did she know she was dying?"

"No," he lied again. "She was positive she'd get better, and until the end, she was making plans for the future."

When he saw the relief in her eyes, he was glad he'd lied. He couldn't deliberately hurt her, and the truth would have been more than she could bear. Maybe before last night he could have. But not now that he'd made love to her.

Gaiety quickly caught the lone tear that escaped past her lashes with the back of the hand that held the flowers. He wanted to comfort her but knew now wasn't the time.

She sniffed and took a deep breath. "When we get back, I'd like to go with Papa to Lilac Hill and stay there until we leave at the end of the week. I realize it no longer belongs to us, but—"

"You're wrong, Gaiety," he interrupted her. "It belongs to you and Titus."

Her eyes searched his face and anger over the senselessness of it all shuddered through him. "Damn it, Gaiety, did you really think I wanted that farm for myself? Hell, I have other means to water my cattle." He took a step toward her. "I wanted that land for Titus."

Gaiety gasped, clearly stunned by his revelation.

Thunder rumbled in the distance, checking Aston's anger, changing his mood. "We better go, or you'll be standing in the rain." He took hold of her arm and helped her into the carriage.

As the carriage bumped forward, Aston's thoughts were troubled. He didn't want Gaiety to be just another face, just another memory, just another woman he'd once spent the night with. He'd had too many of those in his life. Far too many.

Gaiety hugged the tin box to her breast as if she were afraid someone might steal it away from her as she left Aston standing by the carriage and made her way up the incline to the cemetery. The flowers she held tightly in one fist had already begun to wilt. Aston had kept his word and stopped the horse several yards from the gravesite.

A breezy wind whipped at her cheeks and blew the ribbon of her bonnet across her face. The sky had turned dark and rumbling since they'd left the house. She refused Aston's suggestion that they wait until the weather looked better. Gaiety was bent on seeing her sister's final resting place today. The rain wouldn't bother her. It would only match her stormy inner feelings.

There were numerous headstones in the Rutledge family plot, some more elaborately carved than others, she noticed, as she continued on her way over to the one Aston had pointed out to her. It didn't surprise her that her sister's appeared to be separated from the others.

For a few moments she stood looking down at Theodora's marker. It wasn't large or fancy, but a rose had been carved in each corner, giving it a simplistic beauty. Somehow, that small thing made her feel better. The only inscriptions were Theodora's name and the date of her death. It bothered her that she didn't feel the great loss she'd felt when she'd visited her pa's and Josh's grave. Maybe hearing the news that Titus was alive and that she'd be able to see him had at last started the healing.

Gaiety lifted her skirt and knelt beside the grave, her knees resting on the cool earth. Still hugging the tin box to her chest with one hand, she laid the flowers beside the gray stone.

As she looked at the tombstone, she realized she had only a few memories of Theodora, but that didn't seem to matter, now that she knew her sister hadn't suffered and that she'd died happy, planning her future, looking forward to life with her baby.

She set the box down in front of her. Once she opened it the anticipation of the treasures it held would be over. With trembling fingers she lifted the latch and opened the lid.

The first thing she saw was a small pocket-size knife that she recognized as belonging to Josh. A smile crossed her face as she picked it up and fingered it. She was so happy to have it. She laid it in her lap and looked back into the box. There was a length of black ribbon with a satin rose pinned to it, the choker Theodora had worn many times. Gaiety pressed the ribbon in her hand, caressing it between her palms. Theodora had loved it.

On the bottom of the box lay a small silver brooch that had belonged to her mother. Gaiety's breath caught in her throat as she picked it up and laid it out in her palm. Even though it had tarnished, the beauty of the piece showed. She had long forgotten about the pin, but now, as she looked at it, she remembered how Theodora would wear it to church on Sundays. She remembered begging Theodora to let her wear it just once, but Theodora had never let her.

Gaiety held the brooch to her chest as her shoulders shook with emotion. The brooch belonged to her now. The wind picked up, thunder rumbled, and the first drops of rain fell upon her skirt.

Thirteen

Gaiety looked out the window to the noisy street below as she waited for Aston's knock at her door. From her vantage point she saw hustling men and women making their way along the crowded boardwalk. She watched and heard the clinking and clipping of horses and carriages as they traveled down the dusty road in front of the hotel. The main street was lined with saloons, dressmaker shops, and a variety of stores displaying china, pottery, furniture, and fabrics from countries all over the world.

The journey to the southern Alabama port city on Mobile Bay had not been an easy one. The roads between Savannah and Mobile were not as well traveled as the ones from Savannah to Connecticut. The bumping, rattling, and shaking were enough to make anyone sore for days. She was glad she had insisted her father not make the trip after having so recently traveled to Connecticut. The rough ride would certainly have caused a flare up in his rheumatism.

At each tavern and inn where they'd spent

the night, Aston had been able to acquire a separate room for her and Mimi. The first night Mimi questioned her about the sleeping arrangements, but Gaiety had cut her off short the same way she had when the maid had asked why the two of them were going back to Lilac Hill the day after her wedding. Gaiety refused to talk with anyone about that, including her father.

During the long days of the trip, Aston would read newspapers and booklets he'd bought from other travelers. Gaiety and Mimi worked on their knitting and stitching. Josie spent most of his time sleeping.

A shout of anger from across the street caught Gaiety's attention, and she watched and listened while two men had a heated argument. Within a couple of minutes the men appeared calmer. One of them, obviously tired of the conversation, threw up his hands in an annoyed gesture and stomped down the street.

Gaiety's thoughts turned to the reason she was in the port city. After years of futile searching and wondering about Titus, she was now less than a day away from seeing him. Tonight she and Aston would have dinner in the dining room downstairs, then she would come back upstairs and sleep. Tomorrow morning they would hire a carriage to take them to the Franklins' farm on the outskirts of the city.

A knock sounded at the door and Mimi jumped up from where she knelt on the floor, digging through one of Gaiety's trunks. "That'll be Mr. Aston for you. I'll get it."

Gaiety followed Mimi to the door and met Aston, although she had to force herself not to let her gaze linger on his eyes. Often on the journey she'd found Aston watching her, staring at her, and that unsettled her. She couldn't help but wonder if he was remembering their night together. She'd relived each touch, each kiss, each softly whispered sigh a thousand times. It had been impossible to push that night from her memory.

Aston stood handsomely dressed in a freshly pressed suit of clothes. He'd shaved, too, something he hadn't done every morning on their journey. But in truth, she hadn't found his slight growth of beard unattractive. Actually, she'd decided that roguish look was rather appealing. It bothered her that after all that had happened between them, she was still drawn to him. She continuously had to fight remembrances of her night in Aston's arms, in his bed. Even now, as she looked at him, instead of thinking of her reunion with Titus, as she should be, she wanted to relive that night with Aston over and over again.

"I'm ready," she said, refusing to meet his eyes as she stepped out into the hallway. She turned back to Mimi. "Are you sure you'll be satisfied with the sandwiches that were sent up earlier?"

"Oh, yes, Miss, and the tea is still warm. I've already checked the pot. I'll be fine." Mimi smiled graciously.

Gaiety returned the smile and nodded, then walked down the corridor beside Aston. When they reached the top of the stairs, he put his hand to her elbow to help guide her. His touch was warm, comforting, protective. She wanted to accept it, savor it. But Gaiety knew she had to fight those feelings, so she moved away from him and took hold of the banister. He didn't try to touch her again.

Street noises drifted in from the open windows on the front wall of the dining room. The brightly lit room felt hot and muggy from the early evening heat. Gaiety was glad she'd dressed in a lightweight cotton blouse and pale-brown-and-cream-striped skirt. Five tables crowded the floor space, making passage difficult. Gaiety nodded to a couple seated at one table as they passed, then murmured an apology as she bumped the chair of one of the women seated with an older man at another table. After she and Aston were seated, a dainty-looking woman with a pert smile and a starched apron came over to them.

"We have a choice of two plates tonight," she said with a friendly smile, resting her hand on the back of Gaiety's chair. "We have a stew made of beef and vegetables, or chicken with boiled eggs and cornbread dumplings. I'll serve you bread and water with either, at no extra charge."

Gaiety looked up at the woman and smiled. "I'll have the chicken."

"Make it two," Aston said.

After the woman left, Aston laced his fingers together, laid his hands on the table in front of him, and said, "I sent a letter to the Franklins, telling them of our expected arrival date, but with the trouble in getting mail delivered we could very well get there before the letter."

Gaiety wished he hadn't put his hands on the table. She liked his hands. She liked the masculine strength she saw in them. She liked the way they had felt on her skin. She liked the way they could lightly caress or firmly massage. Denying the wayward thoughts, she forced her gaze up to Aston's eyes and asked, "Do you see that as a problem?"

"Not really. I just wanted you to know that they could be surprised to see us."

"Did you tell them in your letter that you were bringing Titus's sister?"

"No, only that I was coming for a visit and that I'd be bringing my wife."

A warmth spread over her when Aston referred to her as his wife. Why did she find it so hard to fight her attraction to him?

"I thought," Aston continued, "You might want to see Titus and talk with him before you decide whether or not to tell him who you are."

Her eyes rounded in shock. "How can you say that? I don't have to decide whether or not to tell him. Of course I will. That's why I'm here."

"Do you think he'll recognize you?"

"I—I don't know," she said, but was sure he wouldn't. "He was only four the last time I saw him. Probably not. But that doesn't mean I don't want him to know who I am."

"Would you recognize him?"

"Well—" she said, remembering the sorrow at not being able to put a face to the little boy who sat on the floor with outstretched arms, crying. She picked up her water glass and sipped, feeling suddenly hot. "Not unless he looks a lot like Josh or Papa. I—I'm ashamed to admit I can't remember his face," she whispered softly.

The look in his eyes told her he understood, but she wondered if he really did. Did he understand what all this had done to her? Did he understand that she had rights?

"That's not surprising. You were what? Eight or nine years old?"

Gaiety nodded and with shock realized she didn't feel that knot of bitterness and vengeance that had always clouded her when she thought of that time. Maybe at last the hurts of the past had started to heal.

"Gaiety, I don't want to upset you, but you need to be prepared for some things I think you may be overlooking. I guess one of the most important is that Titus won't be a four-year-old little boy. He's almost sixteen."

Gaiety straightened in her chair, regaining her aplomb. "I understand that. You needn't talk to me as if I were still a child."

Aston's expression was serious. "Are you prepared to understand that he may not want to go back to Lilac Hill with you?"

"What?" A shiver of fear crawled up her back. "I'm his sister. Of course he'll want to come with me."

"Not necessarily. Gaiety, he's lived here almost twelve years. This is his home, probably the only home he remembers. The Franklins have raised him like a son. He may not want you upsetting his life."

A lump formed in her throat, in her chest, in her stomach. Her hands made tight fists as they lay motionless in her lap. "No, you're wrong about that." Her voice was husky with denial. "I'm his sister. He'll want to come home with me. I'm sure of it." She paused as a thought struck her. "Unless you know something about his life here that you're not telling me."

"No." Aston shook his head. "I haven't seen him since he left with the Franklins. I hear from them about once a year. And last I heard, all was well."

She breathed a sigh of relief. "Good."

Aston leaned back as the proprietor placed steaming bowls of a thick soup with boneless pieces of chicken and cornbread dumplings in front of them. The food smelled wonderful, but Gaiety didn't know if she'd be able to eat very much. She was nervous about seeing Titus, about being with Aston. If only she could have continued to hate him as she had before she'd met him. Why did he have to be a nice man? Why had he loved her so thoroughly she couldn't keep him off her mind?

"I'll give you a few minutes to eat, then I'll bring you a slice of sweet potato pie and cup of strong coffee. I make the best in the city," the woman said without arrogance. Her eyes sparkled with pride. "How does that sound?"

"I'm sure we'll enjoy it," Gaiety told the friendly woman.

Aston smiled at the hotelkeeper and thanked her before he and Gaiety picked up their spoons.

The soup was thick, hot, and salty. Gaiety allowed the warmth of it to soothe her. After a few bites, she looked up at Aston and asked, "Exactly how did it come about that you took Titus away from the orphanage? Was it before or after the fire?"

Aston licked his lips, then wiped his mouth with a napkin before answering. "I felt responsible for you and Titus after Theodora's death, so I went to the orphanage to get both of you. You had already been adopted. The Franklins had worked for us and wanted to move westward and buy their own land. They were childless, so I asked them if they would take Titus with them and raise him as their son. I knew them to be good people. The orphanage caught fire and burned down a month later."

"And all the records with it. That's why Papa and I couldn't find Titus. And no one seemed to know exactly where Mrs. Conners had moved to, either. But I'm confused about something . . . why would Mrs. Conners allow you to take Titus away from the orphanage, then give him to someone else?"

His green eyes seemed to pierce her for a moment. "Gaiety, I was the only one left in the county who even knew his name. You had already been adopted, so I assumed whoever had you didn't want Titus. Mrs. Conners knew I'd married Titus's sister. For her, he was just one less child to look after. Quite frankly, she didn't care what I did with him after I took him away."

What he said was probably true. She was convinced Mrs. Conners had deliberately misled Lane and Mary Smith, making them think the brother she cried for was her dead brother. Her gaze stayed on Aston's eyes, but from her peripheral vision she saw the people from one of the tables rise and leave. They chatted noisily as they passed by and walked out the door. It was becoming uncomfortably warm in the dining room, and Gaiety wondered how Aston could look so cool, so calm, so handsome.

"You didn't want to keep him and take care of him?" she asked, after they'd been quiet for short time.

He paused before he answered, then said, "No. I thought it would be better if he–grew up somewhere else," before giving his attention back to his soup. He wasn't eating. Like Gaiety, he'd started pushing the chunks of chicken around in his bowl.

"You never went to see him?" She was thankful her tone wasn't accusing, only searching.

"No. I thought it best if he not be reminded of the past."

"Does he know who you are?"

He put his spoon down and pushed away from the table. "Not as far as I know. I suggested the Franklins tell him as little as possible about what happened twelve years ago."

"You didn't want him to know about his real family?" Her tone was suddenly accusing.

He gave her a hard look. "I didn't want him to grow up surrounded by the gossip connected to the Talbot name. I don't believe you would have wanted that for him either."

Gaiety lowered her head. Aston was right about that.

"Look, I just don't want you to be too disappointed if Titus doesn't want to come home with you."

Gaiety couldn't even accept the possibility of that happening. "How could I not be gravely disappointed if that were the case?" she asked earnestly. "Besides Papa, he's the only family I have left."

He nodded. "I understand, Gaiety. Try to remember the Franklins and what they'll be going through when you tell them their son is your brother and you want to take him away from them. Even if Titus agrees to go with you, they may not want to give him up."

Gaiety touched her napkin to her lips. She'd been hurting for twelve years. "Believe me, I know what the Franklins will be going through, but I can't let that stop me. He's my brother.

They've had him all these years. Now it's my turn."

"I'm only telling you these things so you can prepare yourself for whatever might happen."

Frustration over the truth of Aston's words made her angry. "And whose fault will it be if Titus doesn't want to come home with me?" she asked, trying to hold her voice down. "Yours," she stated firmly. "You started this damning chain of events when you slept with my sister and got her pregnant."

Aston half rose out of the chair and leaned over the small table. His green eyes sparkled angrily at her. "I never touched your sister, and I'm tired of telling you that."

"Then don't tell me, because I don't believe you. Guilt is what made you go to the orphanage and seek us out to place us in other people's homes."

His fingers spread wide on the table, he leaned closer. "You're right about one thing." He held his teeth together as he spoke. "It was guilt that made me go to that orphanage, but it had nothing to do with the fact your sister was pregnant. *That baby wasn't mine.*"

Gaiety rose from her chair and leaned forward, bringing her face dangerously close to his. "Then why did you marry her?"

"Your father and Josh were holding a gun to my head. I was seventeen years old, and damn it I had two choices. Die or marry your sister."

"Papa wouldn't have shot you!" she said,

knowing she couldn't deny the truth she sensed with him.

"No, but Josh was young, and foolish enough to pull the trigger. He's the reason they were killed."

"He's not! Your father's men killed them in cold blood."

He grabbed her arm and jerked her closer to him. The dishes on the table rattled between them. "When my father's men burst through the door, Josh raised his rifle to shoot."

"You're lying," she said with trembling lips, but knew her words lacked conviction.

"You know, Gaiety, I might feel sorry for you for what happened, but you're making me angry, because I see you don't want to know truth. You don't want to believe anything other than the warped ideas you have of what happened."

"You're wrong! You're a liar and I hate you!"

"You hate me? Really?" His voice softened. "Think about our wedding night, then tell me that without lying to me or yourself."

She gasped. "You're horrible. It's horrible of you to make me want you when you know I've sworn to hate you," she whispered truthfully.

"Excuse me, Miss, is there a problem here?"

Gaiety snapped her head around. One of the men from the other table had walked over. She jerked her wrist out of Aston's hand and gave a nervous smile to the nice-looking stranger. "Not at all. Everything is fine." She cut her eyes back around to Aston. He was pulling on the tail of his waistcoat.

"You sure?" he asked, giving Aston the once-over.

Aston glared at the man as he said, "This is none of your concern."

Fearful that Aston was hot enough to take the man to task for inquiring, she quickly said, "Oh, my, yes, everything is fine. I'm afraid my husband and I were having a little argument, but we've settled it. Thank you."

After a warning look to Aston and a smile to Gaiety, the man nodded and walked away.

When Gaiety turned back to Aston, he surprised her by completely ignoring the incident with the stranger and saying, "Thank you for at least admitting that you want me." He pulled on the cuffs of his shirtsleeves. "Stay for pie and coffee, if you like. I'm going down the street for something stronger to drink and someone easier to talk to."

Filled with anxiety, Gaiety stood on the front porch of the Franklins' small clapboard house. Her blue bonnet matched the color of her dress and was securely tied underneath her chin, and a short, wide-collared cape fell from her shoulders. Her drawstring purse dangled from her wrist as she twisted her black gloves between her hands.

Standing quietly beside her, Aston raised his hand and knocked twice. Gaiety looked around while she waited for the door to open. The yard was well tended. Colorful flowers and neatly trimmed shrubs outlined the house and steps. A weathered high-backed rocker with a multicolored quilted cushion in its seat sat on the far side of the porch. Matching curtains hung at all the front windows. The Franklins' love for their home showed. That made her feel better. If they loved their house, surely they would have loved her brother.

While she waited for someone to come to the door, she thought back to the days she'd spent at the orphanage. She remembered it was always dark in all the rooms there, even during the daytime. She remembered hearing crying, sharp, disciplining voices, leather straps hitting bare backs. She remembered fighting, scratching, biting, hitting.

Gaiety squeezed her hands together tightly and closed her eyes, forcing herself to push those memories aside and recall only the good things she remembered about her past, like Josh laughing as he threw her over his shoulder. All four of them playing in the shallow water of the pond, splashing each other. She took a deep breath and opened her eyes. She was very happy Aston had taken Titus out of the orphanage and given him this well-cared-for home. Now she had to ask herself if she was ready to forgive Aston and trust him.

Her search was moments from being over. Maybe after she talked with Titus she'd be able to put the past behind her, where it belonged, and start a new life with Titus to fuss over and worry about. The handle of the door turned and Gaiety's last thought before it opened was that she had to decide where Aston fit into her new life.

The door opened slowly and a woman Gaiety's height looked at them with small greenish-brown eyes. Her dark brown hair, streaked with strands of gray, had been fitted into a tidy bun at the back of her neck. Her complexion looked healthy and smooth, except for a tiny mole near her left eye. The one thing that surprised Gaiety the most was that there was no smile on her thin lips or in her eyes. A house this well cared for should have a woman with a happy smile and friendly face to welcome visitors. This woman looked sad.

Aston took a step forward and spoke. "Mrs. Franklin, I'm Aston Rutledge, do you remember me?"

"Of course I do." The woman's voice was deep and carried a no-nonsense tone. "I've been expecting you. Got your letter yesterday."

"I'd like to introduce my wife, Gaiety."

Gaiety cleared her throat and said, "How do you do, Mrs. Franklin? It's nice to meet you."

"Nice to meet you, too. I hope you had a good trip. This place is a long way from Southern Oaks. Come on in."

Mrs. Franklin stepped back and allowed Gaiety and Aston to enter. Gaiety had agreed with Aston on the way over that he should do most of the talking. She wanted him to question the woman immediately about Titus, but knew manners dictated he wait until pleasantries were over.

"I've been baking this morning. Just took teacakes out of the oven," the woman said as they followed her through the parlor and into the hallway.

Once Gaiety had stepped inside some of the anxiety of expectation eased. She walked behind Aston so she could look over the house, hoping to see something that would tell her Titus was at home. Inside, the rooms were larger than it appeared they would be from the outside. The parlor had a warm, cozy feel to it. The furniture wasn't expensive, but it was in good condition. The room had that same well-cared-for look of the outside.

As Gaiety entered the hallway, she smelled the homey scent of fresh baked bread. Yes, she thought, as she made her way to the kitchen following the slightly built, cleanly dressed woman, this would have been a good house for Titus to grow up in.

"I guess you heard you missed all the rain we've been having," Mrs. Franklin said as they entered the kitchen. "Rained every day for more than a week. Some of the roads are still too dangerous to travel on. Guess you didn't have any problems, though, seeing as you made it here when your letter said you would. Have a seat at the table and I'll reheat the coffee."

"Thank you," Aston answered, as he pulled out a heavy wooden chair for Gaiety. "We didn't have a problem. We must have been traveling a few days behind the storm."

With still no sign of Titus, Gaiety looked around the kitchen. It was a large room. All the windows were open, but it was still hot from the lit fireplace. A kettle of stew bubbled on a spit over the fire. She watched Mrs. Franklin place the coffeepot on a wire grill near the edge of the fire.

It suddenly dawned on Gaiety that at age sixteen, Titus would either be in school, or out in the fields with Mr. Franklin. No wonder he wasn't home. Her eyes caught a glimpse of Aston's face and she thought she saw concern in his features.

"How's Mr. Franklin?" Aston asked, as Mrs. Franklin put a loaf of fresh bread and a dish of cooked pears on the table in front of them.

She glanced up at Aston. "Jacob's all right. He won't be home 'til late in the afternoon. I send ham and biscuits with him in the mornings, so he doesn't usually come home till he's through for the day. I've got a rabbit stew cooking for supper. I'd be happy for you to stay and share it with us."

Aston looked at Gaiety, then said, "Thank you. But we came mainly to see Titus."

Mrs. Franklin stared down at Aston with that blank expression she'd had on her face when she'd opened the door. "I know that."

"We'll he be home for supper with Jacob?" Aston asked the all-important question.

Gaiety sat stiffly, holding her hands together

tightly in her lap. The waiting was putting her on edge.

"No, sir."

Gaiety's eyes widened as she stared at the plainspoken woman. Her chest grew tight. A hollow feeling developed in her stomach. In that instant she knew something was wrong. She didn't want to know what it was. She wanted only to see Titus.

Remaining calm, Aston asked, "When is he due home?"

"I don't know."

"Mrs. Franklin, what is the problem?" His tone of voice changed abruptly, letting his irritation over her vague answers show.

She gave Gaiety a quick glance before looking over at Aston with sorrowful eyes. "I know you been sending money each month, just like you have all these years."

Gaiety sat forward in her chair. Aston never mentioned that he was paying the Franklins to care for Titus—and for twelve years!

"We'd already talked about letting you know. We just kept hoping things would change for the better and Titus would come home."

Aston pushed away from the table and stood up. "The money's not important right now. Tell me what's going on. Why don't you know when Titus will be home?"

Tears sprang to the woman's eyes and she picked up the tail of her apron and wiped them. "He ran away more than three months ago."

Gaiety jumped up from her chair, visibly shaken by the news. She couldn't believe this. Her hands made fists at her side and her bottom lip trembled. She refused to accept that she'd come all this way only to find Titus gone. Panic rose up in her.

"No! That can't be. I've waited too long to see him. You must be wrong," she accused out of fear.

Mrs. Franklin's nose reddened and she poised backward. "I guess I'm the one who knows what happened. It nearly killed me and Jacob. Do you think we wanted him to leave home?"

Aston moved to Gaiety's side and slipped his arm around her waist. "I know this isn't what we expected, Gaiety, but calm down."

Gaiety felt some reassurance from Aston's touch, but she couldn't calm down. Where was Titus?

Aston turned his attention back to Mrs. Franklin. "Tell us what happened," Aston said again. "Why did he run away?"

She sniffled, rubbing her reddened nose. "Jacob always let Titus go into town with him. When he was old enough, Jacob would let him go down to the docks and play with other boys. As he got older, he made some new friends." She wiped her wet eyes again.

"We didn't think too much of it at first, but he started wanting to stay the night in town with his friends. It really didn't matter during the winter, when there wasn't much to do in the fields, but later, when it was time to plant, Jacob needed him. They had words one day and Titus didn't come home with him." The sadness in the woman's face carried over to her voice. "We raised him right, Mr. Rutledge. Took him to church at least once a month. It's just that these older boys were able to turn him away from us because we had rules and they didn't."

"Do you know where they're living?" Aston asked, not relaxing his hold on Gaiety.

She shook her head. "No—we need to find him before the—" she stopped.

"What?" Aston prodded her.

"We need to find him before the sheriff does. Jacob's heard he's running with a group of young men who are robbers."

"No!" Gaiety whispered earnestly. She felt as if her chest were crashing in on her heart. Not Titus. Pushing away from Aston, she said, "You must be wrong."

Aston took hold of Gaiety's arms and forced her to face him. "Calm down, Gaiety, and let me handle this. It's clear this woman is as upset as you are. Get hold of yourself."

Gaiety knew what Aston said was true. Mrs. Franklin was very upset. She took a deep breath and forced herself to stay calm on the outside, even though she was breaking up on the inside.

Aston gave his attention back to Mrs. Franklin. "Tell us why the sheriff thinks Titus may be involved with these young men."

"According to the sheriff, he fits the description of one of them. They rob men and women as they come out of the gaming halls and saloons down on the lower side of town, close to the docks. Last week they found a dead man. He'd been stabbed. They assume it was the street gang, as the sheriff calls them, who did it."

Gaiety gasped and took an imploring step toward her. "Do you believe Titus would be involved in anything like that, in murder?"

"No, I don't want to believe it. But I never believed he'd take a swing at Jacob, either."

"Why haven't you done something?" Gaiety asked, still not wanting to believe this was true.

"Don't you think we tried to bring Titus home?" Mrs. Franklin's voice grew loud with emotion. "Do you think we wanted him running in the streets, drinking, playing cards and gambling and God only knows what else?" Her voice suddenly softened. "I've prayed for his return. If I knew where he was, I'd tell you. If I had the words to say that would bring him home, he'd already be here. I've tried. Nothing worked."

Gaiety lifted her shoulders, her chin, and blinked back tears as she looked at Aston and said, "I want to go back to town. I'm going to find my brother."

"Your brother?" Mrs. Franklin asked, startled.

Aston sighed. "Why don't you get Gaiety a cup of that coffee, Mrs. Franklin. We've still got a lot of talking to do. We need to know all you can tell us about Titus."

Fourteen

Aston stood outside Gaiety's hotel room door trying to decide exactly what he should say. It was a hell of a thing to have happened, coming all this way and not finding Titus. The Franklins had never been obligated to let him know anything about Titus, so he couldn't blame them. He should have done a better job of keeping up with the boy, but he had no reason to suspect anything had gone wrong.

Maybe he should have checked into Titus's life before he'd told Gaiety he knew where her brother was. But at the time the only thing he'd wanted to do was hurt her the way he'd been hurt by her deceit.

Now he knew he didn't feel that way anymore. Aston Rutledge, the man who'd sworn never to marry now found himself married. The truth was that he loved Gaiety. That's why he'd forgiven her for trying to trick him into marrying. He understood her reasons. And now, damn it, he wanted her to love him.

Aston sighed heavily. That seemed like an

impossibility. They still had so many things between them to overcome. If only he could change her mind about him. Maybe a start would be in finding Titus for her. He reached up and rapped on the door a couple of times.

Mimi opened the door. "Good evening, Mr. Aston," the maid said cheerfully.

"How is she?" he asked.

"Not good, sir. I can't get her to talk or to eat anything. She just sits in front of that window and stares at the street below. It's as if she's looking for someone or something."

"I'd like to talk to her alone. You go stay in my room until I return."

"Yes sir."

Mimi walked out and Aston walked in and closed the door behind him. Just as Mimi had said, Gaiety sat on a chair in front of the window, still dressed the way she'd been that morning, although she had shed her bonnet and cape. She didn't bother acknowledging him. That angered him a little.

Aston looked around the room. It was spacious, but held little furniture. There were a bed, a cot, two chairs, and a dresser with a mirror attached. A covered tray sat on the top of the small chest. He walked over and lifted the napkin. There were several bite-sized tea biscuits, a bowl of honey, and a pot of tea. Aston put his hand to the belly of the china pot. The tea was still warm. He poured some into the cup, added a spot of cream, and walked over to Gaiety.

"Drink this," he said. His voice was harsh and he hadn't intended it to be, but he didn't like her ignoring him.

Gaiety turned and looked up at him with her beautiful blue eyes but didn't take the cup.

"Mimi told me you haven't eaten anything since we returned early this afternoon. Now drink this." His voice softened. "It will make you feel better."

She took the cup and looked into it. "I wasn't hungry," she said, then turned back to look out the window.

Aston snapped the slat-backed straight chair around to face him and straddled the cane seat. "While you've been moping—" Her head whipped around as he'd hoped, and she gave him a sharp look. At least she still bristled when he said something she didn't like. He continued, "I've been thinking. I want you and Mimi to go back to Southern Oaks tomorrow. I'll stay here and talk with the sheriff and see what I can find out about all this."

Her gaze flew to his. "I'm not going back to Southern Oaks," she said, pushing to the edge of her chair. "I can't believe you'd suggest such a thing."

"Drink your tea," he said, "and listen to me." He waited for a moment, then motioned with his hand for her to drink. He knew he'd do anything within his power to find Titus for her. He'd do anything to take away her hurt. But she didn't know either of those things.

Gaiety relented and sipped the tea while he

talked. "I'm serious about this, Gaiety. I want you to go home. There's nothing you can do here. I promise I'm going to do my best to find Titus and bring him back to Southern Oaks with me."

"What can you do here that I can't?" she asked, looking up at him again. "This is a big city. There're so many people here. If the sheriff can't find him, how can you?"

"I don't know, but the first thing I plan to do is talk to the sheriff and see what he's done to try to capture these wayward boys. Maybe I can hire someone to search for Titus." Aston paused when he saw that Gaiety was looking at him so intensely. He wanted to take her in his arms and kiss her and tell her how badly he felt about what had happened, tell her that he knew how disappointed she was. But he knew she didn't want that, so instead he smiled teasingly at her, hoping to make her feel better. "Hell, if I have to, I'll dress up and act like a drunken gambler myself and be a decoy. If that's what it takes to find the hellions, I'll do it."

All of a sudden, Gaiety's eyes lit up with excitement. She set the cup on the windowsill and clasped her hands together at her breasts. "Aston, that's it . . . you and I will do it. We'll go out at night and find him ourselves. We'll pretend you're a wealthy gambler, and I'll be your—ah—you know, your lady for the evening."

Aston started shaking his head before he spoke the one word. "No."

"Wait," she cautioned, holding out her hand as if to stop him from saying more. "It will work. Even if we don't find Titus, maybe we'll make contact with someone who'll know him and can take us to him."

Aston rose from his chair, a frown on his face. He didn't like this idea at all. "Gaiety, you're not talking about nice young gentlemen who will gladly escort you to your brother. These guys are robbers, maybe murderers. That means they hold a gun to your head or a knife to your throat." That thought angered him, and his voice rose. "There's no way I'll put you in that kind of danger. And there's no way in hell I'm letting you dress up like a doxy. You're not going to get mixed up in this. End of conversation."

Gaiety rose and took a step toward him. "Well, it may be the end of the conversation for you, but not for me. For your information, I wasn't moping when you came in here. I was thinking, trying to come up with a plan to find Titus. However, I was thinking along the lines of putting an ad in the local paper asking him to contact Avalina Talbot, but I knew it was a longshot because I'd have to depend on him reading the paper. Your idea is the perfect solution. We'll go after him rather than wait for him to come to us."

"You were right when you said *my* idea. And,

I said I'd dress up. I didn't say anything about you."

"Mrs. Franklin said they were robbing men and women. I'm sure they pick couples because they think a man will be less cautious if he appears more interested in the woman on his arm than in who might be following him."

"She also said that a man was found with a knife in his gut not two weeks ago," he argued emphatically.

"The authorities aren't sure who killed that man. His death might not have anything to do with the group Titus is living with."

Aston's stomach knotted. Gaiety didn't know what she was asking him. He couldn't put her in danger. And she didn't seem to realize that the boy might be in more trouble than he, Aston, could get him out of. He took a step toward her, a soft expression on his face. "I won't take the chance on you getting hurt, Gaiety. I can't."

Her eyes implored him. She took a step forward, too. Her voice trembled slightly as she said, "And I didn't come all this way to leave before I find my brother. I'll look for him without you if I have to. I'll walk the streets day and night until I find him or he finds me. I'm not leaving this town without him."

Aston placed his hands on her upper arms, knowing he needed to touch her. He expected her to pull away from him, but she didn't. A bond seemed to be growing between them and he wanted to pursue it, instead of having to argue with her. They'd done enough of that. He immediately felt better for having touched her. She was warm, soft. He ached to pull her into his arms and hold her.

"You may have to," he said in a calm voice. She needed to be aware of every possibility. "We don't know how much trouble he's in. I think the first thing we need to do is go see the sheriff. We need to know what information he has that might help us and exactly how involved he thinks Titus is in all this. If the sheriff has reason to believe he might have had anything to do with that murder down at the docks, he won't allow him to go home with us, even if Titus should want to."

Gaiety lowered her head and whispered, "He wouldn't have been involved in a murder. I'm sure of that."

Very slowly Aston wrapped his arms around her waist and lightly pressed her against his chest. He didn't want to frighten her and cause her to pull away from him. He held her close without putting pressure on her. If she tried to step away, he wouldn't stop her.

She didn't. Instead, she seemed to melt and mold herself into his arms, laying her head on his chest. Aston gloried in the feel of her in his arms. He felt as if he could make things right with Titus, make things right with Gaiety. She felt so good in his arms he gently kissed the top of her head. Her hair smelled fresh as rainwater. He breathed the scent in deeply, relishing her essences. He wanted to kiss her but was afraid she'd reject him, and he felt too insecure to go through that right now. He needed too desperately to hold her.

All of the sensations from their wedding night rushed through his mind to haunt him. Aston closed his eyes and remembered every caress, each kiss, each small sigh. He needed those feelings again. As with a will of their own his lips slid over her hair and down her forehead to graze over the rise of her cheek. She closed her eyes and snuggled closer to his chest. Hope soared. Aston accepted that small gesture as consent to his advance and kissed her lids.

"Hold me tighter," she whispered softly.

Aston's pulse raced, his heart hammered violently. It was the first time she'd asked him to hold her, and it did crazy things to him. Could it be that she was finally ready to accept any part he might have played in her past? If only she'd ask for more, his home, his love, his life, all those things he would gladly give her. But first she had to forget the past.

Hungry for her, he put all that aside, intent on enjoying this moment so close to her. He wanted to kiss her roughly so he could feel the pressure of his lips on hers. He wanted to crush her to his chest and demand that she respond, but somehow, he knew that even though that's what he needed, she needed to be held gently and kissed softly and touched tenderly.

With parted lips he left feather-light kisses

on her eyes, her cheeks, her nose, and her forehead. Her skin felt soft beneath his lips. She moaned invitingly and his desire for her grew. He wanted somehow to make her see that she belonged to him and he'd never be able to give her up.

When he couldn't stand the buildup of passion in his loins any longer, he lifted her chin and gently placed his lips over hers. They were warm, inviting, responding. He grew hard fast. Trying to think of her need instead of his, he slowly slipped his tongue into her mouth. He wanted to make love to her so badly he hurt.

Gaiety continued to respond to his kisses, allowing him to caress her breasts and kiss her neck and the fine plane of her shoulder. He knew he might be taking advantage of her. She was emotionally drained from the day's events, but he couldn't make himself stop. How could he deny himself the pleasure? As long as she was willing to accept his loving, he was going to kiss her, caress her, make love to her, but he'd stop if she gave the signal.

"I want to thank you for sending money to the Franklins for Titus's care all these years," she mumbled against his lips, as her hands spread up and over his shoulders.

Aston wasn't in a mood to talk, but he wanted to please her. "I was glad I could do it for him." Need forced him to kiss her a little harder, press her closer. His hands ran up and down her back and over her shoulders, down the front of her dress to cup, massage, and fondle her breasts. He was a fool for ever thinking he didn't love this woman. He loved her and he vowed that one day she would love him.

"You don't know how much I wanted to see him," she said, when his lips left hers and started down her neck, leaving moist little patches in their wake. "Or how many years I've wondered what happened to him."

"I do know," he answered huskily, trying to keep his mind on two things at once. "I'm sorry you had to go through that." His body was on fire for her. It was torture to go this slowly when what he really wanted was to throw her down on the bed and love her the way his body ached for him to.

Feeling, as if he were at the point of bursting, he whispered, "Gaiety, let me love you."

His words must have been like cold water in her face. Gaiety took a deep breath and pushed away from him. Aston cursed himself silently and let her. His breathing was painfully fast, and his desire showed haltingly beneath his trousers.

"I'm sorry I didn't mean to take advantage of you when I asked you to comfort me," she said.

He chuckled ruefully. "I'd hardly call it taking advantage of me. I'm the one who wanted more. I knew you only wanted comfort."

"Thank you for saying that, but it's not right for me to ask that from you."

"Why? I'm your husband."

"Yes, but we had an agreement, and I fulfilled my part of it and gave you your wedding night. Please don't—"

"Stop, Gaiety, don't say it. All right? I may have forced you into my bed that night, but I was angry with you. I have no intention of doing that again." He also knew he had no intention of giving her up, but now wasn't the time to tell her that.

She looked as if he'd rebuked her instead of her rejecting him. "Aston, can we do it?"

Hope rose in his chest.

"Can we work together to try to find Titus, or must I do it on my own?"

Aston felt like a fist had hit him in the gut. For a moment, he'd thought she wanted to make love to him, make their marriage real. "No. We'll do it together." He'd do this for Gaiety. She deserved to be reunited with her brother.

A grateful smile lighted on her lips and in her eyes. "Thank you."

He took a deep breath. "I'll send Mimi back over to get dinner for you. I'm going out for the evening. We'll go to the sheriff's office first thing tomorrow morning."

He walked out without acknowledging her appreciation.

Early the next morning Gaiety sat quietly in the sheriff's office and listened to Aston tell him that they wanted to find Titus.

Gaiety watched Sheriff Andrews with interest. He was a balding, heavyset man with small gray eyes and little or no eyebrows. His cheeks were rounded, with jowls hanging over his tight shirt collar. He appeared to be listening closely to Aston's story of how Titus had come to live with the Franklins and how Gaiety was now trying to find him.

As Aston told the story, Gaiety's thoughts drifted back to last night and how she'd felt after Aston had left her. She'd hardly slept for wondering if he'd found a woman to keep him company. Could she blame him if he had? She'd turned him away knowing that he wanted her, knowing she'd wanted him, but also knowing she'd have to admit that she was ready to forget the past, and she wasn't sure she could do that just yet.

"Mrs. Franklin told us how she feared he'd taken up with a gang of street kids and that she and her husband had spoken with you about it."

"I remember talking to the Franklins. Nice people." He shifted in his chair. "Of course, neither of us has any proof this is so. Certainly he hasn't been caught with them. However, one victim gave us good descriptions of the three who robbed him, and Titus Franklin fit one of them."

Gaiety tensed when she heard the sheriff refer to her brother as Franklin. He should carry his father's name, and as soon as she found him, she would talk to him about that.

"And that description could fit at least ten

other young men in this town, too, isn't that right, Sheriff?" she asked, still not wanting to believe Titus had anything to do with the robberies.

"Oh, yes," he answered quickly, letting his eyes roam freely over her face. "But the Franklins are the only ones who've been in asking about a runaway."

Aston cleared his throat and sent Gaiety a clear message with his eyes. He wanted to do the talking.

"We heard they hit two or three times a week. Is that right?" Aston asked.

The sheriff nodded, lacing his fingers together and laying them on his stomach. "The buggers are a real problem all right." He reached up and scratched behind his ear. "Until a couple of weeks ago, we weren't that worried about them. They weren't bothering anyone too bad, just lifting a few dollars off the riffraff down by the docks, and recently they've moved uptown a bit and started going after decent folks. Then, last week, we found that dead man. Knife wound to the stomach," he added. "Appears he was a vagrant. We can't find anyone who knows his name. Still, it makes the townfolks uneasy when there's been a killing. Something has to be done for sure."

Gaiety didn't like the sheriff's seeming disregard for the dead man. Murder was wrong whether or not the dead person was a respectable man.

Giving Gaiety a quick, reassuring glance, Aston asked, "Do you know for sure these boys are the ones who killed him?"

The sheriff shifted in his chair again. "No, we don't. All we know is that most of the time the boys work in teams of three. Two of them carry knives, and the other one holds a gun. Always before, the victims handed over their money when they were told and the kids ran away. I call 'em boys cause I'm hearing that most of them look like they haven't started shaving yet. But no one's sure."

A little annoyed that the official seemed to be rambling, Gaiety said, "But getting back to Aston's question, do you agree that someone else could have killed this man?"

Sheriff Andrews sat straighter in his chair and cleared his throat. "Could've been, yes," he answered. "And this man could have been the first to refuse to turn over his money and then got the knife."

"But they'd never hurt anyone before. What makes you think they killed this man?" Aston asked.

"'Cause they're the only ones we've had any problem from. Just last week one of the boys sliced a man's arm when he tried to take the knife away from him."

Gaiety winced.

"What are you doing to try to find these young highwaymen?" Aston asked, sounding irritable.

"I put another man on patrol. That gave me two walking the streets. I need more, but I don't have the money to pay for more. The way I see it is, they're going to mess around with the wrong man one day and one of them will be killed. That'll scare them and they'll go back where they came from."

"So you don't have a problem with us trying to find her brother?"

"No. No," he said. "Be happy for you to. 'Course, I'll expect you to bring him by here and let me question him, if you do. I might be persuaded to be lenient on him if he comes clean with what he knows."

"Lenient?" Gaiety asked worriedly.

"If he's running with the gang, he's breaking the law, young lady. I'll have to consider it carefully."

"We understand," Aston said. He rose and the other two followed him. "If we find him, we'll bring him in."

Aston shook the sheriff's hand as Gaiety stared in astonishment. She didn't understand.

"What on earth were you thinking, to say such a thing to the sheriff?" Gaiety asked, as soon as they walked outside.

He took hold of her upper arms. "I said what the sheriff wanted to hear. I think we should find Titus as soon as we can and take him and run. I have a feeling the sheriff is looking to catch one of the kids and make an example out of him. It'll make him look good to his townspeople, and it will make the other boys think twice about attacking others if he comes down hard on one of them."

Gaiety relaxed. "Thank goodness we agree. I was thinking the same thing."

"There's no way the sheriff would let Titus go if he really thought Titus was involved with that man's death. And, Gaiety, you haven't seen Titus in twelve years. You have to prepare yourself for that possibility."

Fifteen

Gaiety stood in the middle of her hotel room dressed in a low-cut red satin dress, the neck and wide straps trimmed with black lace. A red-and-black satin bow was pinned to her hair, which she'd swept back into a loose chignon. Aston stood quietly staring at her, his hands stuffed in the pockets of his trousers, lightly tapping one foot.

"I don't think I can let you leave the hotel in that dress, Gaiety. Couldn't Mimi have found anything less revealing than that?"

Aston's outrage made Gaiety smile a little. It was nice to know that he cared enough to worry about how she was dressed. In fact, she and Mimi had worked fast to add a row of lace at the neckline—breastline, really—to cover a little more of her skin. She'd thought the same thing when she first saw the dress, but she wouldn't let Aston know that. He was looking for an excuse for them not to go out tonight and search for Titus. She didn't intend to let him off the hook. The frock was overtly revealing, showing more than a fair amount of her breasts.

She looked him in the eyes and said, "I'm not supposed to be dressed like I'm going to church. Besides, I'll be perfectly safe as long as I'm with you." A soft smile played on her lips.

He slowly walked toward her, a slight sway to his shoulders. "Did it ever cross your mind that you may not be safe *from* me?" He stopped just inches from her and lowered his voice to a husky whisper. "Lord knows you're desirable enough dressed in your regular clothes, but there's something extremely provocative and alluring about you in that dress. It's so out of character for you that it makes me want to forget you're my wife and—"

Gaiety's breaths came fast and choppy. His words, his tone, and the smoldering look in his eyes had her senses clamoring for more of what he was saying. Her heated skin ached for his touch and started a hunger of desire in the pit of her stomach. But she had to hide those feelings. Aston didn't know it, but she wanted him to find her downright tempting. She needed to be loved again the way he had loved her on their wedding night.

He reached out and ran the backs of his fingers down her cheek. Gaiety wanted to close her eyes, press his hand to her cheek with both of hers, and kiss his palm, but instead she asked, "And what?"

Their eyes met and held. Tension heightened between them. He cupped her chin, letting the pads of his fingers caress her skin. "And pretend you're a woman I've paid to spend the night with so I don't have to have permission to take you to bed."

She had to do something, say something, to counter his draw on her. Like the harlot he wished her to be, she wanted him to make good on his words and take her to bed, without asking permission.

"Is it different?" she asked, with curiosity showing in her voice and her expression. "The way a man treats his wife in bed, as opposed to the way he treats a paid woman?"

His hand slid down her neck until his open palm rested on her chest. The warmth from his hand thrilled her, comforted her. She tried to imagine Aston touching her any way other than with the loving tenderness he'd shown her. And if any woman had ever experienced that wonderful sensation, could she ever settle for anything less?

"In some ways, it's exactly the same," he answered, looking dreamily into her eyes. "But in others, it's worlds apart. I can tell you that it won't be easy for me to keep my hands off you tonight."

Gaiety moistened her lips. She didn't want him to keep his hands off her, but how could she tell him that? How could she let him know without becoming the woman she was dressed to be? And that brought another thought to her mind—did he want her touch as much as she wanted his, or did he just want to touch a woman? She pushed away those intruding thoughts and said, "I think I can trust you to keep your mind on the business at hand and off my body." She picked up the loosely woven black shawl and wrapped it around her shoulders and breasts, not really concealing anything.

"Is that better?" she asked, knowing she was using a seductive voice, but sure she hadn't intended to. She needed to put a stop to this forward banter and go in search of her brother. She couldn't let the feelings Aston had breathed life into control her. Those had to be denied.

"Not a hell of a lot, no," he said in an irritable tone, and moved away from her. "I think you need to put on another dress."

"Aston, we're only playing a part, and only for a short time. I'm hoping someone will try to rob us tonight so we can ask about Titus."

Aston looked at her and chuckled lightly as he adjusted his embroidered waistcoat. "You make it sound so easy, Gaiety, and it's not. Damn it, I don't like the idea of other men looking at you in that dress and thinking what they're going to be thinking."

Suddenly feeling somewhat devilish, she decided to tease him. "And what *is* it they'll be thinking?" she asked.

Aston looked away as if he wouldn't say, but then turned back to her and answered huskily, "The same thing I'm thinking right now. That you're a hell of a fine-looking woman and that dress makes you look hot and ready for a man to take you to bed."

The soft smile faded from her face and she wrapped her shawl tighter about her shoulders. She hadn't expected Aston to be so blatant. Gaiety was sure of one thing: she didn't want any man except Aston looking at her and wanting to take her to bed. Aston, who'd saved her sister's treasures. Aston, who'd taken care of Titus all these years. Aston, who'd taught her how a man loves a woman. Aston was the only man she wanted.

She lifted her chin. "You look like a very handsome rogue," she said in a light voice, wanting to dispel the heavy overtones of the conversation. "No doubt I'll have to fight off several women who will be seeking your favors tonight."

Much to her delight, Aston smiled and chuckled a little. She meant what she'd said. He was handsome. He'd shaved everywhere except a fine line just above his top lip. The thin, closely cropped mustache gave him a dangerous look that made him wonderfully appealing. He'd also shed his dark brown coat for a white evening jacket and exchanged his cravat for a black bow tie. He would definitely turn heads tonight. Hers was just the first.

As she looked at him, she recalled the night she hadn't been able to forget. Her one night in his arms, in his bed. She remembered last night, when he'd realized she needed to be held and comforted. Did he know how much it meant to her when she backed away and he didn't push her for more? Did he know how overjoyed she was to have her mother's silver pin, her father's land, Josh's pocketknife, and now, the promise of a reunion with Titus? Aston had given her all those things.

Now she knew that even if her memory someday failed her and she no longer remembered their faces, she had a part of her family to cherish always. At first she'd been too overwhelmed by the knowledge that Aston knew where Titus was, that he'd wanted Lilac Hill for her brother and not for himself, to realize all he'd done for her family. She remembered all those years she'd hated him. But not anymore. She didn't fully understand the feelings she had for the man she knew today as Aston Rutledge. But now she could separate him from the man she'd hated for twelve years. How was she going to let him know?

As she watched him check his pocketwatch, she wondered if Aston knew that tonight she needed his loving again. She needed him in her bed with his hands loving her, helping her to understand all the new and wonderful feelings he'd opened up for her. Did he have any idea how she felt? If not, did she have the courage to tell him, to show him after they found Titus?

"We'd better get started," Aston said, breaking the silence that had fallen between them.

"It's a long ride to the other side of town. Where's Mimi?"

"She went downstairs to get her supper."

"All right. Before we go, I want to make sure you understand one thing: if I tell you to do anything, you're to do it immediately and with no argument."

She nodded.

"I need more confirmation than that, Gaiety. You must obey me. It might mean our lives."

"I understand. I know how dangerous this is."

"A couple of other things. Don't smile at any man. Don't even look him in the eyes. He'll think you're giving him the eye and that you're for sale to the highest bidder. I'll have a hard enough time watching men look at you. I don't want to have to kill anyone tonight."

The thought of that made Gaiety shiver. "I won't give any man reason to think I'm interested in him."

Aston looked into her eyes for a moment longer then opened the door. "All right, let's go."

Gaiety stood behind Aston with her arm resting on his shoulder. He sat at a card table with three other men in a crowded, smoke-filled saloon on the south side of Mobile. She'd often wondered what went on behind the closed doors of gaming rooms. Now, after spending more than an hour in the noisy place, she wondered why men enjoyed it so much. Their plan was to spend an hour or so in a bar, then take a stroll before going to the next one.

The room was darker than she'd expected it to be, but not as large as she'd expected. Although several lamps were lit, smoke from the cigars, pipes, and dimly lit oil lamps added to the hazy atmosphere. When she'd first entered the room, she'd caught sight of the painting hanging over the bar. A bare-breasted woman lounged against an ornately carved chair with a red cloak draped across the lower half of her body. Gaiety quickly averted her gaze, but not before a heat of embarrassment crept up her neck and over her cheeks.

Loud voices of men talking and laughing mixed with the clinking of glasses and scraping of chairs on the wood floor. The room smelled of liquor, smoke, leather, and horse, a mixture she found almost offensive. Gaiety wouldn't have been comfortable in the room under any circumstances, but dressed as she was made it worse. From her peripheral vision she saw heads turn and eyes stare, though she was careful not to look directly at anyone.

There were four other women in the room, all clothed in a fashion similar to Gaiety's dress, with feathers and bows pinned in their hair. Two of the women were so busy talking, drinking, and laughing with some of the men that they paid her no mind. One woman occasionally looked at her with disdain in her expression, but the last had caught her attention a number of times. That one looked as uncomfortable as Gaiety felt. She couldn't help but wonder about the young woman and what had happened to bring her into the saloon.

Aston was holding his own at the table, winning as many games as he lost. One man lost every game he played and soon excused himself from the table. They'd all shared the bottle of whiskey that sat in the middle of the table. She noticed Aston had been careful to drink only a little.

When the bottle was empty, one of the men threw a coin toward her and said, "Hey, sweet thing, get us another bottle, will you? And this time, why don't you bring a glass for yourself? You look thirsty to me." He gave her a cunning smile and winked at her.

Gaiety tensed. Aston picked up the coin off the table and tossed it back to the man, then reached up and took hold of Gaiety's arm as if to hold her there. He didn't have to worry; she wasn't going anywhere.

"She's mine, and she doesn't do errands for anyone but me," Aston said.

The gambler's gaze flew to Aston's face. "Did you pay her for the whole night?"

"Let's just say I've bought up all her time." Aston kept his face serious and his tone low.

The man's gaze shifted from Aston to her, then back to Aston. Gaiety didn't like the way the man's eyes roamed over her face and down her body. She remembered what Aston had said about men wanting to take her to bed, and she cringed inside. She realized she hadn't really considered what it would be like to have men look at her and think she could be bought for the night.

Remaining as serious as Aston had, he said, "Name your price."

"She's not for sale." Aston's voice was deadly calm. His eyes never left the other man's face.

"Everything's for sale. For the right price." The gambler chuckled. "Name yours."

Gaiety could see that he was making a game out of this, and by the look in his eyes, she knew he wouldn't give up easily. She wondered if she should say anything, or just leave it to Aston.

"If you want your whiskey, go get it. We'll wait for you. If you don't, shut up and deal."

"Yeah. Deal," the other man at the table said irritably.

The gambler threw a coin over to the man and said, "This doesn't concern you. Go get us a bottle. You can keep the change."

The card player picked up the coin and looked at it. He shrugged his shoulders, pushed back his chair, and headed for the bar. Gaiety's heartbeat sped up. Fear eased into her veins, Why wouldn't this man give up?

He picked up the deck of cards and started shuffling while keeping his gaze on Aston. "We've won about the same amount of games. I'd say our skill and luck runs about even.

What do you say to just the two of us playing for the right to spend the night with her?"

Aston pushed back his chair so quickly it scraped loudly against the floor and caused Gaiety to stumble backward. The room suddenly grew quiet as everyone stopped what they were doing and saying to watch and listen. He rose and glared down at the man. "I don't play cards for women. Either lay your money down, or find another table."

The card player paused in the middle of his shuffling. He looked around the room, then back to Aston. He took four coins off his stack and laid them in the center of the table.

"No reason to get mad." One corner of his mouth lifted in a grin. "It doesn't hurt to ask, does it? Sit back down. We'll play for money." He laid two more coins in the center of the table and started dealing the cards.

Aston glanced back to Gaiety before taking his chair again. She saw that his chest was heaving with anger. She hadn't wanted to cause trouble. All she wanted was to find her brother.

After winning three straight games, Aston threw his cards into the center of the table and said, "I'm out." Without another word he rose, took hold of Gaiety's arm, and ushered her away from the table.

"I need some fresh air," he mumbled. "How about a walk outside?"

"I'd love it," she said, wanting to get away from the leering troublemaker. Gaiety felt safe with Aston's warm touch. She hooked her arm through his as they walked out the door, leaving the noisy crowd behind.

The night air had a warm muggy feel to it, indicating rain was on its way. Gaiety looked up at the heavens as they walked along the creaking boardwalk and saw deep purple-black clouds racing against a midnight blue sky, blocking starlight from her view. From various directions along the street she heard loud talking, pealing laughter, and somewhere in the distance, a badly played piano.

"I would liked to have put my hands around that bastard's neck and taught him how to address a lady," Aston said, as soon as they left the area of the saloon.

Gaiety pressed her breast against his upper arm, wanting to soothe him. "Aston, you can't blame him. He thought I was a paid woman."

"Doesn't matter. A gentleman knows when to accept no for an answer. He was trying to impress you with his interest in you."

"Well, he didn't. Now, let's forget about him. I don't consider him worthy of conversation. Besides, don't you think you should be staggering, or doing something to pretend you're drunk? Mrs. Franklin said the kids usually attacked drunken gamblers."

Aston chuckled and bumped his body into hers, knocking her sideways. She squealed delightedly and hit him across the arm with her beaded drawstring bag, then picked up her skirts and took off running down the boardwalk. He caught her easily and pulled her into his arms and kissed her so thoroughly that Gaiety was breathless. She responded instantly to his embrace. She loved the feel of his arms around her, his lips on hers, his tongue in her mouth, her breasts pressed against his chest. All of him made her heady with excitement. She felt young, happy. She felt free to enjoy this frolicsome time with her husband.

Wanting to play, Gaiety pushed away from Aston again and ran. This time he let her run farther down the darkened street before grabbing her arm and gently pushing her up against a wall. She breathed hard and laughed. "You almost didn't catch me."

He looked down into her eyes, smiled, and said, "You can't run away from me, Gaiety. I won't let you get away."

Gaiety took his words as a promise. A small slice of starlight fell upon his face and the warmth buried inside him glowed. Gaiety knew she wanted to spend the rest of her life with Aston. Could she forget the past and look to a future with this man? She reached up, slid her arms around his neck, and plowed her fingers into the back of his hair. With gentle pressure to his head, she pulled him down to meet her. Their eyes closed. Their lips met. They kissed. They hugged.

Aston enfolded her into his arms, pressing her with his body against the wall as his mouth claimed hers in a sweet, gentle kiss. She breathed in the scent of him, the mixture of shaving soap and whiskey. Her hands pressed his cheek, then moved around to the back of his head, where her fingers played in his hair.

His kiss became bruising, his ardor increased. His hands and body became frantic with movements as he tried to get closer to her. She couldn't remember him ever kissing her so hard, his tongue probing so deeply into her mouth, his hands squeezing her so hard, running over her almost viciously.

For a moment, she was shocked he would treat her so roughly. But shock gave way to desire building inside her. She realized he was only demonstrating his hunger for her. Knowing that he wanted her that desperately increased her own passion, her demand for his kisses and caresses. Aston lowered his head and kissed the swell of her breasts. He massaged and caressed her shoulders, pulling her straps down to give him better access.

Gaiety kissed Aston's cheeks, along his jawline, and down his neck, occasionally letting her tongue graze his skin to taste the trace of shaving soap, to feel the faint growth of beard.

She might have been able to resist him if she hadn't experienced the pleasures he could give her. Wanting to show him how much she needed him, she let her hand slip down the front of his trousers to fondle that part of him she most wanted to feel again. The bulge was stiff, hard against her palm. Heat seared through Gaiety as if she were on fire.

In one quick, easy motion, Aston grabbed hold of her wrist and carried her hand up to his heaving chest. Her eyes popped open and she stared into his passion-filled eyes.

"You're supposed to stop me, not encourage me," he said in a raspy voice.

Her breathing was ragged. "I was doing what seemed natural, what felt right," she answered honestly.

"This is not going to work, Gaiety," he said, his voice fading to more of a sigh. He bent his head and laid his forehead against hers. "Our spending so much time together. Whenever I'm around you I want to kiss you. I want to do more than kiss you. Gaiety, I want to make love to you." His breathing was labored, his voice earnest. "I can't stand here in this street and treat you like a whore when I know that I want you for my wife in every way."

Gaiety gasped, then swallowed hard. How did she feel about that? Did she want to be his wife for all time? Is that what all these magical feelings meant? And did he really mean what he was saying, or was he looking for his own form of revenge against her for the way she'd tricked him into marrying her?

From over Aston's shoulder Gaiety caught a glimpse of a man approaching rapidly. She was about to say something to Aston about it when she realized the man's arm was raised to strike. She screamed and pushed against Aston's chest, hoping to get him out of harm's way. Not reacting quickly enough, the handle of a gun struck Aston on the forehead above his eye. He winced and slumped to the ground.

Gaiety saw the gambler who'd wanted to buy her for the night. She opened her mouth to scream but he slammed her against the wall. He shoved his hand over her mouth and jammed the barrel of his gun into her ribs.

"Scream and I'll kill both of you. Do you doubt me?" he asked, in a whispered low voice.

Worried about how badly Aston might be hurt and fearful for his life, she shook her head furiously.

Slowly he removed his hand but kept the gun pressed deeply into her side, making her wince from the pain. "I wouldn't have had to hit him if he'd just let me have you. I've never seen a man think so highly of a whore." His gaze roamed over her breasts. "You must be something special. I decided if he wanted you that badly, there must be a reason."

"I'm his wife—"

His hand flew to her mouth again, crushing her lips painfully against her teeth. "I'll do the talking. I'll do the poking. Your job is to stand there quietly, spread your legs, and take what I have to give you. I don't want to hurt you, but I will if I have to." He pressed the gun harder into her ribs. "Do we understand each other?"

He looked so vicious as he ground out the whiskey-coated words that Gaiety trembled. Oh, God! What was she going to do? She managed to cut her eyes over to where Aston lay. He wasn't moving. Panic rose within her. She couldn't worry about herself. Aston needed her help. She tried to move her face away from the bruising force of his hand against her mouth but he only held her tighter.

"Do we understand each other, sweet thing?"

Her gaze returned to Aston. He lay facedown on the boardwalk. The barrel of the gun dug painfully into her side. The only way she was going to get away from this man was to let him do what he wanted so she could see to Aston. She swallowed hard and nodded.

The gambler smiled as he raised the short-barreled pistol to her chest and placed it in the valley between her breasts. He removed his other hand from her mouth and placed it on her breast. "I've wanted a piece of you all night. I've never had a high-and-mighty-acting whore. Something tells me you're going to taste real good."

Unable to hold still, Gaiety tried to squirm away from him. Her muscles tightened. "No, I—"

He grinned and pulled back the hammer. The clicking noise was so loud she thought she might faint. Would he really kill her if she fought him? Gaiety had to make some decisions. She'd be of no use to Aston or Titus dead. She had to obey this man. Later she could learn how to live with what was about to happen to her. Taking a deep breath, she did her best to calm herself and relax against the wall.

"That's better." He smiled.

Still holding the gun, he leaned toward Gaiety and buried his lips in the soft skin between her neck and shoulders. Gaiety sank her teeth into her bottom lip to keep it from trembling, telling herself that she had the strength to get through this. He held her arm with the hand that held the pistol, the barrel pointing toward her face. She cringed from fear, from disgust at the man's touch.

With his free hand he rubbed her shoulder before letting his hand slip down to her breasts. He pressed his lower body against her again and again, pumping his hips against her softness. She tried to close her mind to his groping hands, seeking lips, probing tongue, and foul taste. But she couldn't. She felt every dreaded touch, every breath.

She remained passive, just as he'd demanded, until he raised her dress and pulled on her drawers. Knowing she couldn't submit without a fight, Gaiety came alive. She bit his lip, pushed against his chest, and brought her knee up between his legs with all the strength she could muster. The man doubled over. Gaiety turned to flee, but his hand caught her arm and jerked her backward. A fist caught her under the chin and slammed her into the wall. Her breath left her lungs, stars swam before her eyes.

"Hey, Duncan, look." The young man pointed to the other side of the street. "There's a man roughing up a whore."

"Where?"

"Over there, in that dark corner."

"Yeah, I see. Wonder what she did?"

"She probably won't let him have what he wants."

Duncan laughed, took his hat off, and scratched the top of his head, then resettled the hat. "Yeah. What's that on the ground?"

The two young men walked closer. "It's another man. Guess they were fighting over the woman."

"Yeah." They slowed their steps as they drew near and lowered their voices. "I bet he has some money in his pockets."

They smiled at each other. "I'd bet they both do. Guess there's only one way to find out."

Duncan pulled a pearl-handled gun from underneath his waistband and the other young man pulled a knife. "Same as always?" he asked.

"Yep. Who would've thought we'd get lucky when we were just walking home? The gang should be right proud of us after this."

The two eased up on the struggling man and woman. The younger one with the knife fanned out to the left of the couple. Duncan stood directly behind the man. Grasping the handle with both hands, he pointed the gun at the man's back and yelled, "Give me your money or I'll shoot."

The man whirled around, pointing a pistol at Duncan. Both guns exploded.

Titus watched in horror as fire flew from

the tips of both guns as the balls were hurled from the chambers. He yelled, but to no avail. Both men staggered, staring wildly at each other before they fell to the ground.

The blast of gunshot jerked Aston awake. He rolled over and came up on his hands and knees quickly, trying to assess the situation through blurred vision and a splitting pain in his head. Gaiety leaned against the wall. A young man holding a knife stood looking at two men on the ground with gunshots to their chests. His mind was fuzzy, but a quick glance told him both men were dead. What in the hell had happened?

Wide-eyed, Gaiety stepped forward and whispered, "Titus. You're Titus. I know you are."

The young man nervously pointed the knife toward her. "Who are you? How'd you know my name? I don't know you." He looked from side to side. "Why did he kill Duncan? No one was supposed to get—"

Aston didn't wait for him to finish as he dived for the young man's legs, knocking him off his feet. The knife went flying from his hand. "Get the knife!" he shouted to Gaiety.

Gaiety grabbed the knife as Aston continued to wrestle the young man. His head was hurting like hell, but with two dead men lying in the street, he didn't have time to think about his injury. He rolled the kid over on his stomach, twisted his arm behind his back, and shoved it up toward his neck. Titus cried out as Aston yanked him to his feet.

Fighting a wave of dizziness he said, "We have to get out of here before someone comes."

"Titus," Gaiety said holding the knife limply at her side, refusing to respond to Aston's demand. "You look just like Josh. I'm your sister . . . Avalina."

"Avalina?" he asked softly.

"Yes," she whispered with a tremulous smile.

"Avalina?" Suddenly his face reddened and he struggled against Aston's hold. "You're a whore!" he shouted at her. "You're a goddamned whore!"

"No!" she pleaded. "No, I dressed up like this to try to find you."

Gaiety looked like she might faint because of her brother's fierce accusation. Aston knew someone would be rounding the corner any second. They needed to get away from the two men lying in the street.

"Gaiety, we have to get out of here before the sheriff comes or you'll never be able to get Titus out of this mess. Now go. *Hurry!*"

With understanding lighting her eyes, Gaiety turned and fled. Aston followed, forcing Titus to run ahead of him.

Sixteen

Shaking with fear, with relief, with worry, Gaiety followed Aston and Titus into the small tavern where Aston had rented a room for the night. Over to the far side of the taproom, two men sat at a table drinking a tankard of ale and gave them no more than a passing glance as the three hurried up the stairs to their room.

As soon as the door shut behind them, Aston shoved Titus into a slat-backed chair beside the fireplace and said, "Don't move." He struck a match and lit an oil lamp that sat on a low chest in front of him.

Titus lowered his head and hid his face in his hands. "I can't believe Duncan's dead. No one was supposed to die." His head popped up, his eyes wide with fear. "I have to get out of here. I need to go tell the others."

"Stay put. You're not going anywhere," Aston said, then turned to face Gaiety. "Where's the knife?"

She pulled it from the folds of her skirt and handed it Aston. She shivered as he took it from her. Her hand burned when she released it because she'd held the handle so tightly. It was still hard to believe that Titus had been carrying such a deadly weapon, robbing people, threatening them. How could he? What had happened to make him do such things?

"Hey, that's mine," Titus said, rising from the chair.

"Sit down and shut up," Aston barked, as he pointed a stern finger at him. "Or I'll take you straight to the sheriff, where you belong." Aston grabbed hold of the back of his head. "Damn!" He blinked rapidly several times before sliding the knife into his boot.

Protectiveness surged through Gaiety. How could she have forgotten that Aston had been hurt? "Aston, please," she said, taking hold of his arm and forcing him back toward the bed. "Sit down and let me take a look at your head. You took quite a hit from that man's gun. Your ears are probably still ringing."

"I'm fine," he said, but allowed her to help him to the bed as he kept his scowling gaze on Titus.

Titus threw his head back, flinging his long brown hair out of his eyes, and crossed his arms across his chest in defiance as he huffed loudly.

"Then you won't mind if I have a look." She poured some water into the basin and wet a cloth. Carefully she wiped the dried blood off his forehead. "It doesn't look too bad," she said.

"That's not the one that hurts. It's back here. I must have hit my head when I fell."

She gently placed her fingers in his hair and looked for his wound. His hair was softly textured. She sifted through it lovingly, letting the pads of her fingers glide effortlessly over his scalp, searching for the injury. A strong desire to press his face against her breasts and hold him engulfed her, and she had to fight herself to remain aloof. There were so many things to tell Aston, so many things to thank Aston for, she didn't know where to begin. But too many other things needed to be settled first.

"What happened out there?" he asked, in a soft voice that only she could hear.

Gaiety squeezed her eyes shut for a moment. Remembering all that had happened, she trembled. If only she could somehow have prevented the killings. Aston reached up and took hold of her hand. She swallowed hard and looked down at him. Keeping her voice low, she said, "The gambler hit you over the head with his gun and he—he attacked me."

His eyes probed hers. "Did he hurt you?"

Looking into his eyes made her feel better. "No, I'm all right."

Aston touched the corner of her mouth with the tips of his fingers. "Your lip is cut."

"He put his hand over my mouth so I couldn't scream." She looked away. She didn't want to have to tell Aston the horrible man had kissed her and touched her. "While I was struggling with him, Titus and the other young man approached us and yelled for him to hand over his money. He—he still had his gun in his hand. He turned around and they shot each other." She took a deep breath and stepped away from him. She didn't want him asking more questions. She didn't want to relive the details of the shock on their faces, the blood on their shirts.

Wiping her hands down her dress, she said, "You have a goose egg on the back of your head, but the skin doesn't seem to have been broken. It will probably be sore for several days."

Aston lightly touched the large knot that had formed underneath his scalp. "It gave me one hell of a headache," he said, rubbing it gently.

"I don't have anything—"

"Hey, Avalina, if that's who you really are . . . when you get through with him, I'd like some answers," Titus interrupted her in a belligerent tone of voice.

"He's going to be a handful," Aston whispered to Gaiety.

"I won't turn my back on him no matter what he's done. He's my brother."

Aston's features remained serious. "He's a thief who carries a large knife. He may be beyond your help."

A sharp pain stabbed Gaiety in the side. She'd never agree with that; never. "No," she whispered earnestly. "I won't let you be right about that." She turned away quickly and looked at Titus. His blue eyes, so much like hers, had dark circles under them. Oil had collected in his hair, making it stringy and a dirty shade of brown. He wasn't much taller than her. His lanky frame didn't fill out his dusty, worn clothes. Looking at him, she knew the only thing he needed to straighten up his life was her love. She could see him through this and into a better life.

Gaiety walked back over to him and stood in front of him. "I am your sister, Avalina Talbot Rutledge. Do you remember me?"

"I remember your name."

She turned to Aston. "This man is my husband, Aston."

"Yeah, I've heard his name before, too."

Gaiety tensed. "You have?" Did Titus remember that Aston was once married to Theodora?

"Mama usually said a prayer for him when we went to church, but I don't know why." He ran his fingers through his hair, pushing it away from his face. His expression seemed to be challenging Aston to deny his claim or explain it.

Aston remained quiet.

Little needles of fear pricked Gaiety's skin. "How much do you remember about your life in Georgia? How much have the Franklins told you?"

"They told me shi—"

"Watch your mouth," Aston interrupted him. "If you don't know anything about how you came to live with the Franklins, just say so."

Gaiety clasped her hands together tightly and held them in front of her. She felt stiff, tight. She didn't want to be considered the peacemaker between her brother and her husband. Aston was making it clear he wasn't going to be sympathetic to Titus. And Titus made it clear he didn't like Aston.

Titus rolled his eyes around in his head before settling his gaze on Gaiety. He scratched his nose with the back of his palm and sniffed. "I know my name is Titus Talbot, even though everyone else thinks I'm a Franklin. I know I was taken from an orphanage when I was four or five, and I remember I once had a sister named Avalina. That's about it."

"Do you remember Josh or Theodora? Papa?" she asked, wanting him to remember some little thing about them so they could share their memories and make them stronger, make them last a lifetime.

"I assume I had a papa before Jacob Franklin," he said sullenly. "And I know there were other kids in the family."

The lump in Gaiety's throat grew bigger. "Do you remember our farm, Lilac Hill?"

"Nope." He spread his legs out before him and crossed his feet at the ankles, showing little concern for her questioning. "Look, one of my friends got killed tonight. I was roughed up by your husband. I don't feel like talking right now. Can I just have something to eat and go to sleep?"

Titus seemed so young to her at that moment, so in need of her compassion. Did he fully understand what he'd been doing on the streets of Mobile Bay?

"Ah—well, I'm sure the kitchen is closed downstairs. I have some small biscuits Mimi packed for me. Those will tide you over until morning." Gaiety rummaged through her purse and found the biscuits wrapped in a white cloth and gave them to Titus. He took them from her without giving thanks and greedily popped a whole one into his mouth. She looked at him and a warmth of love spread throughout her. He'd been wrong to do what he was doing, but she felt sure her love would change him.

Titus looked up from the napkin. "If you are Avalina, why does he call you Gaiety?"

"I was adopted, too. My new parents renamed me. I go by Gaiety now."

Without responding Titus returned to his biscuits.

"Gaiety."

Aston's voice cut into her thoughts, and she turned to him.

"We need to talk and make some decisions," he said.

Aston took her by the arm and they moved to the far corner of the room. "I think he should be told the whole story, but not until we get him home."

"I agree," she said, thankful that Aston still held her arm. His touch was comforting, and she desperately needed that right now.

"I'm afraid we could have big trouble. Do you think anyone saw us at the scene where those two men shot each other?"

"I—I don't think so. I didn't see anyone. No one came running to help us."

"Good. If no one can connect us to the scene, we shouldn't even cross the sheriff's mind. But to be on the safe side, we need a plan."

"What? I'll do whatever you say."

"What I'd like to do is take Titus to the sheriff and let him scare the hell out of him."

"Aston!" she gasped.

"But I won't. The sheriff wouldn't let him go with just a warning. Our only hope is that seeing his friend killed shook him up enough that he'll think twice before he tries stealing for a living again."

"Oh, Aston, I know if we can get him home, away from the influences here, he'll change. I know he'll want Lilac Hill once he sees it."

"I hope you're right, Gaiety, because neither of you will like the alternative."

No . . . Gaiety wouldn't allow herself to think about that. It wouldn't happen; she'd see to it. Titus was going to turn out to be a fine young man.

"As soon as he goes to sleep, I'm going to go arrange for a carriage to take us to pick up Mimi and Josie at first light. We'll drive to the next town and take the stage from there."

"That sounds like a good plan to me."

"There's one other place I want to go before we leave."

"The Franklins'?" she asked softly.

Aston sighed. "I think they have a right to know we found him and are taking him with us."

She nodded, remembering the plainspoken woman with the well-cared-for home.

Gaiety looked up at him with concern in her eyes. "Do you think the sheriff will ever come to Georgia looking for Titus?"

"I doubt it. He didn't really seem that concerned about the problem."

"I hope you're right."

"The sheriff has what he wanted—an example. With one of the young men getting killed tonight, maybe that'll make the others think twice about their thievery. Maybe it'll make Titus realize how lucky he is. He could have very easily been the one that caught that bullet."

Gaiety cringed from the truth of his words. All three of them had come close to having their lives destroyed tonight. She'd come to realize something else, too—she loved Aston. She'd couldn't deny the feeling any longer. She wanted to spend the rest of her life with him. She wanted to live with him at Southern Oaks and have his children. But how did she go about telling him all these things?

Aston slipped his arm around Gaiety's waist and they walked over to Titus. He looked up at them with rebellious blue eyes.

"What's the matter?" he asked, looking up from his meal. "Don't you like the way I eat?"

"It's like this, Titus," Aston said. "You've got two choices: you can go back to Georgia with your sister and learn how to lead a decent life, or I can turn you over to the sheriff and you can go to jail." Aston's voice was deadly calm. "Which is it going to be?"

"Jail? You call that a choice? The only place I intend to go is back to my friends," he grumbled obnoxiously.

"That's not a choice."

"I need to tell them about Duncan."

Aston remained firm. "No one can help your friend. The others will find out soon enough."

"Titus," Gaiety said, stepping forward. "You have a farm, your own land waiting for you in Georgia. Don't throw it away," she pleaded.

For the first time that evening, Titus seem to perk up and really look at Gaiety; but then, as if realizing he looked interested in what she said, he slouched farther down into the chair. "Yeah, all right. I'll go, but I'm not promising I'll stay."

Seventeen

After closing the door to Titus's room, Gaiety stood outside in the dimly lit upstairs hallway of the gracious mansion of Southern Oaks, shoring up the courage she needed to go back downstairs and talk to Aston. She leaned against the wall and watched the flickering flame in the lamp at the top of the stairs. On the opposite wall a mirror threw the reflection of the light down the long hallway.

Returning to Southern Oaks had been very much like the trip to Mobile. Mimi and Gaiety sewed, Josie and Titus slept, and Aston read the papers and talked with other travelers. Gaiety was sensitive to every look and word that passed between Aston and Titus. Her brother made it clear he didn't like Aston telling him what to do. More than once she interceded between the two during the week-long journey.

The long days had given her time to think and mull over her relationship with Aston, her feelings for him, and his connection to her past. Finding Titus and dealing with his youth and immaturity had helped her understand something her father had tried to tell her months ago. Aston was young when he married Theodora and might have made some mistakes, but she'd never let that excuse him of any blame, even though she'd believed he was telling the truth when he'd said Theodora's baby wasn't his. What she hadn't realized was that it made *him* a victim, too. It was time she let him know she'd come to love him and trust him.

There was a tightness in her chest and stomach every time she looked at him. Now she wanted to clear the air and start over with nothing between them. She wanted to be his wife and his lover, but she wasn't sure Aston still wanted the same thing. He'd remained respectful but cool on the trip home.

It was early evening when they finally arrived at Southern Oaks. Everyone was hot, tired, and irritable. They had eaten only one meal about mid-morning that day, so Mimi and Gaiety helped Alma prepare a quick dinner of cheese, bread, cooked plums, and piping hot tea.

Gaiety couldn't help but notice Aston ate only a little before he excused himself, took his cup of tea, and went into his office to check his mail and paperwork. She agreed to allow Mimi to see Hank after Mimi promised she wouldn't be out very long.

Titus had grumbled about the meager meal, and trying to placate him, Gaiety promised him a bountiful feast tomorrow. After he finished off the cooked fruit with the last bit of bread, she offered to show him the house. His disposition hadn't changed much during the trip or upon arriving home. The only thing he wanted to see was a bed, so while Alma went to get him one of Aston's extra nightshirts, Gaiety took him up to one of the guest bedrooms and turned back the covers. She was sure that with enough love and kindness, Titus would change his attitude and come to love her as she loved him. She had to believe it. She decided that tomorrow would be soon enough to talk to Titus about their family. Tonight she had to talk to Aston. And there was no need to wait longer to do it.

Taking a deep breath, she lifted her skirts and started down the stairs. Somehow, she had to find a way to tell Aston that she'd changed her mind. She no longer wanted to live at Lilac Hill. She wanted to live at Southern Oaks with him. But more than that, she needed to tell him she loved him and wanted to be his wife, to have his children. When she'd married Aston, her heart had been so full of deceit and revenge she'd denied her initial attraction to him, the warm feelings she'd had before she knew who he was. Now her heart was open to those wonderful feelings. She felt full of love and gratitude, and she wanted him to know.

Her soft leather shoes made no sound as she made her way down the long, wide corridor to Aston's office at the back of the house. She knew he'd be busy, that he had a lot of work to catch up on, but this was important, too. Even if he no longer wanted to make a home life with her, she had to let him know how she felt.

As she walked through the doorway, he glanced up from his desk. He looked at her for a few seconds with those beautiful green eyes before he rose and said, "Gaiety, come in."

She was nervous. Her heart hammered like an ironsmith at work. "I'm sorry to interrupt," she said, as she walked into the room and stopped in front of his desk, thankful her voice didn't show her nervousness.

Aston rubbed the back of his neck and down his shoulder. "You're not. I'd just decided to wait until tomorrow to look at the rest of these letters. I'm simply too tired to bother with all this tonight." He stretched out his arm and swept it over the stacks of papers on the top of his oak desk.

He did look tired, she noticed. He'd taken off his jacket, waistcoat, and cravat, but his white shirt was still buttoned tight at the throat. His trousers looked in need of a pressing, and his hair was attractively rumpled and curling upward a little where the ends fell below his shirt collar. But to her he'd never looked more handsome than he did at this moment. Her heart overflowed with love for him. It felt wonderful not to have to deny it to herself.

"That's probably a good idea," she answered softly. She paused, then added, "I don't want to keep you long, but do you mind if we talk for a few minutes before you go upstairs?"

He smiled. "Not at all. Let's go over to the sofa and sit down."

Gaiety wasn't sure she wanted to sit. Her nerve endings tingled. In fact, she wasn't sure she could be still, she was so tense. Aston walked from behind the desk and she joined him at the Windsor-styled settee which stood against the far wall. Making himself comfortable, Aston leaned back and stretched his legs out in front of him. In contrast to his relaxed position, Gaiety sat on the edge of the settee, keeping her back straight, her shoulders and chin erect. The skirt of her peach-colored gown flared out around her legs. She folded her hands in her lap and laced her fingers together, hoping they wouldn't show how nervous she was about this talk. She was more convinced than ever that it'd been her destiny to marry Aston.

"Did Titus give you any trouble about going to bed?"

She cleared her throat. "None at all. He's exhausted. I don't think he's eaten or slept properly since he left the care of the Franklins. I told him we'd have a long talk tomorrow. I think once he knows the whole story about our past he'll realize how wrong he was to take up with those ruffians and he'll settle down."

"I hope you're right."

"I know I am," she said earnestly, leaning toward him. "He'll learn to take life more seriously and be responsible for himself and his actions. He'll be sorry he was ever involved in robbing people."

Aston reached over, placing his fingertips under her chin. "What about your life? What are you going to do, Gaiety?"

Was he asking her to tell him what was in her heart? His eyes watched her face lovingly. She looked into his eyes and knew she wanted to tell him she loved him. The past belonged behind her. It was time to start over with him. But to tell him so would leave her open to rejection, so she tempered her first inclination and said, "That depends a lot on you."

"Me? I don't think so."

His voice was husky. His eyes continued to search her face. He was so serious she felt sure her heart skipped a beat. Her breaths came in short little gasps. Maybe he no longer wanted her for his wife. Maybe she'd waited too long. Fear inched its way up her back and she looked away from his penetrating gaze to stare at her clasped hands.

Aston continued, "I made my decision when I decided to marry you, Gaiety. I haven't changed my mind."

Her lashes flew up. Their eyes met. She had to be truthful. "I've changed. I married you only because I wanted to upset your life, to hurt you. I—I wanted to make you pay for all the horrible things that happened to my family."

"You succeeded in all those things, Gaiety. You are a formidable woman."

But do you think you can ever love me? her heart

cried out for her to ask, but instead she reached over and took his hand and held it in both of hers. Touching him gave her strength, courage.

"Aston, I need to tell you that I'm so very grateful you helped me find my brother. If there is any way I can repay you, I will."

His expression quickly changed to one of irritation. "I don't want your gratitude." He pulled his hand free of hers and shifted in the settee. "And I've already been paid, rememember? You gave me my wedding night in exchange for Titus." He said the words tightly, as if holding back anger.

Too late she realized he misunderstood her. She wasn't handling this right. But she had no experience at telling a man she loved him.

"Let me say this another way. Aston, now that we've found Titus, I need to know you've told me the truth about what happened between you and Theodora. That you've told me everything that happened and there's no more to say. I need to know I can finally let go of the past and enjoy tomorrow."

He simply looked at her for a moment as if trying to decide what to say. With an anxious look on his face, he took hold of her upper arms, pulled her toward him, and he said, "All I've told you is true. There is no more to tell. You can forget the past and look toward the future."

Relief washed over her, but still fearful of

rejection and life without Aston, she asked, "Are you going to be in my future?"

"It has to be your decision, Gaiety. Do you want me there?"

"Oh, yes, Aston. I want to live here at Southern Oaks with you as my husband. I want to have your children. I'm sorry I doubted you about Theodora's baby. I'm sorry I misjudged you all these years."

Aston crushed her to his chest, giving her a short, fierce kiss before looking back into her eyes. "Thank God! I was so afraid you were going to tell me that we'd both fulfilled our end of the agreement and that we should part in the morning."

She kissed the base of his throat. "No. I haven't wanted that for a long time. In spite of everything I've tried to do to keep it from happening, I've fallen in love with you."

He chuckled lightly and hugged her to him. "I love you, too, my beautiful wife. Like you, I didn't want to love you. My pride didn't want me to love any woman after what Theodora did to me. But it was no use. Your strength, your loyalty, your caring won me over, and I was lost to your charms, your shrewdness. I not only love you, Gaiety, I admire you for fighting for what you believed was right."

She was unaccustomed to his words of praise; her heart swelled with pride. She trembled with happiness. "Aston, I love you so much. I want to do everything in my power to make you happy."

"You have made me happy by coming in here tonight and telling me you believe me, you love me."

They smiled lovingly at each other and kissed again.

"I don't think Titus is mature enough to live at Lilac Hill with Papa. Would you mind if he stayed here with us?"

"He's welcome at Southern Oaks."

Gaiety's heart filled to bursting with love for her husband. Even knowing her brother had been a thief, he was willing to let him stay at his home.

She looked up into his handsome face and whispered, "Thanks for giving Titus a second chance. Thanks for giving me a second chance."

"How could I not? You bewitched me that day by the pond. I wanted you in my arms that day, and I still do." He kissed her passionately. "Let's go to bed," he murmured against her lips.

Gaiety nodded.

A few minutes later, in the dim light of the oil lamp, Aston slowly undressed her, then himself. They lay down on the bed, arms and legs entwined, facing each other. Gaiety was afraid to let go of him, afraid the wonderful feeling of hearing that Aston loved her would disappear.

She ran her fingers through his hair and gently massaged his temples. "Does that help you relax?" she asked in a low voice as his hand made a slow caress over her back and up and down her hip.

"Mmm." He closed his eyes and breathed deeply. He pulled her closer to his naked body, allowing her no escape. "Just being here in bed with you helps me relax. I spent most of my time on that stage tense and stiff as a board."

"Because of Titus?"

"No, because I was trying to figure out some way to keep you with me. I didn't care if I had to bribe you or lie to you. I couldn't bear the thought of you living at Lilac Hill."

Gaiety stiffened a little. "You didn't, did you?"

"What?" he asked softly, kissing the sensitive skin behind her ear.

"Lie to me. Everything you said to me tonight was the truth, wasn't it? You meant it when you said you loved me?"

Aston slid his arms underneath her and rolled himself on top of her, gently settling his body on hers. "Oh yes, my darling, I meant everything I said."

Gaiety rose up and met his lips with hers. The kiss was tender at first, but as their mouths opened and tongues explored, passion grew and the kiss became ardent, urgent, showing their hunger for each other. She yielded to his overpowering kisses, exhaling unevenly as she sought to match his fervor. All thought of talk fled her mind. She gave herself up to the glorious feelings of her husband's loving. At last she was free from all entanglements. She was free to love Aston, and it felt wonderful.

She relished the feel of his hands on her body, his eyes on her face, his breath against her lips. He touched her skin as if she were made from the finest silk, and she responded by touching him with worshipful hands.

She was filled with a desire she'd only recently come to understand, a desire she knew would stay with her the rest of her life, a desire so intense it made her tremble. She loved her husband and wanted to please him. Tenderness welled up inside her. Everything had been resolved. She could accept the love she was feeling for Aston.

With practiced ease he ran his hand down her back over the swell of her hip to caress her inner and outer thigh. Gaiety stroked his back, the spare line of his shoulders, down his side to his hip, feeling every hard-ridged muscle beneath her hand.

"I've wanted us to do this again ever since our wedding night," she whispered against his ear as he kissed her neck.

"I'm glad I wasn't the only one who missed this. So many times I wanted to say to hell with what you wanted and simply take you. You were my wife. You were mine, but I couldn't have you."

"And now you can. All night."

He looked down into her eyes adoringly. "For the rest of our lives."

"Yes," she answered. "I love you, Aston Rutledge."

"And I love you."

When they were both beyond restraint, Aston showered her with fiery kisses and caresses as he fit his body inside hers. They continued their loving until they both sighed with contented pleasure.

Afterward he kissed her slowly, gently, as if they had all the time in the world to enjoy each other. And they did.

Later that night, Aston lay in bed wide awake, knowing he was the worst kind of liar. He'd lied to the woman he loved above all others. And not once. Twice. The oil lamp had burned low, night air had cooled the heated room, and the moon threw shadowed light across the foot of the bed. Gaiety lay sleeping peacefully with her cheek pressed against his chest.

He reached over and lightly caressed the soft skin of her shoulder. He hadn't lied when he'd told her he loved her. That soothed his conscience somewhat. If he'd told her the truth about Theodora, would Gaiety have believed him? She was always quick to defend her sister, her family, who, no matter what she thought, were not blameless in what had happened. He was afraid if he told her what Theodora had done it would not only destroy her sweet memory of her sister, it would destroy any hope he had of building a solid relationship with her, too. He wasn't willing to take the chance of losing her. Theodora had meant nothing to him. Gaiety meant everything to him. The truth would hurt her, maybe destroy what they had together. He wouldn't let Theodora come between them again.

Reluctantly, he thought back to the night Theodora had died. He'd always tried to push that time from his memory. Even now, he didn't want to remember the shadowed room where Theodora had lain in bed, screaming in pain from her injuries suffered in the fall and from a baby that was trying to be born. He saw her sweat-soaked body thrashing about; she was begging for help one moment and damning him to hell the next. Trying to soothe her, he'd placed the pearls she'd wanted around her neck, but in the end, nothing helped. She grew too weak to fight, too weak to breathe. He turned his head and shied away from those memories.

Who had been in the room with him that night? The doctor, his father, and Alma. His father had died, and the doctor had retired to a small farm on the other side of Savannah. Not much chance of Gaiety running into him. But Alma might one day be persuaded to talk. First thing tomorrow morning, before Gaiety awoke, he'd have a talk with Alma. Gaiety must never know what had gone on that night.

He wrapped his arm around his wife and pulled her closer. She snuggled and mumbled in her sleep, fitting her nose into the crook of his neck. At last they could both put what happened twelve years ago behind them. It bothered him to have lied to her. She would never know it, but his lies would protect her from a much deeper hurt.

Mimi paced from one side of the back porch to the other, occasionally stopping to brush her hand down the skirt of her best dress. She'd sent word to Hank by Josie, telling him she was back and for him to come see her at the usual time.

It was a pleasant night, with many stars twinkling in the dark sky. A quarter moon did little to brighten the night. She'd missed Hank's kisses and talking to him. And he never got tired of listening to her.

As she looked up at the sky, she remembered their last night together. Hank hadn't wanted her to leave, but there was no way she could have refused to go with Miss Gaiety. Gaiety had picked her out of a group of fifteen young ladies, all wanting the job of being her maid. At the time, having been recently orphaned, Mimi needed the job desperately. Mimi had known she wasn't the most qualified person who'd applied for the position, but she was eager to do a good job, and it must have shown. Gaiety chose her.

She tried not to think about the possibility of someone taking her place with Hank while she was away. Mimi clasped her hands together at her breast and looked up into the heavens.

The minutes dragged on, and she prayed Hank had waited for her return.

When she was about to give up hope that he'd come, she heard running feet. She strained to look down the road to the carriage house. At last she saw him appear out of the darkness. Mimi squealed with delight as her heavy heart lifted. She grabbed up the tail of her skirt and ran down the back steps, eager to meet him.

Hank caught her up in his arms and hugged her tightly to his chest, swinging her around a couple of times before setting her on her feet. Their lips met in a sweet, welcoming-home kiss that ended all too quickly for Mimi. She wanted him to kiss her forever.

His sandy brown hair fell across his forehead as he raised his head and looked down into her eyes. "I missed you," he whispered. "I thought you'd never return."

She settled into his embrace, enjoying the feel of his arms around her. They swayed gently back and forth. "I've missed you, too, Hank. I didn't think we'd ever get back home."

He placed his hands on either side of her face, his touch gentle. "I hope Mr. Aston and Miss Gaiety took care of all their business, because I don't want you ever to leave me again." He gave her a short, hard kiss.

"Hold me tighter, Hank," she whispered into the collar of his shirt. "I don't want you to let me go."

He hugged her close for a moment, then said, "Mimi, I want you to marry me."

Mimi went still. Shock washed over her. "Marry you? I—don't know."

His hold on her loosened. An almost frightened expression clouded his face. "You do love me, don't you?" he questioned.

She held onto his upper arms as she thought back to the first day she met him. Yes, she'd always loved him. "Don't even ask it. You know I do." But even she had to wonder why she hesitated when this was something she shouldn't have to think twice about.

"Well, why did you say you didn't know? Why didn't I get a yes? Is it that you'd rather live here in this big house instead of the small room I have in the carriage house?"

"Oh, no, Hank, no," she said, aghast he'd think such a thing. "I don't mind that at all. This house is pretty to look at, but I'm never real comfortable in it, always afraid I'll break something."

"Are you afraid I can't take care of you?"

"Of course not. It's not that, either. Besides, I've got a little put away myself for when I marry. Mr. Lane always paid me good money."

"Then why not say yes?"

Mimi pressed her lips to the warmth of his neck. "I'll have to think about it because I have to consider Miss Gaiety. I've been with her a long time. I don't know what she'll say about this."

"Since she just got married, I'd think she'd be real pleased for you."

Mimi shook her head. "I don't know what's

wrong, but their marriage isn't what it's supposed to be."

"What do you mean?"

"They don't even sleep together most nights."

"I guess what you're trying to tell me is that you think Miss Gaiety still needs you?"

"Yes."

Hank smiled. "I don't mind you working for her. Maybe she'll let you take care of her during the day while I work for Mr. Aston. The only difference is that at night you'll come down to the carriage house and sleep with me."

That sounded like a wonderful dream come true, but she still wanted to talk with Miss Gaiety before she gave Hank an answer. "I promise I'm going to think about this long and hard and let you know soon." She smiled up at him and pressed her body close to his. "In the meantime, can we go somewhere and just kiss for a little while? I've missed you."

He hugged her to him. "I know just the place."

Eighteen

"I'd like to talk to you alone, Alma," Aston said, as he walked into the breakfast room the next morning. Last night had made him sure of one thing: he loved Gaiety more than he'd ever thought possible, and he'd do anything in his power to keep her from being hurt any more by the past.

Alma nodded to the darkie who was helping her set up the breakfast buffet. "Go out to the cook house and check on the biscuits for me. I'll call you when I'm ready for you to come back inside."

After the other woman shuffled out the door, Alma turned to Aston and asked, "Would you like for me to pour you a cup of coffee?"

"Yes, thank you."

Aston walked over to the double windows, and pushing the drapery panel aside, looked out over the spacious west lawn. The earth was alive with greenery, dotted with colorful flowers. The air was clear with the quiet of morning, the sky beautiful with sunshine. It was strange; he felt good and bad at the same time. Lying to Gaiety was the only thing he could have done under the circumstances. Now he not only had to protect her, he had to protect his lie and somehow learn to live with what he'd done.

"Here you are." Aston took the flower-painted cup from Alma. "Would you like to sit down, or should we stand here by the window?" she asked.

"Here's fine." He sipped the hot coffee, then looked at her. "For a particular reason, I'd like to tell you about something I don't think you're aware of."

"Yes, sir." Her voice trembled, and a worried expression clouded her features as she folded her hands together in front of her.

Aston realized he'd upset her. "Relax, Alma. You haven't done anything wrong."

"Thank you, sir."

"Gaiety is Theodora's sister."

Surprise lighted her eyes. She placed her open palm against her chest. "No, sir. That can't be." Her words were breathy.

Aston tried to keep all emotion out of his voice as he said, "Yes, it's true. Gaiety's name was Avalina Talbot when Lane Smith took her from the orphanage and adopted her. The youngster upstairs is their brother, Titus. Gaiety and I didn't go away on a wedding holiday as most people suspected. We went to Mobile to find Titus."

"I—I don't know what to say, sir. Miss Gaiety

is nothing like Miss Theodora." She shook her head disbelievingly. "How did you find out about all this? When?"

"There's no need to go into the details that no longer matter." He sighed with resignation. "I'm telling you this much because you were in the room with me the night Theodora died."

The housekeeper winced and turned her face away from him. "It's a cross I still bear that I couldn't help that poor girl's suffering."

Knowing how she felt, Aston sipped his coffee, hating to relive those torturous hours, hating Theodora, yet not wanting her to suffer and die. It had taken him years to get over those mixed feelings for Theodora. So many times he'd wished so many things could have been different.

"It's very important to me that Gaiety never know the truth about that night."

She glanced up at him. "The truth? I don't understand. What else is there to tell but the truth?"

"I told her Theodora didn't suffer. That until the end she thought she was going to live. I didn't tell her the truth about the stairs. I think it's best she never know about that."

"I understand. I'm glad you told me this. Miss Gaiety has already questioned me a couple of times about your first wife. I had no idea she was asking because Theodora was her sister."

A heaviness filled Aston's chest. He gripped

the handle of the cup tighter. "What did you tell her?"

"Not much. Thank the good Lord, she didn't ask about that night specifically, so I didn't mention it, either. But you don't have to worry, Mr. Aston. I wouldn't have breathed a word about that anyway. You didn't even have to say anything. You and your father made it very clear that what happened that night wasn't to go any further, and it never has."

Aston relaxed a little and sipped his coffee again, grateful Alma had been so loyal. Suddenly, out of the corner of his eye, he thought he saw a shadow pass across the doorway. He tensed as he spun around. There was no one there. An uneasy feeling washed over him. He walked over to the doorway leading into the dining room, but saw no one.

"Did you see one of the maids pass by?"

"No, sir."

He gave her a half smile. "Good. And Alma, thank you. I knew I could count on you."

Gaiety was disappointed to awaken and find Aston gone from their bed. She lay quietly in bed for a few minutes and remembered their wonderful night of lovemaking before she rose and dressed for the day. She didn't know when she'd ever felt better, and she'd never been happier. Gaiety Rutledge had everything in the world she could want–Aston, her brother, and her father close by. After so many years of trying to get even, she'd finally realized what she needed to do was forget the past and leave it behind, where it belonged. Because of Aston and all he'd done for her and Titus, she could do that.

Downstairs, she found Alma, who told her Aston had gone to his office at the sawmill, but he hoped to be back before too long. In the breakfast room, splattered with stripes of sunshine, she saw Titus sitting at the table, finishing his meal. She could never thank Aston enough for giving her back her brother.

"Good morning," she said cheerfully, walking into the room with a light heart and big smile. "I hope you feel rested today."

"I'm all right," he said, cutting his eyes around to her as he lifted a forkful of egg into his mouth.

Gaiety served herself a peach tart and cup of tea and joined Titus at the breakfast table. "Have you seen Aston this morning?"

He hesitated. "Ah—no. He was already gone when I got down here. Why?" He didn't look up from his food.

"No reason."

In the warm morning sunlight, Gaiety looked at her brother. He needed new clothes, his hair trimmed, and more meat on his bones. He needed love, too, and she'd been storing it up for years. She had plenty of that to give him.

"One of the things we can do today is get

you fitted for a new suit of clothes. Would you like that?"

The corner of his mouth curved upward in a half-snarl. "I had plenty of clothes, if you and *Assston* would have let me go back and get them."

Gaiety bristled. She couldn't have missed his slur on Aston's name if she'd wanted to. She started to let it go, but on second thought, realized she couldn't. If Titus thought he could be disrespectful to her husband and get away with it, she'd never have any control over what he said. She had to be firm now and stop his inappropriate attitude.

"Titus, I don't appreciate you mispronouncing my husband's name. And it's in very poor taste for you to be so disrespectful to a man who's done as much for you as Aston has."

"He didn't do anything for me," Titus came back quickly, as he pushed his empty plate aside. "I didn't ever get any of the money he sent the Franklins each month."

"Of course you did. It helped buy your clothes, send you to school, and feed you. It helped give you that nice house you grew up in."

With his thumb and middle finger he thumped a crumb across the table. "Whatever you say."

Gaiety decided not to overdo the lecture. Maybe it would be best to do everything in little doses. She cut into her peach tart and took a generous bite. The fruit was a bit tangy and the pastry slightly sweet. Delicious. She wouldn't let Titus run over her, she thought, but she had to be easy on him. She remained quiet, knowing she needed to get her thoughts together while she ate breakfast and drank her tea. Titus remained at the table with her, brooding. She was desperate for his attitude to change so they could have a true brother-and-sister relationship. But before that could start, she had to fill him in on the missing pieces of his life.

When her teacup was empty, she turned to him and said, "Why don't we take a walk outside? There are some things I'd like to tell you."

"I just ate. I'm too full. Maybe later." He slouched further into the seat of the chair.

His biting words stung, but she decided to ignore them this time. She could accept his obnoxious behavior better when it was directed at her rather than at Aston. "It will do you good. Come on, you can walk off some of that food."

He looked at her and asked, "Can we just go in the room that has the green sofa and talk there?"

He didn't want to walk, but he was willing to talk. That was progress. Not wanting to argue the point and realizing he was seeking a compromise, she agreed. "All right, let's go." Maybe being firm was a good way to counter his ill-temper and boorishness.

Once in the parlor, Titus didn't take the

green sofa. He plopped down in the ornately carved armchair. His stringy brown hair fell in his eyes and he slung his head back rather than brushing it away from his face with his hands. Gaiety smiled at him and made herself comfortable on the sofa.

"Can you tell me why you left the Franklins and took up with that gang, Titus?"

"Yeah. It was exciting."

"Ex—exciting?" She stumbled over the word. Maybe for some people it was exciting to walk the streets with a knife in their pockets. She considered it horrifying.

"Nothing ever happened on that farm. We were miles from anyone. I either worked or went to school every day. When Papa took me into town and let me have a little freedom, it was fun. I liked it; I wanted to be on my own. So when I was old enough, I left."

Gaiety stared at him in a reproachful manner. "You thought it was fun to rob people?"

"No," he said in a loud voice, giving her a sullen look. "Being on my own. I only went along with the robberies because I had to when I joined the group. We had to have money to eat, didn't we?"

She relaxed a little, thankful to hear him admit he really didn't like thievery. She was also glad to hear he hadn't run away because the Franklins had done anything harmful to him. His problem appeared to be a case of a young man with wanderlust in his heart. Maybe they'd caught him in time. She gave a silent prayer that she would be able to help him change.

She took a deep breath and asked, "Do you want to talk about your first family?" she asked.

He shifted restlessly in the chair. "Sure. Yeah. Why not?"

"You told me in Mobile you didn't remember very much."

"Yeah, that's right."

"You don't know what happened that led to your adoption by the Franklins, is that right?"

Titus stretched and yawned as if he couldn't have been less interested in the conversation. "I know what Mama told me, but I doubt it's the truth." He looked directly into her eyes. "I discovered people don't like to tell the truth."

His words and expression made Gaiety uncomfortable. Surely he didn't think that after all these years she was going to lie to him.

"Tell me what they told you, and I'll tell you whether or not it's the truth."

A smile lifted one corner of his mouth. But it wasn't a nice smile, it was a warning smile. "As if you'd know. Are you sure you've been told the truth, sister?" He chuckled.

He was deliberately trying to make her uncomfortable, but she wasn't going to let him. She squared her shoulders and said, "Just tell me what you've heard."

"I was four when my father and brother were killed in a gunfight. Too bad they didn't win. At the time, my sister Theodora was married to a wealthy man, but she died shortly after the wedding, during childbirth." He slung one leg over the arm of the chair and swung his foot back and forth. "You were adopted right away and I was left to rot in the orphanage until a *kind* man by the name of Aston Rutledge found me and asked the Franklins to take me away with them. They needed a son to help them work, so they agreed to take me." He looked into her eyes, challenging her to dispute his story.

"What you've heard is true."

"As far as you know," he said, then quickly added, "I've always wondered why I wasn't adopted by the same people who adopted you."

Gaiety wasn't surprised that he'd been scarred by his feelings of rejection. "There's no one to blame but the woman at the orphanage. She didn't tell Lane and Mary Smith that I had a brother there. By the time I was able to make Papa understand I had a brother at the orphanage, it had burned down, no records were saved, and Mrs. Conners couldn't be found. We looked for you for three years," she finished on a soft note.

He became very still and stayed quiet. For a moment she thought his eyes were going to mist.

"Yeah, well, I did all right without you." He started swinging his leg again.

But he hadn't. He'd resorted to stealing, and that wasn't right at all. It was wrong, but she wasn't going to take him to task over that now. There'd be time for that later.

She shored up her courage and asked, "Do you know who Theodora married?"

That warning smile that had chilled her before flashed across his lips again. She wouldn't be daunted by him.

"Let me guess. Aston Rutledge." He thumped his finger into the air.

"That's right," she said, wondering how he'd picked up on that bit of information. "Do you know why they married?"

"No. Tell me what you've heard."

His cunning voice bothered Gaiety. This wasn't going to be easy. Titus's flippant attitude made it difficult for her. It was best to tell him now and get everything out so he could learn to deal with the past. Her best approach was to try to keep it simple.

"Before the age of fifteen, Theodora became pregnant. She told Papa and Josh that Aston was the father. He wasn't, but at gunpoint they forced him to marry her. Aston's father's men rushed into the church and when the gunfire stopped Papa and Josh were dead. The sheriff sent us to the orphanage and Aston brought Theodora here to Southern Oaks with him."

"Why didn't he let us come live here with our sister? Why did we have to stay in the orphanage?"

"I suppose he didn't feel responsible for us at that point. He was young, not more than a year older than you are now. He made some mistakes, too," she said gently.

"Yeah, you're right about that." Titus rubbed

the back of his neck and asked, "And what have you been told happened to Theodora after she came to live here?"

Gaiety cleared her throat. "A couple of weeks before her baby was due, she fell down the stairs, killing herself and the baby. She lived for a short time, but she and the baby weren't strong enough to make it through."

He brought his leg down from the chair arm, landing it with a thud to the floor, and moved to crouch on the edge of the seat. "I suppose *Assston* told you all this?"

She squared her shoulders and lifted her chin, her expression firmly set with disapproval. "His name is Aston, and yes, he told me about Theodora's death."

Titus chuckled ruefully. "And you believed him?" He shook his head as if he couldn't believe she'd been so gullible. "How'd you end up married to him?"

She wasn't prepared to tell him that story right now, and maybe never. "I love Aston." That was all he needed to know, and she never wanted Titus to doubt that. Gaiety leaned toward her brother. "Titus, if you remember anything about Papa, Josh, or Theodora, you need to tell me. It will help us if we share our memories and keep them alive. We owe them that much."

Titus unfolded his lanky frame and stood up. He looked down at her, his hair falling around his face, his lips set in a grim line. "We owe them to find out the truth."

She rose to stand beside him. "I just told you—"

"You told me the shit *Assston* told you," he interrupted her. "That's not the truth."

Gaiety gasped, then turned angry. "How dare you speak to me with such vile language? You are free to speak your opinion, but I demand that you do it in a respectful manner, and never mispronounce my husband's name again."

"Or you'll what?" he asked loudly. "Send me to bed without any supper? Well, I don't care. He lied to you. He's a lying son-of-a-bitch, and I—"

Gaiety's hand flew out and she slapped him across the face. She was immediately appalled by her behavior but refused to let it show. Titus had to know she demanded his respect. He appeared shocked by her violence. He blinked several times and looked at her, his mouth agape.

"You hit me?" His voice was whispery with surprise.

She took a deep breath and tried to calm her racing heartbeat. He might never forgive her for striking him, but she couldn't apologize. "I will not let you speak that way about Aston."

Titus reached up and rubbed his reddening cheek. "Maybe I deserved that for my language, but I'm not lying. Ask him. I overheard him talking to that gray-haired woman this morning. I don't know what went on, but he lied to you about what happened to Theodora the night she died."

A chill shook Gaiety. Her stomach knotted. "What are you talking about? I know you and Aston don't get along, but—"

"But I'm not lying about this. I heard him telling that woman never to tell you what really happened to Theodora. She said you'd already questioned her but she didn't tell you anything."

Gaiety folded her arms around her waist and hugged herself. Pain filled her. This couldn't be true. Just last night, Aston had sworn he'd told her the truth about the past, about Theodora. She'd believed him.

Shaking from fear, from the slightest possibility Titus might be right, she insisted, "You have to be wrong." She whispered, "I love Aston. He loves me."

"He lied." Titus's voice rose in pitch. "How else would I know that you'd questioned that woman about Theodora if I hadn't heard it this morning? You can love him if you want to; I don't care. But soon as he gets back, I plan to find out exactly what happened to my sister."

"Titus is right. I lied."

Gaiety gasped, then slowly turned open-mouthed, wide-eyed, to glare at her husband standing in the doorway of the parlor. She couldn't move. She looked at him and knew she loved him for so many reasons. How could he have lied to her? Even after he admitted it, she didn't want to believe him. How could she believe the man she loved with all her heart had lied to her?

He should have known it wouldn't work. Aston felt like a fist had hit him in the stomach as he walked farther into the room. Even as he'd lied to Gaiety he'd had the feeling she'd find out the truth one day. Had it been wrong for him to have wanted to spare her the truth? Even now he could refuse to tell her what had really happened, but would they ever have a complete marriage as long as this was between them? Maybe it was time she knew the whole truth and learned how to deal with it.

"See, I told you," Titus proudly stated, slinging his hair back.

"No, Aston, I can't believe you lied to me. *You promised.*"

He walked closer to her and took hold of her hands. They were cold, trembly. "Gaiety, it's true. I was only trying to spare you the—"

"Spare me!" She jerked away from him. "After twelve years of searching for the truth, wanting to know everything, how can you say you wanted to spare me? That wasn't your decision to make. I deserved to know the truth."

"*We* deserve to know the truth," Titus corrected, as he moved to stand protectively beside Gaiety. "And you can start by telling us why you lied about getting Theodora pregnant."

Aston's temper snapped. To hell with their feelings. Today would be the last time he was accused of getting that girl pregnant. "I never *touched* your sister!" He spoke roughly as he advanced on Titus. "I have never lied about that."

"Yeah, and birds don't fly," Titus sneered.

Aston wanted to hit the bratty, smart-mouthed kid. "Whether or not you believe me is your choice." He quickly turned to Gaiety. "I never lied about that, Gaiety. I never touched Theodora before we were married or after."

She looked stricken, sad, and his heart went out to her. He wanted to pull her into his arms and comfort her. How could he expect her to believe him about anything, now that he'd admitted he'd lied about part of it? He wanted to tell her he wasn't sorry for keeping the truth from her because he knew how it was going to hurt her. He was sorry that now he had to tell her the truth.

"The only thing I lied about was her death."

"Yeah, right. We're supposed to believe that."

Aston was about to lose his temper with Titus. "Why don't you stay out of this?" He turned to Gaiety. "Let's discuss this alone."

"Like hell."

"Titus, please, watch your language." Gaiety admonished him before Aston had the chance. "Titus stays. This concerns him as much as it does me." Her words were stiff and emotionless. She wouldn't meet his gaze. She didn't want him to see how badly she hurt. "Just please tell me the truth this time, Aston. Don't let me have to go through this again. No more lies," she whispered earnestly.

"Yeah, tell us why you wouldn't let Theodora bring us here to live with her in this fancy house."

He refused to look at the kid again. He was afraid if he did, he'd hit him. He kept his gaze on Gaiety, although she wouldn't look into his eyes. "Theodora didn't want you to live here."

"Liar."

"I'm not lying. Twice Mrs. Conners came to see Theodora and asked her to take you. I managed to get my father to agree, but Theodora said no. Theodora's mind was sick. It would have to have been so. She had no tender feelings for you or Titus."

"That's not true, Aston. I lived with her for eight years. We laughed. We played together. Why are you saying these things? Why are you trying to hurt us so?" she asked, even as a little voice reminded she'd often wondered why Theodora hadn't come to visit them at the orphanage.

Titus was almost dancing around the room with outrage. Gaiety hardly moved a muscle. Her eyes blinked, her hands and teeth were clinched.

"Don't listen to him, Avalina. You've been fooled by him before. Theodora probably begged him to let her bring us with her. She would have wanted us with her since Papa and Josh were gone. Believe him? No thank you. He was probably responsible for her death, and that's what he's hiding." Titus spat his words with vehemence.

All the old feelings Gaiety had put to rest resurfaced. She'd always known there was more to Theodora's death than what she'd been told, but she'd allowed her admiration and love for Aston to sway her away from what she'd known to be true. She advanced on him.

"Just last night you told me—" She stopped as her voice broke emotionally. She swallowed hard as she remembered his words. 'I'd bribe you or lie to you to get you to stay with me.' No more lies, Aston. Tell me the truth."

His throat tightened as he tried one more time to shield her from the pain. "You don't want to know it."

Gaiety was so frustrated, she wanted to strike out at him and force him to tell her. How could he think she didn't want to know the truth?

"Now," was all she managed to get out.

A mask of resignation stole over his face. His chest heaved with a heavy sigh. "Theodora threw herself down the stairs. She wanted her baby to be born dead. She didn't want it to live. When she was screaming with pain, she admitted she hadn't fallen by accident. She was trying to kill the baby, not herself."

Earlier she had been shocked, angered, but now she was devastated. An overwhelming grief settled upon her. Could Theodora have been that selfish? Maybe she no longer wanted her brother and sister in her life, but how could she not want her baby? Slowly she shook her head. "No," she whispered breathlessly.

"Liar!" Titus hissed, nearly jumping off the floor. "You're a goddamned liar!"

Aston pointed a straight finger at Titus. His eyes narrowed and his voice remained low. "Don't call me a liar again. I'm sick and tired of hearing it." Aston's gaze darted from Titus to Gaiety. "You asked for the truth. I told you you wouldn't like it."

Gaiety was speechless. She closed her eyes and drew a painful breath. An overwhelming grief settled upon her. She'd lost Aston. She'd opened herself up to him and planned for their future together. She'd loved him. How could he have done this to her?

"You bastard! You got her pregnant, then killed her and her baby," Titus yelled again.

"No!" Aston's voice grew louder as he swung around to point a finger at Titus again. "Your sister was a lying, selfish whore who killed herself trying to kill her baby!"

Gaiety rushed to lash out at Aston, but Titus beat her to him. He swung, hitting Aston with an upper cut under the chin, snapping his head backward. Aston kept his footing and landed a hard fist into Titus's midsection. He coughed and doubled over.

"Stop this!" Gaiety exclaimed, stepping between the two, shaking with fear, with outrage, with pain.

"Get out of my way," Titus said, looking up from his bent position. "I'll kill him!"

"Titus, stop this madness," Gaiety said, pushing him away as he moved to pass her. "I want you to go to the barn and ask Hank to prepare a carriage for us. We're leaving right away."

"Not until I—"

She was shaking so badly she could hardly stand. She felt raw, exposed. "Go. Now. I'll be right out to join you. We'll go to Lilac Hill."

After another deadly look at Aston, Titus turned away. Gaiety saw that Alma, Josie, and Mimi stood in the doorway. They parted to let Titus through. She cleared her throat, hoping to give her voice more strength than she felt she had. "Mimi, go pack a small case and meet me outside. Alma, Josie, would you please excuse us?" She didn't know how she managed to stay so polite.

"Are you all right, Mr. Aston?" Josie asked.

Aston wiped the corner of his mouth with the back of his hand. "I'm fine. Do as Gaiety asked."

The servants cleared the doorway, and after taking three deep breaths that did nothing to calm her, Gaiety turned to face Aston. She needed to hold herself together long enough to say what had to be said and get out of the house. A red bruise had already formed on Aston's chin. She loved him and it hurt her deeply but she had to say, "I can't believe the things you say about my sister."

"I know. That's why I never wanted to tell you the truth."

"I have to leave."

He grabbed her upper arms, his fingers pressed into her skin. His heart thudded painfully in his chest. For a moment, he wanted to shake her. Was there no way to escape the past? Would what Theodora had done to him twelve years ago destroy his life again? Would he never be free from her damning lie?

"No. Damn it, Gaiety, I don't want your pity, but would you stop to think about what all this has done to me? I was seventeen years old. I've never forgiven her for what she did to me, but I didn't want her or her baby to die like that. I told you the truth about her death."

"Which time?" she asked softly. "Just now, or weeks ago?" His intake of breath let her know her words hit their mark, but she felt no victory. How could she, when even now she wanted to forgive him but couldn't?

A coldness settled over her. "I don't know what to believe. Each time your story gets more muddled. I thought I could trust you, but now I'm not sure I can."

Slowly Aston turned her loose and backed away.

Without another word Gaiety turned and walked out the door.

Nineteen

Titus walked ahead of them, fishing pole in hand, as Gaiety and her father followed him on the path that led to the pond at the north end of Lilac Hill.

Late afternoon sunshine glistened around them, filling the beautiful day with warmth. The sky, a light shade of blue, was dotted with puffs of white clouds. A gentle breeze stirred the leaves on the hardwood trees. In the distance, Gaiety heard the occasional squawking of blackbirds as they flew from limb to limb, searching for the right perch. A pretty yellow-and-orange butterfly fluttered along the path in front of them.

"It's good to have you back, Gaiety," Lane said, as they ambled along slowly. "And Titus's disposition certainly seems to have improved over the last three days."

She looked at the back of the lanky youth walking ahead of them. He seemed so carefree. Gaiety didn't want to tell her father about Titus's problems with the authorities. Maybe one day, but not right now. Aston was on her mind.

"He is doing better. He's settled down a lot since we arrived at Lilac Hill. I think he realizes this is where he belongs."

"I haven't pressured you to talk since you've been here, but I'm worried about you. You're much too quiet. I thought surely once you'd found your brother you would wear a smile to match the name I gave you so many years ago. Are you never to be happy?"

She cut her eyes around to him, hoping her bonnet shielded most of her face. She felt bad about not measuring up to her father's expectations. He'd done everything in his power to make her happy. Lane had allowed her to do things no other father would have, and she would always be grateful to him.

"My unhappiness has nothing to do with you, Papa."

"Oh, I know that, dear."

She would be blissfully happy right now if Aston hadn't told those vicious lies about her sister. Theodora had her faults. She knew that now. But Aston's accusations were unforgivable. Even now it hurt to remember the things he'd said to her. Had he really expected her to believe Theodora could be so cruel as to want her baby dead? She had to wonder if he was still seeking his own kind of revenge for what she did to him, or for what Theodora had done to him?

Gaiety smiled at her father, a weak smile, she

knew. "I'm so very happy we found Titus. You know that, Papa. And I want you to know that I left Mobile with the feeling that I would make my marriage to Aston work." A lonely feeling lingered around her, and she tried to shake it. "For so many good reasons, I've fallen in love with him."

"Gaiety?"

"It's true," she said. "I know it's unthinkable, a seeming violation to all I've held dear these years, but Papa," she placed a hand on his arm. "From the very first time I saw Aston I was attracted to him. Even when I wanted to hurt him, when I felt I had to hate him, I was attracted to him. You can't know how desperately I fought it, and I'm still fighting my love for him."

He patted her hand, then fitted it in the crook of his arm as they walked. "Nothing would make me happier than for you to make your marriage work. Aston's a good man. Do you want to tell me what happened?"

"Come on! Catch up," Titus turned around and called to them.

Gaiety motioned for him to go ahead. "Papa can't walk as fast as you," Gaiety answered. "Don't wait for us. You can dig for the bait while we catch up."

Titus waved his agreement to her and took off, the fishing poles held tightly in his hand. His shoulders swayed gently back and forth, giving a flowing motion to his easy stride. His long hair fanned out to caress his shoulders.

Gaiety smiled. She would always be so very grateful to Aston for finding Titus.

"I thought I'd resolved all those haunting feelings about the past, about Aston's role, but now I'm thinking maybe I was letting my tender feelings for him overshadow what I knew to be true. I know Aston is a good man, an honorable man. And I was willing to believe the first story he told me about Theodora."

Lane grunted as they started down a slope and he had to walk faster. Gaiety held tightly to his arm and helped shoulder his weight until the ground leveled again. "Which was?"

"The baby wasn't his. He never touched her. He said Theodora wanted to marry him because his father was the wealthiest man in the county. I hated to think she'd do that, but it seemed possible."

"I agree. Are you saying that you no longer believe he told the truth about that?"

In the distance, she saw the gently rippling water. Titus had dropped to his knees and was digging around the soft bank for wigglers. She stopped and faced her father. His eyes were clear and understanding. "I don't know what to believe anymore. He's told me so many different things. Papa, he told the most horrible story." Her hand squeezed his arm as her heart broke all over again. "Aston said Theodora didn't want Titus or me to live with her at Southern Oaks. He said that she—" She swallowed hard, trying to suppress the feelings of outrage that wanted to surface. "That Theodora threw herself down the stairs. She admitted on her deathbed that she'd wanted to kill her baby and had ended up killing both of them."

Lane's color heightened at the news. "Good Lord! That's terrible."

"Yes, and it can't be true. I can't accept that horrible lie as the truth," she said, with determination. "Theodora may have tricked him into marriage. I can believe that, for I tricked Aston into marriage, too. I can even believe she wouldn't want us with her at Southern Oaks. I don't think she ever cared too much for us, but I can't believe she would want to kill her baby." She shook her head in disbelief, in sorrow that Aston had said such a thing.

"Wait, wait," Lane said, holding up his hand to stop her. "We have some things to clear up. First, Aston wasn't tricked into marrying you. He married you because he wanted to."

Gaiety felt a tightening in her chest. "What do you mean, Papa? You told him if he wanted the land, he'd have to marry me."

"Ah—well, yes, I did the first time we talked." He sighed. "I might as well tell the truth. When I came back from Connecticut, I told Aston I'd changed my mind about the marriage proposal and that I was withdrawing my offer."

"You what? Papa, you didn't." Stunned by this news, she felt light-headed.

"Yes, because I thought it would be best for you. But it doesn't matter now, because Aston wouldn't agree. He was quite adamant about marrying you. You both seemed to want the marriage, so I didn't stand in your way."

She hadn't tricked him. Aston wanted to marry her. That thought thrilled her and made her heart sing with gladness. She had hidden her true identity from him, but it was his choice to marry her.

Lane took his hat off, ran an open palm over his head, and smoothed his hair. "Now, this story about Theodora . . . why is it so difficult to believe? If it's a lie he tells, what's the reason? Why would Aston come up with such a gruesome tale?"

"He wanted to hurt me," she answered, the only reason she'd been about to come up with.

"Why? If he wasn't tricked into marrying you, why would he want to hurt you?"

A moan of distress escaped Gaiety's lips. "I don't know, Papa," she said, realizing this new information confused her all the more. "Maybe he wanted to get back at Theodora for lying about the baby. Maybe he wanted to tarnish her name in my eyes."

"Gaiety, Theodora has been dead for twelve years. He has no motive for wanting to do that."

The sun was sinking lower. Gaiety untied the ribbon under her chin and pulled her bonnet off. "I don't know, Papa. You may be right. I only know if I believe Aston, I have to believe my sister was a murderer. How can I do that?"

Her voice was barely a whisper. "I need some time to think about all this."

"That's a good idea. When you've thought it all through, I believe you're going to see that Aston was telling the truth."

"Hey, are you two going to join me, or are you going to talk until it's dark?" Titus called to them in a grumbling manner.

"We'd better join him," she said, ignoring his comment as they started walking again.

"There's something I'd like to tell you, and now is as good a time as any. While you were away, I went into Savannah and rented a house from a family who's going to take an extended tour of Europe. They could be gone for a year or longer. That should give me plenty of time to find a house of my own."

Gaiety reeled from this latest news. "Papa, no. You *know* we want you here with us!"

He chuckled lightly and wrapped his arm around her shoulder as they headed down the last few yards to the pond. "Gaiety, the country is fine for a time, but I'd like to live in town. Titus is a young man now, and Lilac Hill rightfully belongs to him. It's not mine, not Aston's. What you need to decide is if this is your rightful place. Is it here, or is it with your husband?"

She felt a quickening in her heart. A lump in her throat made her voice husky as she said, "You're right; I have to decide."

"Hey, are you two ever going to get here? I've found a bed of worms and put one on the line," Titus called, as he waded out into the pond, whipped the pole backward, and cast the line into the water. Gaiety remembered seeing Josh do the same thing when he was Titus's age. The late afternoon sunshine shimmered on the water, and as she watched it glistening, she was transported back in time.

Gaiety was a little girl with long, stringy hair, playing in the shallow water. Josh had waded in the water up to his waist and was fishing. Gaiety turned back toward the bank and saw Theodora. She was angry. She was shouting and pointing her finger at Titus, who sat on the ground crying, his arms reaching for her. She turned away from him. Titus cried and crawled after her. He pulled on the hem of her dress. Theodora turned around and struck him across the face. He fell backward, screaming. She hit him again and again. Gaiety started running toward them.

"No, no," she whispered.

"Gaiety, are you all right?"

Her father's voice brought her back to the present. She was shaking, deeply disturbed by the flashback of memory. Why had she remembered that? Had it been true, or had Aston's cruel words prompted her to imagine it?

"I'm sorry, Papa, what did you say?"

"I said I'm going back to Connecticut for a visit in a week or so. Would you and Titus like to join me? It will give you time to think about all that's happened—your marriage, finding Titus, and what Aston's told you. You might decide he's not lying, or if he is, that he had a good reason."

She couldn't think. She was too distressed by all she'd learned today. What she needed was some time alone to sort through what her father had told her, what she'd just remembered, and her feelings for Aston.

Looking back at Lane, she said, "Papa, you haven't been back from Connecticut much more than two months. So much traveling isn't good for you."

"You worry too much. I feel good. Besides, I told Mrs. Taylor I'd come back for a visit. I'd rather go before I settle into the house in town."

Gaiety placed her hands on her hips and stared disapprovingly at her father. "You told her you'd go in August or September, not June. Papa, you know how I worry about you on a long trip."

"I'm not going to crawl in a hole and stop doing what I want just because I have a few aches and pains." He reached down and picked up one of the fishing poles Titus had left on the bank. "You certainly don't have to make a decision about going with me right now. Just add it to all the other things you have to think about."

Lane walked off to join Titus. Gaiety would think about traveling with her father. Titus might enjoy it. She watched the waning sunshine shimmer on the water and remembered Aston's kisses, his touch, his loving. She loved

Aston; that she couldn't deny. But what was she going to do about it?

"Miss Gaiety, it hurts me a lot to say this, and I know you're going to be mad with me and maybe a little disappointed, too. I'd like to think you'll be disappointed, anyway."

"Mimi, please just tell me what you want to say." Gaiety stood before her mirror, brushing her long hair.

"I won't be going with you to Connecticut. I'm going to have to quit your employ."

"Mimi!" Gaiety exclaimed in surprise as Mimi set her breakfast tray on her night table. "Whatever are you talking about? What have I done? I won't hear of you leaving."

"Oh, you haven't done anything, Miss Gaiety. I love working for you and I'm going to miss you, but Hank proposed last night and I accepted."

Gaiety dropped her brush to the dresser and rushed over and hugged Mimi tightly. "That's wonderful news. I'm so very happy for you." Gaiety felt tears of happiness gather in her eyes and she wiped them with the tips of her fingers. "I didn't know you and Hank were that serious."

"I knew he was the one for me the first time I saw him." Mimi's eyes turned dreamy, and she hugged herself. "He was so handsome. We've talked about getting married before and decided we'd wait for a while longer, but when you decided to go to Connecticut with Mr. Lane, Hank said he didn't want me to go. He missed me too much while we were in Alabama, and he doesn't want me to go away like that again. I missed him a lot, too."

"I'm sure you did." Gaiety smiled as her own heart ached. She knew how Mimi felt. She missed Aston. Her heart cried out for her to go to him and tell him the past was over and she was ready to look to the future with him, but she couldn't bring herself to do it. She hoped going back to Connecticut would help her come to terms with all that'd happened.

"I'm sure Hank missed you and wants you with him. And, Mimi, I understand."

"But I'm going to miss you, too, Miss Gaiety." Mimi's bottom lip quivered. "I'll never find anyone to treat me as good as you and your papa, except Hank. I'd forsake anyone for him."

Mimi's words touched her heart and caused her to pause. "As it should be. You've been a good friend as well as my maid. I don't know what I'll do without you. Even though I'm happy for you, I'm going to miss you terribly."

"I feel the same way. I always thought I'd get to bounce your children on my knee. Now I guess someone else will do that."

Gaiety was aware of a pain deep in her heart. She wanted to have children to love and take care of. For a few days she had hoped that her last night with Aston had given her a child, but it hadn't been so. She shook off those sorrowful feelings and said, "I won't be gone long, Mimi. Surely, we'll be able to see each other from time to time, even if Hank doesn't want you working for me."

"Oh, it's not that Hank doesn't want me working for you, Miss Gaiety. He just doesn't want me going away, and I know you need someone to go with you. We'd hoped you would be going back to Southern Oaks to live with Mr. Aston so I could work for you during the day and go home to Hank in the evenings, but I guess that won't happen." She hung her head.

Wanting to get the conversation off herself, Gaiety asked, "Does Hank have a place for you to live?"

"Oh, yes, Miss." Mimi's eyes brightened. "He has a big room in the back of the carriage house. It's a nice room with furniture. He said maybe Mr. Aston can find a job for me on Southern Oaks so we can save our money and one day build a house of our own."

Gaiety felt an unusual sting of jealously that Mimi would be at Southern Oaks with the man she loved, and Gaiety would be all alone. She admonished herself for the envious feelings. "Aston likes you very much. If he has a place, I'm sure he will hire you."

Mimi clasped her hands together and held them to her breasts. Her eyes sparkled with renewed hope. "Oh, I'd like that, Miss Gaiety. Will you be all right?"

"I think I can manage by myself. In fact, taking care of my own clothes and hair will give me something to do. I think I'll enjoy it for a while. Besides, I'll have Papa, Titus, and Maine with me. If I decide I need anyone else, I can always bring Jeanette along, so don't worry."

"Thank you, Miss Gaiety. And I know it's not my place to say it, but I hope you and Mr. Aston work things out. I can't imagine living anywhere without Hank. My place is with him."

Gaiety folded her arms across her chest and turned away. Mimi's words were true: a woman's place was with her husband. Suddenly Gaiety knew what she wanted to do. All it had taken was a few well-chosen words from her maid.

She'd been gone from Southern Oaks for the better part of a week and Aston hadn't tried to get in touch with her. If he'd loved her, wouldn't he have wanted to talk to her again? Or had she hurt him too badly?

She walked over to the window and looked out. Once again she closed her eyes and remembered her last night with Aston.

"Good riddance," Aston said aloud, as he poured himself a generous portion of his finest brandy. No matter that it was only mid-afternoon, he was in need of a strong drink. He held the glass in one hand as his other balled into a tightly shut fist. He tried to deny the sense of betrayal he felt, but it was too consuming. Damn it, he was trying hard not to care.

He took two more swallows before he calmed enough to refill the glass and plop down in the chair behind his desk. He propped his feet up and leaned back in the chair. The brandy stung his tongue and his stomach. Aston was thankful the brandy burned. It gave him a reason to wince. He breathed heavily as he thought about the possibility of getting drunk. Why the hell not? Maybe if he got rousing drunk he wouldn't think about what Gaiety had done to him. Maybe he wouldn't think at all.

He should have lied to her. Damn it! He knew Gaiety didn't want to know the truth. That's the reason she wouldn't believe him. She didn't want to. He'd never intended to tell her what had really happened to Theodora. Damn, he hoped that girl was in hell for all the misery she'd caused him. Not only did she ruin his life and kill her baby, she'd destroyed Gaiety's life, too.

"Gaiety." He said her name softly and swallowed hard. He should have lied to her. He was wrong not to continue the lie, even though Titus had overheard him talking to Alma. In time, he could have made her doubt Titus.

When she'd left for Lilac Hill, he'd wanted to follow her immediately, but decided she needed some time to come to terms with what he'd told her about her sister. In her overwrought state, she would only have refused to see him. He felt she needed to adjust to a lot of things, including the attitude of her newfound brother. And Aston had wanted a few days to get in touch with the doctor who could corroborate his story and start the search for the woman who had managed the orphanage. Mrs. Conners would confirm that she'd come to Southern Oaks twice and asked Theodora to take her brother and sister.

It had never occurred to Aston that Gaiety would take off to Connecticut with her father without even trying to work things out with him. He could have broken a branding iron in two when Mimi told him Gaiety was leaving, but she was staying and marrying Hank.

He should have lied to Gaiety. Damn her. He missed her in his home, his life, his bed. He enjoyed her companionship and wanted her with him.

The day was already warm. The brandy made him hot. With one hand he removed his cravat and collar and unbuttoned his shirt. Maybe too many things had happened to Gaiety too quickly. He couldn't blame her for not wanting to believe the truth. If he hadn't been in Theodora's room when she'd admitted throwing herself down the stairs, he wouldn't have believed it. Theodora should have known she was endangering her own life as well as her baby's.

Aston rubbed his forehead, his temples, his eyes. He laughed bitterly as he thought about the selfish, self-centered Theodora.

If Gaiety had truly loved him, she wouldn't

have left without a word to him, he decided, his thoughts quickly jumping back to his wife. It was all clear now; she'd never loved him, had never planned on living with him.

"Drinking so early in the afternoon, Aston? Is that what marriage will do for a man?" Fredrick asked, from the doorway of Aston's office.

"Your humor has always been inappropriate, Fred." Aston swung his legs down and his feet hit the floor with a thud. He was in no mood for his cousin. "Join me if you like. Help yourself."

"Thank you. I don't mind if I do." Fredrick walked over to the side table and poured himself a drink.

"What can I do for you?" Aston asked, hoping to get rid of him quickly. He couldn't feel sorry for himself in front of anyone.

"Actually, I came to see your wife. Where is Gaiety? I have an invitation to deliver to her." He took a seat in front of the desk and sipped his drink.

Aston set his glass down on his desk. "She's visiting with her father right now," he hedged. "Perhaps you should give the invitation to me. I'll see she gets it."

"Oh, there's no hurry. I was hoping you wouldn't mind if I stayed the night. Surely, she'll be home for dinner. We'd like you and Gaiety to spend the weekend in Savannah. Elaine is desperate for Gaiety to come to the Wilsons' party. We've already arranged it."

In spite of his misery, Aston became amused. Fredrick was fishing for information and didn't even know it. He could refuse to let Fredrick stay the night and prolong the inevitable. But why in hell should he do that? Gaiety wasn't coming back. In fact, he'd just decided he didn't want her to. He'd had it with the Talbots—all of them. That family had plagued him for years, and he was putting an end to it here and now.

He looked up at Fredrick. "You're always welcome to stay the night. However, coming to Savannah won't be possible. Gaiety won't be home today, nor will she be home tomorrow. She's traveling to Connecticut with her father. I'm not sure how long she'll be gone. But do thank Elaine for the thought."

Fredrick's lashes flew up, and his mouth flew open. His hand stopped on its way to his mouth. "My God, Aston . . . surely you jest. You've not been married more than a month. Why would Gaiety leave?"

"Don't question me on my marriage, Fredrick. It's of no concern to you." Aston tried to remain firm but nice.

"Well, I am concerned. Does she have a relative who's ill?"

Aston saw the perfect answer. "No, for reasons I won't go into, she recently found a brother who'd been lost to her for many years. She wanted to spend some time with him, and I heartily agreed."

"How generous of you." He sipped his drink.

"After Elaine and I marry, I hope I'll be as understanding with her as you are with Gaiety."

Understanding, hell, Aston thought, as he smiled and nodded to Fred. Deep inside him, a burning passion of anger filled him. Gaiety wasn't the person he'd thought she was. He was better off without her. A thousand times he wished he'd kept his vow and not married. But even as he thought these things, a little voice inside him said, "You should have lied to her."

Twenty

It was early in the evening by the time Titus pulled the horses to a stop in front of the mansion at Southern Oaks. It had been almost two weeks since Gaiety had left the plantation. During that time, Aston had been on her mind constantly. She'd alternated between hating him and loving him, believing him and distrusting him. It had all started coming together when her father had told her Aston hadn't been tricked into marrying her. He'd wanted to marry her. Mimi had helped, too, when she'd reminded her a woman's place was with her husband. Gaiety's place was with her husband—the man she loved.

She'd finally come to terms with the fact that she had to believe Aston. How could she have accepted what Aston had said as the truth without giving it proper consideration? When all the pieces had been put together, she knew Aston was telling the truth about her sister. Even though it caused her great pain, she had to believe him. If she hadn't been so horrified by what he'd told her that day, she'd have realized Theodora was capable of what he'd said. Gaiety didn't know how it happened, but Theodora had cared only for herself and what she wanted. She'd have preferred to have remained oblivious to the truth. She wanted to believe Theodora had died thinking she and her baby were going to live.

Gaiety finally understood, as Aston had said, that he'd withheld the truth about Theodora's death because he hadn't wanted to hurt her. Now, with all that behind her, she wanted to be with her husband.

Titus helped her step down from the carriage to the front lawn. She turned to look at the house with its six Doric columns rising three floors as he unloaded her baggage. The dark shades of evening twilight enhanced the whiteness of the house, making it look majestic. She'd missed everything about Southern Oaks, but most of all, she'd missed its master. How was he going to receive her? That worried her.

Her father left earlier in the day for Connecticut. Titus would be staying at Lilac Hill with Jeanette and Helen to look after him. She no longer feared he'd run away to Mobile. She'd remained patient, kind, and encouraging, and it had paid off. Titus was beginning to understand that at the age of sixteen he had his own farm and it was up to him what he did with it and with his life. He seemed quite satisfied with the roots Lilac Hill gave him.

Lane appeared happy about her decision to return to her husband. He'd never wanted anything more than her complete happiness. Titus had said a lot of things, but the most important was that it was her life. She would continue to build a relationship with her brother, but it'd have to be done from Southern Oaks.

After several conversations she'd tried to get him to agree to live at Southern Oaks with her and Aston for a year or two, but he wouldn't agree.

"Want me to take these inside for you?" Titus asked.

"Oh, no." She whirled away from the house and faced Titus. "I'll have someone come get them for me," she said.

The front door opened and Josie came out carrying a pitcher. "Miss Gaiety . . . I'm glad you're back. Mr. Aston has been as irritable as a bear fighting honeybees since you been gone."

Gaiety laughed softly, although her stomach was quaking uncontrollably. She wasn't sure at all that Aston would welcome her back into his home. She turned to Titus. "Are you sure you're going to be all right? You know I'm going to worry about you."

"I know how to take care of myself. And don't worry, Gaiety. I'm not going to run away. I told you . . . I don't want to go back to Mobile or the kind of life I had with the street gang."

She smiled and patted his cheek. "Let me know if you need me."

He nodded and answered, "You let me know if you ever need me, too."

"I will." She reached up and gave him a hug, and for the first time he responded by lightly touching her back with a soft pat. She was thrilled to have that small response. Reluctantly, she let him go. He climbed back up on the carriage and waved goodbye.

Gaiety turned and hurried up the steps to Josie. "I'm so happy to be home, Josie. Where's Aston?"

"Yes, ma'am. He's upstairs in his room, taking a wash. He's been in the fields most of the day. I came down to get him some more hot water and heard the carriage pull up, so I came out to see who was here."

"He's upstairs in the washtub?" she asked, to be sure.

"Yes, ma'am, waiting for this hot water."

Trembling with fear of rejection, she reached for the pitcher. "May I?"

He looked at her, then at the pitcher. A smile spread across his face and lighted in his eyes. "You want to carry this up to him?"

"Please."

He handed her the jar. "Miss Gaiety, are you here to stay this time?"

"Yes, Josie. I'm here forever."

Gaiety's stomach continued to jump and quiver as she made her way up the stairs. She prayed Aston would forgive her for doubting him so long, for blaming him for Theodora's sins. At the top of the stairs, she paused and took a deep breath. She'd been wrong. She had to make it up to Aston.

Pushing the door open with the toe of her shoe, she walked into Aston's bedroom and stood inside the doorway for a moment while her eyes adjusted to the dimly lit room.

Aston lay with his back against the tub, his knees drawn up and poking out of the water. His eyes were closed. His lashes didn't even flutter when she closed the door. He'd wet his hair and slicked it back away from his face and forehead, showing a crown filled with thick, dark hair. Her gaze followed the bridge of his nose down to his finely sculpted lips and over his clearly defined cheekbones. He was so handsome. How could she have doubted him for so long? Her heart cried out for her to rush over to him, wrap him in her arms, and beg him to forgive her for not trusting him and to take her back.

She wanted to tell him she was sorry and loved him with all her heart, but how should she approach him? Face-to-face, she decided, and closed the door. She walked up beside the tub and stood before him. He didn't move or blink an eye. She knew it was crazy, unheard of, but she wanted to disrobe and join him in the tub of gently moving water.

She tilted the pitcher and slowly poured the hot water into the tub. The water made an obnoxious splashing sound as it disturbed the peacefulness of the room.

Aston stirred. "Pour it all in at once, Josie, and get out of here."

When she didn't respond, he opened his eyes and caught sight of her. Surprise showed in his expression for only a second; then he hid it. He stayed relaxed against the tub, but his gaze didn't waver from her face.

"What are you doing here?" he asked in a mean sounding tone. "I thought you'd gone to Connecticut."

His tone surprised her. While she didn't exactly expect him to welcome her with open arms, she hadn't expected the open hostility she heard in his voice. She stopped pouring and set the pitcher on the floor. Whatever happened, whatever he said, she had to remain strong. "I thought about it, but decided I didn't want to go."

He chuckled bitterly, then closed his eyes as if he could care less that she was in the room. "Get out of here, Gaiety, you're interrupting my private time. I have nothing to say to you."

His words and attitude stung like large needles piercing her skin, but she couldn't blame him. She'd been wrong to behave the way she had. Now she was ready to make everything right . . . and she would—no matter how long it took.

"I've done a lot of thinking since the last time we talked."

"So have I."

"I want to put Theodora to rest once and for—"

Aston sat up in the tub so quickly Gaiety jerked back. "Don't mention her name in this house!"

His voice boomed loudly. His fist came down hard into the water and splashed droplets on her face and the front of her dress as water streamed down his hairy chest. His anger didn't frighten her.

"I've had it up to here with Talbot women." He made a slice across his neck with his finger. He stood up in the tub, splashing water over the edge and onto the floor. "I don't need you here. I don't want you here. Now, get out."

He was angry with good reason, but Gaiety found it difficult to take him seriously when he was standing completely naked in front of her with water running down his body.

At first she was reluctant to look at him, but she'd missed him so much she found her gaze sliding down his neck, over his shoulders, and lower. He had a powerful-looking body, and she wanted desperately to touch him.

"I was just beginning to put my life back together after the hell Theodora put me through, then you came along," Aston continued. "Now, I've had it. Get out." He pointed toward the door.

Gaiety remained where she stood. She felt no fear or danger from him. She deserved his anger; she'd been wrong. Now it was time to say the things she should have said then. Forcing her gaze up to meet his, she said, "I'm staying."

"No, you're not. This is my house, and I don't want you here."

Her shoulders hurt from standing so straight, holding herself so rigid. She had to remain so to buffet the pain of his words.

"I'm your wife. This is my house, too. I'm sorry I didn't believe what you said about my sister. It hurt me more than you'll ever know. I didn't want to—"

"It's too late, Gaiety. I'm not interested. The fact is, I don't care anymore. Believe what you want."

A small sound of desperation escaped her lips. He spoke so calmly, it frightened her. Had he lost all feeling for her? If he'd continued shouting so angrily, she could fight with him, but what could she do if his calm words were true? If he no longer cared for her?

"I never wanted to marry, you know that. But you were beautiful, tempting. You were a good woman in bed, but I know a lot of women who are good in bed. And Fredrick can give me an heir for Southern Oaks."

His words hit her so hard for a moment she thought she might faint. "Aston, you said you loved me."

"I lied." He smirked. "That doesn't surprise you, does it? That I'm capable of lying?"

Overflowing with hurt, she turned and ran to the door, but something stopped her from opening it and rushing out. Could it be that he was testing her? Had she hurt him so much, so deeply, he had to be sure of her feelings this time? She tried to stall her trembling lips, her shaky hands. She wouldn't run away again.

She turned and faced him. He was so very appealing, standing in the middle of the tub with the water lapping gently at his legs. She wouldn't give him up without a fight. If what she'd once thought was true, that Aston was her destiny, she'd make him see they belonged together.

Gaiety started unbuttoning the front of her blouse as she walked toward him. "I don't believe you. I love you, and I know you love me. Southern Oaks belongs to our children . . . not your cousin's."

His eyes narrowed as he watched her. "That's not your decision to make. It's mine."

Feeling shaky all over, she took a few more steps toward him and pulled her blouse from the waistband of her skirt. "I can accept you not wanting me back in your bedroom as your wife; that's your choice." She slid the blouse over her shoulders and off her arms and tossed it aside. "But as your wife, this is my home, and I intend to live here."

"And your brother?" he asked, sneering.

"Titus wants to live at Lilac Hill. I've agreed that's what is best for him." She reached behind her and unfastened her skirt and untied the ribbons that held her petticoats around her waist. She shoved them down her legs and stepped away from them, leaving her dressed in her corset cover and drawers. "Papa has rented a house in town where he plans to live when he returns." She took a deep breath, trying to stay calm.

His gaze roamed over her scantily clad body before returning to her face. "What are you doing, Gaiety?"

"Undressing. Do you mind if I take my old room?"

"Why, Gaiety? Why do you want to come back and upset my life again? Haven't you done enough?"

His voice was so earnest she had to hold herself back from rushing into his arms. "I love you. I want to be near you. I'm sorry our pasts were connected by an event neither of us could control, but it's time to forget and start over."

"You're lying."

She gasped. "I'm not. I love you, Aston."

"I don't believe you."

His words were so matter-of-fact they tore at her heart with carelessness. Now she knew how he'd felt when he'd told the truth and she didn't believe him. That feeling of helplessness, that pressing weight against the chest. She didn't blame him for rejecting her. Somehow, she'd make it up to him. She had to.

"I want us to start over," she said earnestly, walking so close to him her knees knocked against the washtub.

Didn't you say those same words to me the last time we were in bed together?"

Her throat ached from trying to hold back

the tears that threatened. "Please, Aston, meet me halfway?"

"All right. Have Josie put your things in your old bedroom. In public we will be husband and wife. If I decide I want an heir of my own for Southern Oaks, I'll visit your bedroom."

She didn't like what he'd said or the way he'd said it. Again she was tempted to walk out and not humble herself anymore, but her love for him bade her to stay and fight for her right to be his beloved wife. If he'd had feelings for her before, he could again.

"You wanted me to forgive and forget the past. I have. Now *you* have to do it."

"What are you talking about?"

"You have to forgive me for doubting you, and you have to forgive Theodora for what she did to you."

His hand made a fist of fury. "I won't ever forgive Theodora for what she put me through. Because of her selfishness, I was forced to watch her and her baby die. Hell, no, I haven't forgiven her, and I don't know how you could, either."

His words tore gaping holes in her heart. She hurt so badly for him, for herself, for her sister. She wanted to comfort Aston, but how could she when he refused her?

"Your love has helped me forgive."

"You're lying again. There's no need. I've already told you you can live here, if that's what you want."

"I'm not lying," she whispered. Again she

was aware of how Aston had begged her to believe him in much the same way as this. In an act of desperation, she bent and unlaced her shoes and stepped out of them. Her heartbeat increased. She lifted her foot and stepped into the tub with him. The water was warm, soothing. If he wanted her out of his bedroom, he would have to pick her up and throw her out.

"After our father was killed, you could have abandoned Theodora. You didn't have to keep her box of treasures when she died. You didn't have to take Titus from the orphanage and give him a good home. You didn't have to go with me to Mobile to find him. You didn't have to put your own life in danger once you realized he was involved in a street gang. How could I not love you?"

Aston remained stiff, refusing to look at her. "If you love me, then it's for what I have done for your family . . . not for who I am."

"No, that's not true. I was attracted to you the first time I saw you at the pond. You were too handsome and arrogant for a poacher."

"And you were arrogant for a woman. Go away, Gaiety," he said, for the third time that night. "I don't want to love you. I don't want to forgive Theodora."

She reached and circled him with her arms, fearful he'd reject her, but knowing she had to touch him, hold him. He didn't push her away. Gaiety let her head fall to his wet chest. She held him tightly. His wet body felt cool to her cheek. How could she have treated him so abominably? She loved him. She'd make it up to him.

"I love you," she whispered. "I love you. Please forgive me for doubting the truth of your words."

"It's foolish of me to trust you again, foolish to love you again. I can't do it," he answered huskily.

She looked up into his eyes. "No, it's right, Aston."

He took hold of the back of her head and held her firmly. "Gaiety, tell me you're here to stay this time."

"I'm here to stay, my love."

"What if you hear about something I haven't told you or neglected to tell you? Will you run away again?"

"No. Never. This is my home. You are my life. Aston, don't turn me away. I love you."

Aston claimed her lips with a desperate kiss that was much too brief for Gaiety.

Looking down into her eyes, he said, "We've been here before, thinking that all was settled between us. I don't want to love you tonight and lose you tomorrow morning."

"You won't lose me. When I told you I'd put everything to rest, I meant it. Even Titus is coming around, and I hope one day the two of you can be friends."

He gave her a noncommittal nod and a shrug of his shoulders and pulled her tighter against his chest.

"I meant it when I said your love had helped

me forgive and forget the past. I want to tell you something else—I now understand you were Theodora's victim. I'm so very sorry I didn't realize that sooner."

Aston looked deeply into her eyes. "And what made you come to that conclusion?"

"I wanted someone to blame, and you were the easy target. My father had no trouble believing you, but I was afraid to admit it to you or myself. I simply didn't want to believe Theodora could have been so cruel or so sick."

Aston stepped out of the tub, picked up Gaiety, and carried her over to the bed. He laid her down on the comforter and fitted his naked body beside her. "I love you Gaiety. I thought I'd go crazy when I heard you'd gone back east."

"I love you, too, Aston." she returned. "Is all forgiven?"

"Yes, my love," he whispered softly, then kissed her on the lips.

It was their destiny to be together, and Theodora had been part of fate's plan to make it so. Someday Aston would realize that.

In the meantime, Gaiety wrapped her arms around his neck and reached up and kissed him passionately, drawing his wet body close to hers. She had missed him, and she intended to show him just how much.

DISCOVER DEANA JAMES!

CAPTIVE ANGEL (2524, $4.50/$5.50)
Abandoned, penniless, and suddenly responsible for the biggest tobacco plantation in Colleton County, distraught Caroline Gillard had no time to dissolve into tears. By day the willowy redhead labored to exhaustion beside her slaves . . . but each night left her restless with longing for her wayward husband. She'd make the sea captain regret his betrayal until he begged her to take him back!

MASQUE OF SAPPHIRE (2885, $4.50/$5.50)
Judith Talbot-Harrow left England with a heavy heart. She was going to America to join a father she despised and a sister she distrusted. She was certainly in no mood to put up with the insulting actions of the arrogant Yankee privateer who boarded her ship, ransacked her things, then "apologized" with an indecent, brazen kiss! She vowed that someday he'd pay dearly for the liberties he had taken and the desires he had awakened.

SPEAK ONLY LOVE (3439, $4.95/$5.95)
Long ago, the shock of her mother's death had robbed Vivian Marleigh of the power of speech. Now she was being forced to marry a bitter man with brandy on his breath. But she could not say what was in her heart. It was up to the viscount to spark the fires that would melt her icy reserve.

WILD TEXAS HEART (3205, $4.95/$5.95)
Fan Breckenridge was terrified when the stranger found her near-naked and shivering beneath the Texas stars. Unable to remember who she was or what had happened, all she had in the world was the deed to a patch of land that might yield oil . . . and the fierce loving of this wildcatter who called himself Irons.

Available wherever paperbacks are sold, or order direct from the Publisher. Send cover price plus 50¢ per copy for mailing and handling to Zebra Books, Dept. 4446 , 475 Park Avenue South, New York, N.Y. 10016. Residents of New York and Tennessee must include sales tax. DO NOT SEND CASH. For a free Zebra/Pinnacle catalog please write to the above address.

MAKE THE ROMANCE CONNECTION

Z-TALK *Online*

Come talk to your favorite authors and get the inside scoop on everything that's going on in the world of romance publishing, from the only online service that's designed exclusively for the publishing industry.

With Z-Talk Online Information Service, the most innovative and exciting computer bulletin board around, you can:

- ♥ CHAT "LIVE" WITH AUTHORS, FELLOW ROMANCE READERS, AND OTHER MEMBERS OF THE ROMANCE PUBLISHING COMMUNITY.
- ♥ FIND OUT ABOUT UPCOMING TITLES BEFORE THEY'RE RELEASED.
- ♥ DOWNLOAD THOUSANDS OF FILES AND GAMES.
- ♥ READ REVIEWS OF ROMANCE TITLES.
- ♥ HAVE UNLIMITED USE OF E-MAIL.
- ♥ POST MESSAGES ON OUR DOZENS OF TOPIC BOARDS.

All it takes is a computer and a modem to get online with Z-Talk. Set your modem to 8/N/1, and dial 212-545-1120. If you need help, call the System Operator, at 212-889-2299, ext. 260. There's a two week free trial period. After that, annual membership is only $ 60.00.

See you online!

KENSINGTON PUBLISHING CORP.